THE
LOOKING
GLASS WARS

BY

FRANK BEDDOR

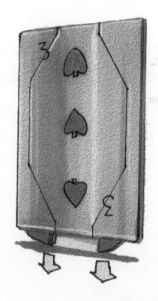

DIAL BOOKS

Dial Books
A member of Penguin Group (USA) Inc.
Published by The Penguin Group
Penguin Group (USA) Inc., 375 Hudson Street, New York, NY 10014, U.S.A.
Penguin Group (Canada), 90 Eglinton Avenue East, Suite 700, Toronto, Ontario,
Canada M4P 2Y3 (a division of Pearson Penguin Canada Inc.)
Penguin Books Ltd, 80 Strand, London WC2R 0RL, England
Penguin Ireland, 25 St. Stephen's Green, Dublin 2, Ireland (a division of Penguin Books Ltd)
Penguin Group (Australia), 250 Camberwell Road, Camberwell, Victoria 3124, Australia
   (a division of Pearson Australia Group Pty Ltd)
Penguin Books India Pvt Ltd, 11 Community Centre, Panchsheel Park, New Delhi - 110 017, India
Penguin Group (NZ), Cnr Airborne and Rosedale Roads, Albany, Auckland 1310,
   New Zealand (a division of Pearson New Zealand Ltd)
Penguin Books (South Africa) (Pty) Ltd, 24 Sturdee Avenue, Rosebank,
   Johannesburg 2196, South Africa
Penguin Books Ltd, Registered Offices: 80 Strand, London WC2R 0RL, England

Logo Design: Christina Craemer
Card Soldiers & Part 2 art: Doug Chiang
Part 1 & Part 3 art: Branislav Hetzel
Front & Back cover: Brian Flora
Map Design: Cold Open
Book Design: Teresa Kietlinski Dikun
Text set in Goudy
Printed in the U.S.A.

10 9 8 7 6 5 4 3 2

Library of Congress Cataloging-in-Publication Data
Beddor, Frank.
 The Looking Glass Wars / by Frank Beddor.
   p. cm.
Summary: When she is cast out of Wonderland by her evil aunt Redd, young Alyss Heart struggles
to keep memories of her queendom intact until she can return and claim her rightful throne.
ISBN 0-8037-3153-1
[1. Fantasy.] I. Title.
PZ7.B3817982Lo 2006 [Fic]—dc22   2006001672

Dedicated to my niece
Sarah
for her sense of wonder

THE LOOKING GLASS WARS

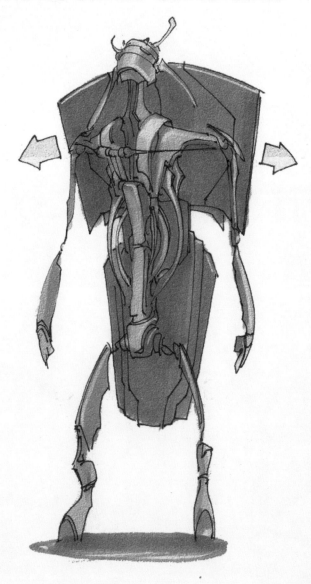

WONDERNATIONS

SNARK MOUNTAIN

VALLEY OF MUSHROOMS

SNARK MOUNTAIN

MOUNT ISOLATION

Redus Fortress

WHISPERING WOODS

WONDERTROPOLIS

The Duck

CHESSBOARD DESERT

VOLCANIC PLAINS

Heart Palace

The Bench

Pool of Tears

OUT

EVERLASTING FOREST

BLAXIK

CRYSTAL MINES

ALYSSIAN HEADQUARTERS

PROLOGUE

Oxford England. July 1863.

Everyone thought she had made it up, and she had tolerated more taunting and teasing from other children, more lectures and punishments from grown-ups, than any eleven-year-old should have to bear. But now, after four years, it had arrived: her last, best chance to prove to them all that she had been telling the truth. A college scholar had thought enough of her history to write it up as a book.

She sat on a blanket on the banks of the river Cherwell, the remains of a picnic lunch in a basket at the Reverend Charles Dodgson's elbow. She held the book in her hands. He had written and illustrated it himself, he said. It had a nice weight and heft, felt substantial. It was wrapped in brown paper and tied with a black ribbon. Dodgson was watching her, anxious. Her sisters Edith and Lorina were hunting minnows at the river's edge. She untied the ribbon, carefully undid the wrapping.

"Oh!" Alice's Adventures Underground? What sort of title was that? And why was her name misspelled? She had told Dodgson how to correctly spell her name, had even written it out for him. "By Lewis Carroll?" she read with growing concern.

"I thought it would be more festive than saying it was by a reverend."

Festive? She had told him little that was festive. Concern was fast turning to alarm, but she swallowed it. What mattered was that he had faithfully recorded her history in Wonderland as she remembered it.

She opened the book and admired its rough-cut pages, the neatness of the handwriting. But the dedication took the form of a poem, in which her name was again misspelled, and she didn't think the lighthearted rhyme scheme appropriate, considering the material it was supposed to introduce. Her gaze caught on one of the stanzas:

> The dream-child moving through a land
> Of wonders, wild and new,
> In friendly chat with bird or beast—
> And half believed it true.

Dream-child? And what did he mean by half believed?

She turned to the first chapter and immediately felt as if her insides had been scooped out, like the half grapefruits Dean Liddell ate for breakfast every morning, after which only raw, pulpy hollows remained. Down a rabbit hole? Where had the worrisome White Rabbit come from?

"Alice, is something wrong?"

She skipped ahead, turned page after page. The Pool of Tears, the caterpillar, her aunt Redd: It had all been twisted into nonsense.

"I admit that I took a few liberties with your story," Dodgson explained, "to make it ours, as I said I would. Do you recognize the tutor fellow you once described to me? He's the White Rabbit character. I got the idea for him upon discovering that the letters of the tutor's name could be made to spell 'white rabbit.' Here, let me show you."

Dodgson took a pencil and small notebook from the inside pocket of his coat, but she didn't want to look. He had indeed said it would be their book, his and hers, and she had found strength in that—strength to suffer the indignities that came from insisting on truths no one else believed. But what she held in her hands had nothing to do with her.

"You mean you did it on purpose?" she asked.

The grinning Cheshire cat. The mad tea party. He'd transformed her memories of a world alive with hope and possibility and danger into make-believe, the foolish stuff of children. He was just another in a long line of unbelievers and this—this stupid, nonsensical book—was how he made fun of her. She had never felt more betrayed in all her life.

"No one is ever going to believe me now!" she screamed. "You've ruined everything! You're the cruelest man I've ever met, Mr. Dodgson, and if you had believed a single word I told you, you'd know how very cruel that is! I never want to see you again! Never, never, never!"

She ran, leaving Edith and Lorina to make their own way home, leaving the Reverend Dodgson—who considered children to be spirits fresh from God's hands, their smiles divine, and who thought there could be no greater endeavor than devoting all of his powers to a task for which the only reward was a child's whispered thanks and the airy touch of her pure lips—shaken, unsure of what had just happened.

He picked up the book, still warm from Alice Liddell's touch, not knowing that it was as close to her as he'd ever be again.

PART ONE

CHAPTER 1

THE QUEENDOM had been enjoying a tentative peace ever since the time, twelve years earlier, when unbridled bloodshed spattered the doorstep of every Wonderlander. The civil war hadn't been the longest in all of recorded history, but no doubt it was one of the bloodiest. Those who had entered a little too quickly into the carnage and destruction had trouble adapting to life during peacetime. When hostilities ceased, they ran amok on the streets of Wonderland's capital city, looting and pillaging Wondertropolis until Queen Genevieve had them rounded up and shipped off to the Crystal Mines—a spiderweb-like network of tunnels carved in a far-off mountainside, where those unwilling to abide by the laws of decent society lived in windowless dormitories and labored to excavate crystal from the unforgiving mountain. Even after these people were taken off the streets, the peace that settled on Wonderland was nothing like that which had existed before the war. A third of Wondertropolis' quartz-like buildings had to be rebuilt. The smooth turquoise amphitheater had suffered damage in an air raid, as had the public works towers and spires sporting fiery, reflective pyrite skin. But the scars of war are not always visible. Although Queen Genevieve ruled her queendom judiciously, with care for the well-being of her people, the monarchy had been forever weakened. The coalition of Diamond, Club, and Spade dynasties that made up Parliament was falling apart. The matriarchs of the families were jealous of Genevieve's power. Each thought she could rule Wonderland better than the queen. Each watched and waited for an opportunity to wrest control from her, keeping a none-too-friendly eye on the other families in case they happened to make a move first.

After twelve years, the daily life of Wonderland had returned to what might be called "normal." Were you to walk Wondertropolis' gleaming streets, enjoying the sight of its jagged crystal buildings and shop fronts, were you to pass the stations where Wonderlanders arrived for work in sleek glass tubes hovering on cushions of air, were you to stop and purchase a tarty tart from a vendor and relish its tarty tart flavor bursting upon your tongue, you would never have known that in certain back alleys, on certain open plains, precautions were being taken: regiments of card soldiers put through

military maneuvers, transports produced, weapons of attack and defense designed and tested. And you would not have been alone.

~

Entertaining no thoughts of war, Princess Alyss Heart stood on the balcony of Heart Palace with her mother, Queen Genevieve. The city was in the midst of a jubilant gala. From the Everlasting Forest to the Valley of Mushrooms, Wonderlanders had come to celebrate the seventh birthday of their future queen, who, as it happened, was bored out of her wits. Alyss knew she could do a lot worse than be Queen of Wonderland, but even a future monarch doesn't always want to do what she is supposed to do—like sit through hours of pageantry. She would rather have hidden with her friend Dodge in one of the palace towers, dropping jollyjellies from an open window and watching them splat on the guards below. Dodge wouldn't like the jollyjelly bit—guardsmen deserved better treatment, he'd say—but that would only make it more fun.

Where *was* Dodge anyway? She hadn't seen him all morning, and it wasn't nice to avoid the birthday girl on her birthday. She searched for him among the Wonderlanders gathered to watch the Inventors' Parade on the cobbled lane below. No sign of him. He was probably off doing something fun; whatever it was *had* to be more fun than being stuck here, forced to watch Wonderlanders show off their silly contraptions. Bibwit Harte, the royal tutor, had explained to her that most of Wonderland took pride in the Inventors' Parade, the one time every year when citizens flaunted their skills and ingenuity before the queen. If Genevieve saw something in the parade that she thought particularly good, she would send it into the Heart Crystal—a thirty-three-foot-tall, fifty-two-foot-wide shimmering crystal on the palace grounds, the power source for all creation. Whatever passed into the crystal went out into the universe to inspire imaginations in other worlds. If a Wonderlander bounced in front of Queen Genevieve on a spring-operated stick with handlebars and footrests and she passed this curious invention into the crystal, before long, in one civilization or another, a pogo stick would be invented.

Still, Alyss wondered, what was the big deal? Having to stand here until her feet hurt—it was punishment.

"I wish Father were here."

"He's due back from Boarderland at any moment," said Queen Genevieve. "But since the rest of Wonderland is here, I suggest you try to enjoy yourself for their sake. That's interesting, don't you think?"

They watched as a man floated down from the sky with what looked like a hollow mushroom cap strapped to his back.

"It's pretty good, I suppose," said Alyss, "but it'd be better if it were *furry*."

And with that, the mushroom contraption was suddenly covered in fur, its inventor falling to the ground with a thump.

Queen Genevieve frowned.

"He's late," Alyss said. "He promised he'd be here. I don't understand why he had to make a trip so close to my birthday."

There *were* reasons, as the queen well knew. Intelligence had indicated that they may have already waited too long. Unconfirmed reports suggested Redd was growing more powerful, outfitting her troops for an attack, and Genevieve was no longer sure that her military could provide adequate defense. She was as keen as Alyss for King Nolan's return, but she had determined to enjoy the day's festivities.

"Ooh, look at that," she said, pointing at a woman wiggling as she walked so as to keep a large hoop swinging round and round her waist. "That looks diverting."

"It'd be more fun if it had fountains of water coming out of it," Alyss said, and immediately the hoop was spurting water from tiny holes all along its surface, the surprised inventor still wiggling to keep it swinging round and round.

"Birthday or not, Alyss," Queen Genevieve said, "I don't think it's nice to show off."

The fur on the first-ever parachute vanished. The fountains of water on the newly invented hula hoop dried up. The power of Alyss' imagination had made them appear and disappear. Imagination was an important part of life in Wonderland, and Alyss had the most powerful imagination ever seen in a seven-year-old Wonderlander. But as with any formidable talent, Alyss' imagination could be used for good or ill, and the queen saw mild reasons for concern. Hardly one revolution of the Thurmite moon had passed since Alyss' last incident: Impatient with young Jack of Diamonds for some childish indiscretion, she'd imagined his trousers filled with slick, squiggling gwormmies. Jack of Diamonds had said he "felt something funny," looked down, and saw that his trousers were moving, alive. He'd been having nightmares ever since. Alyss claimed not to have done it on purpose, which may or may not have been true, Genevieve couldn't tell. Alyss didn't yet have full control of her imaginative powers, but the girl would say anything to get out of trouble.

"You will be the strongest queen yet," she told her daughter. "Your imagination will be the crowning achievement of the land. But Alyss, you must work hard to develop it according to the guiding principles of the Heart dynasty—love, justice, and duty to the people. An undisciplined imagination is worse than no imagination at all. It can do more harm. Remember what happened to your aunt Redd."

"I know," Alyss said sulkily. She had never met her aunt Redd, but she'd heard stories about the woman for as long as she could remember. She didn't bother trying to understand it all; it was *history*—boring boring boring. But she knew that to be like Aunt Redd wasn't good.

"Now that's enough lecturing for one princess' birthday," Queen Genevieve said. She clapped her hands and the parachute and hula hoop passed into the Heart Crystal, much to the joy of their inventors.

An empty pair of King Nolan's boots floated out from behind the balcony door and began to dance in front of the brooding princess.

Queen Genevieve, watching yet another extraordinary display of her daughter's imagination, said, "Alyss."

Something in her tone made the girl stop what she was doing. The boots thudded to the ground, still.

"It's all in your head," the queen sighed. "Remember that, love. Whatever happens, it's all in your head."

It was both a warning and an expression of hope: Queen Genevieve, aware of the dark forces at work somewhere in the wastes of the Chessboard Desert, knew that joy and happiness didn't last forever in Wonderland; sooner or later the queendom would come under attack, and it would require all of Alyss' imaginative powers—and then some—to ensure its survival.

CHAPTER 2

TWO DAYS into their return trek through Outerwilderbeastia, King Nolan and his men urged their spirit-danes at
a gallop along a narrow mountain ridge. Four-legged creatures with bodies that looked vaguely bulldoggish from the
front and tapered to a thin, tail-less rear end, spirit-danes
had flat faces with slow, blinking eyes, fist-sized nostrils, and
a quizzical mouth. They were not the fastest means of getting
around Wonderland, but they proved the most efficient mode
of travel to and from Boarderland—being the only creatures
capable of carrying a man, as well as gifts of wine and crystal,
while making decent time over the irregular terrain of Outerwilderbeastia.

This had not been a journey King Nolan desired to make.
He had done it for the good of the queendom. A last-minute

negotiation with King Arch of Boarderland to establish an alliance between their two nations against Redd. It was of course Genevieve's rightful place to conduct all negotiations, but she had thought it prudent to send her husband in her stead: Boarderland was a kingdom; King Arch didn't believe in queendoms. The seat of power, he often proclaimed, was no place for a female.

King Arch greeted Nolan as if the mere sight of him brought on fatigue. "Why should I form an alliance?" he asked after Nolan had just explained the reasons. "Redd doesn't dare attack Boarderland."

"Because we're neighbors, Arch. If Redd does take control of Wonderland, she's likely to grow more ambitious and look to Boarderland as her next target."

"Oh, I think I can defend myself against any *female*, even without an alliance." Arch snapped his fingers and a shapely courtesan emerged from behind a glittering curtain to massage his shoulders. "Besides, it rather goes against my principles— partnering with a queendom. I don't want the peculiar ways of your nation influencing Boarderland's female population. The last thing I need is the seeds of some so-called greater purpose being planted in their feminine heads, as if they should 'do more with their lives' than is required for their marital administrations."

"I'd be more concerned about the influence a Redd-controlled Wonderland would have on your *entire* population," said King Nolan.

King Arch made a sound deep within his throat, a doubtful grunt. "Frankly, Nolan, I don't have the highest regard for you, letting yourself be bossed around by your wife as you do."

King Nolan did not feel—nor had he ever felt—bossed around by Genevieve. He loved his wife, in part, *because* of her strength, her estimable handling of the very responsibilities that Arch thought should fall only on a man's shoulders. To Nolan, nothing could compare to the love of his kind, strong-willed queen.

"So," Arch said, "you'd receive military support to help defend against your enemies and what would I get? What benefits would the people of Boarderland be able to expect as a result of this proposed nation-coupling?"

"I am prepared to offer you crystal-mining rights within our borders, twice-yearly payments of a million howlite gemstones, and the use of our military should the need for it ever arise."

King Arch stood; the meeting was over. "I'll consider it and send word of my decision in the next week or so."

~

Eager to arrive back at Heart Palace in time for Alyss' birthday, Nolan made a race of the journey with his men, riding at full speed without stopping for rest or food. They were still half a day's ride away. The mountain ridge was far behind them now and they galloped across a dusty plain. At the crest of a hill, with Heart Palace visible on the horizon,

Nolan reined in his spirit-dane. A gust of wind carried with it—or so he imagined, for he was quite a distance from the palace—the sounds of revelry, music, and laughter. His men came to a stop beside him.

"What is it, my lord?"

"She'll never forgive me for missing the party."

"I think the queen would forgive you anything, my lord."

"Not the queen. The princess."

"Oh. With her you'll have trouble."

The men laughed. With Alyss, King Nolan would indeed have trouble, but it would be a pleasant sort of trouble. Even in her pouts, he thought his daughter a delightful creature.

"Hi-yah!" With a refreshed sense of urgency, the king prodded his spirit-dane onward, toward home and family.

CHAPTER 3

BIBWIT HARTE gathered together books and papers in preparation for his charge's lessons the next day. Now that she had reached her seventh birthday, Alyss would begin her formal training to become queen.

"And being a queen isn't easy," muttered Bibwit Harte. "The position comes with tremendous responsibilities. One has to study law and government and ethics and morality. One must train the imagination for the promotion of peace and harmony and the precepts of White Imagination, because Black Imagination is not what anybody wants at all, oh no. And if *that* isn't enough, there's the Looking Glass Maze to get through." Bibwit Harte, alone in the library at Heart Palace, recited from an ancient Wonderland text, *In Queendom Speramus*: "*A unique Looking Glass Maze exists for every would-be queen. The maze must be successfully navigated by the would-be queen if she is to reach her imagination's full potential and thus be fit to rule."* The tutor returned to his usual tone: "And where the Looking Glass Maze is, only the caterpillars know."

Mr. Bibwit Harte was an albino, seven feet tall, with bluish green veins pulsing visibly beneath his skin, and ears a bit large for his head—ears so sensitive that he could hear someone whispering from three streets away. He was rather intelligent, but he had the habit of talking to himself, which more than a few Wonderlanders found strange, particularly members of the Diamond, Spade, and Club families, not one of whom had ever forgiven him for his decades-long schooling of the Heart daughters as opposed to their own. Not that Bibwit paid much attention to what others thought of him. He talked to himself because there weren't many people as learned as he, and he liked to talk to learned people.

"Happy birthday to you, happy birthday to you!"

Bibwit threw open a pair of doors leading to the royal gardens, and the chorus of voices might have become painfully loud to his finicky ears if it had been any other song sung to any other princess. But he found nothing too much when it was in appreciation of Alyss. Among the assembled guests being led in song by the garden's sunflowers, tulips, and daisies, Bibwit spied various members of the suit families (he bowed to the Lady of Diamonds when he caught her eye) and General Doppelgänger, commander of the royal army, who suddenly split in two and became the twin figures of Generals Doppel and Gänger, so as to lend two voices to the song instead of one. Bibwit bowed to the blue caterpillar—that oracle of oracles, sage of sages, wisest of the wise—sitting curled in a corner of the garden, puffing on his hookah while a gwynook—a small creature with a penguin's body and an old man's wrinkled face—waddled about on his back.

"Waddling is an underappreciated art," Bibwit heard the gwynook say to the caterpillar. "Say, let me have a puff of that."

"Ahem hmm hem," grumbled the caterpillar, who never shared his pipe with gwynooks, even on the happy occasion of Alyss Heart's birthday. "Smoking's bad for you."

"It is indeed a special day when a caterpillar comes all the way from the Valley of Mushrooms to partake in the celebration," Bibwit Harte murmured, watching two spirit-danes pull a giant cake toward Alyss, a host of tuttle-birds glowing and flapping their wings in place of candles. Next to the birthday girl stood the queen, and behind her, Hatter Madigan, leading member of Wonderland's elite security force known as the Millinery, and the queen's personal bodyguard. Carrying the backpack common among Millinery men, wearing a long coat and bracelets, and the top hat he took off only in times of violence, he alone in the crowd remained stoic, alert.

The song ended. The guests applauded, and Queen Genevieve said, "Make a wish, Alyss."

"Besides wishing that Father had never gone on his trip," Alyss declared, "I wish to be queen for a day."

Her mother's crown lifted into the air and floated toward her head. The guests laughed—all except Hatter Madigan, who never laughed.

"Hatter Madigan," sighed Bibwit, "even *you* should relax sometimes and enjoy yourself."

"You'll be queen soon enough," Genevieve said to her daughter. The queen's imagination was not exactly weak, and the crown floated back onto her head.

Alyss noticed Bibwit standing at the library doors and decided to have a little fun. It was the least she could do until she found Dodge. She whispered, "Do you want some cake, Bibwit Harte?"

The tutor nodded and she brought him a slice of cake on an edible chocolate plate.

"Happy un-birthday to you," she said. "It's raisin-butterscotch with peanut butter, marshmallows, and gummy wads. It's the best."

Bibwit stared at the cake. "Yes, well . . . thank you, Alyss. But I'm afraid you won't be so nice to me after we begin our lessons tomorrow."

"I won't *need* any lessons," Alyss said. "I'll just imagine that I know everything and then I *will*, so you won't have to give them to me."

Bibwit picked at the cake, examining it, squinting at it. "My dear," he said, "you can't imagine everything because you don't know everything there is to imagine. That's precisely where the lessons come in. Trust me, I know what I'm talking about. I taught your grandmother and your mother when they were your age, and yes, I did try to teach the woman who shall not be named—namely, your aunt Redd—but we won't go into *that*."

Not at all sure that it was the right thing to do, Bibwit put a bit of cake into his mouth. He chewed once, twice, but something was amiss; the stuff in his mouth felt like it was *moving*. Alyss started to laugh. Bibwit spat the half-chewed cake into the palm of his hand and saw that it wasn't cake at all; it had turned into a handful of gwormmies.

"Got you!" Alyss shouted, and ran away.

The gwormmy prank hadn't been nice, not nice in the least, but Bibwit was willing to forgive. Alyss was young, she needed to be *taught*. She might remind him of Redd in certain things, but he was confident that she wouldn't grow up to be like her. He wouldn't let it happen. Besides, he couldn't blame Alyss for needing to occupy herself somehow. There were hardly any children her age at the palace.

He cast a last gaze about the gardens. The blue caterpillar had slithered off somewhere. Frog, the palace's internal messenger, was hopping about in his finest clothes, no doubt longing for some guest to entrust him with a message for another guest. Generals Doppel and Gänger were again in one body and they, or rather he, General Doppelgänger, was conversing with Sir Justice Anders, head of the palace guardsmen. Hatter Madigan, following the queen like a protective shadow, remained as unexpressive as ever.

Bibwit retired to the library, where picture books from Alyss' earliest youth sat on shelves next to a ten-volume chronicle of the civil war, written from various points of view—the card soldiers who'd fought on the front lines; members of the chessmen militia; General Doppelgänger and his sergeants; even Queen Genevieve herself. It came complete with lists of those killed in each of the battles and explanations of the strategies that had called for the sacrifice of Wonderlander lives. Bibwit took down the first volume of the chronicle and set it with the other books and papers he'd collected for Alyss' lessons. The book contained a catalog of atrocities committed by Redd—torture, the slaughtering of prisoners, mass graves. The tutor had always viewed Redd's fall into the diabolical as *his* fault, a failure in her education.

"It's never too soon for a future queen to become familiar with the uglier contingencies of ruling a land," he said to himself.

CHAPTER 4

KING NOLAN and his men left Outerwilderbeastia behind. They passed through a narrow stretch of the Everlasting Forest and were stampeding through the eastern edge of Wondertropolis, the most rural area of the capital, home to farmers and those favoring the quiet country life, when their spirit-danes stopped and reared up on their hind legs, agitated. Speckled across the tranquil landscape, looking harmless, and partly camouflaged by the day's lengthening shadows, were Redd's undealt card soldiers, lying flat one on top of another, each deck fifty-two soldiers thick, awaiting orders.

"Redd's decks are stacked."

So whatever King Arch decided, it would no longer matter; Wonderland didn't have the luxury of waiting for his answer.

"We have to warn the palace," said King Nolan.

One of his men removed a looking glass communicator from his saddlebag and began tapping out a coded message on its keyboard. If the soldier had had time to hit the Send button, his message would have appeared on a crystal viewer in the Security Oversight Room of Heart Palace. But with a sound akin to the metal blades of scissors rapidly opening and closing, an unseen deck hidden in nearby underbrush fanned out and surrounded the king and his men. The air filled with adrenaline-induced war cries from Redd's soldiers, agony-infused moans from the throats of King Nolan's men. The looking glass communicator fell against a rock and shattered, its owner dead before the device hit the ground.

The Wonderlanders were outnumbered five to one. At the center of the skirmish, slashing his sword this way and that, was King Nolan, still atop his trusted spirit-dane when a figure in a scarlet cloak passed through the fighting, untouched, and stabbed him through the heart with her pointed scepter.

"My queen . . ." he moaned, slumping into death, blood leaking from the corners of his mouth. "My queen . . ."

CHAPTER 5

GOT HIM, *I got him, I got him!* A laughing Alyss left Bibwit Harte frowning at the half-eaten gwormmies in his hand and ran into the palace's Issa Room, where (finally!) she found Dodge Anders standing to attention, waiting for her. He looked as if he would have waited for her all his life, if necessary.

"I was wondering where you were," she said, breathless. "I thought you were ignoring me."

"I had to get you a present, didn't I? Why're you running?"

"No reason."

"Uh-huh." Dodge knew she must have been up to something, she was always up to something, but he let it go. He handed her a small box tied with red ribbon and bowed. "Happy birthday, Princess."

"Cut it out."

Alyss didn't like her best friend bowing to her and he knew it. Hadn't she told him so countless times, saying she didn't care if he was a commoner, she just didn't want him doing it? He was her elder by three years and four months. Did he like bowing to a younger girl? And what was so bad, or lowly, about being a commoner anyway? It gave Dodge the freedom to venture out beyond the palace grounds, and Alyss wouldn't have minded *that*. For all her rebellion and free spirit, she had never been outside the luxurious confines of Heart Palace.

She opened the present and stared down at a gleaming, sharp, triangular-shaped tooth resting on a bed of puff.

"Jabberwock tooth," Dodge said.

"You didn't kill the beast yourself, I hope?"

Jabberwocky were huge, ferocious creatures living in the Volcanic Plains—a land of active volcanoes, lava rivers, and geysers of noxious gas, extremely dangerous for any Wonderlander to enter. But you never could tell what Dodge might do. Ever since the age of three, when he toddled into the coat of his father's guardsman uniform and saluted, the direction of his life had been known. Dodge wanted nothing more than to be like his father, Sir Justice Anders, who had distinguished himself with his bravery in the civil war and been awarded his current position by the queen herself. Dodge now stood before Alyss in his own guardsman uniform, complete with fleur-de-lis badge.

"No, I didn't kill the jabberwock," he said. "I bought that in a shop."

"I'll keep it forever," Alyss said.

She slipped the tooth onto her necklace. She had grown up with Dodge, couldn't remember a time in her life when he *hadn't* been her partner in adventure. By her bed, she kept a holographic crystal that showed him, at four years old, kissing her cheek as she sat in her royal baby carriage. Officers of the court stood frowning in the background. What their problem was, Alyss never understood, but she cherished the crystal all the same.

Dodge became embarrassed whenever she showed it to him, so she showed it to him often. He knew why the court officers were frowning: the importance of class distinctions, of consorting with your own kind. Alyss might not care about such stuff, but Sir Justice had explained the situation to his son and Dodge understood that part of being a successful guardsman meant abiding by what was considered *proper*, by not allowing his affections for anybody—especially Alyss—to compromise his duty.

"You can never marry the princess, Dodge," Sir Justice had explained, sympathetic, even a little proud that the princess had taken a liking to his son. "She will one day be your queen. You can show your affection by serving her to the best of your ability, but she has to marry someone from a suit family, and Jack of Diamonds is the only boy of proper rank close to her age. I'm sorry, Dodge, but you and the princess . . . it's not in the cards."

"I understand, Father." But this had been only half true; Dodge's head understood, his heart did not.

"Don't you have to practice any military exercises?" Alyss asked now.

"I can always use more practice, my princess."

"Stop calling me that. You know I don't like it."

"I can never forget who and what you are, my princess."

Alyss clicked her tongue. Sometimes Dodge's seriousness could be tiresome. "I have a new military exercise for you," she said. "We must pretend we're enjoying ourselves at a party. Music is playing, there are mounds of delicious food, and you and I begin to dance." She held out her hand.

Dodge hesitated.

"Come on."

He put an arm around Alyss' waist and moved with her in gentle circles. He had never touched the princess before—not like this. She smelled of sweet earth and powder. It was a clean, delicate smell. Did all girls smell like this or only princesses? A potted sunflower in the corner of the room began to serenade them.

"This isn't a military exercise," he said, making a weak attempt to free himself.

"I order you not to go anywhere. While we're dancing, Redd and her soldiers crash into the room. It's a surprise attack. People are screaming and running. People are *dying*. But you stay calm. You promise to protect me."

"You know I'd protect you, Alyss." He felt warm all over

and a little dizzy. He was holding the princess close. He could feel her breath on his cheek. He was the luckiest boy in the queendom.

"And then you battle Redd and her soldiers."

He didn't want to let her go, but he did, brandishing his sword. He jousted this way and that with his imaginary foes, spinning and ducking in imitation of Hatter Madigan, whose military workouts he often watched and studied.

"And after many close calls," Alyss narrated, "your life in danger every second, you defeat the soldiers and stab your sword into Redd."

Dodge looked the picture of intensity as he plunged his sword into the air where he envisioned Redd to be. He made a show of eyeing his handiwork, his vanquished foes littered on the ground before him. He returned his sword to its scabbard.

"I'm saved," Alyss continued, "but I'm shaken by what I've just witnessed. You calm my nerves by dancing with me."

The sunflower in the corner again began to serenade. Without hesitation this time, Dodge took Alyss and spun her about the room. He had loosened up despite himself, despite what he knew his father would think of his behavior. He was reveling in feelings he should not have allowed himself to feel.

"Will you be my king, Dodge?"

"If it pleases you, Princess," he said, trying to be nonchalant, "I—"

32

"You there, clean my boots!" a voice shouted from the corridor. "Servant, do my bidding!"

Dodge immediately stepped away from Alyss, stood stiffly to attention.

"Wash my waistcoat, make my bed, powder my wig!" the voice shouted.

Ten-year-old Jack of Diamonds, heir to the Diamond family estate, marched into the Issa Room. He stopped when he saw Alyss and Dodge.

"What are you doing?" Alyss asked him.

"I'm practicing being a royal personage. What does it look like I'm doing?"

Jack of Diamonds would have been a handsome boy if not for his bullying personality and for the fact that he had the biggest, roundest rear end in Wonderland. It looked like he carried an inflated cushion in the back of his trousers. He also had the silly pretension of wearing a long, white powdered wig because he'd heard that the well-to-do in other worlds wore powdered wigs. He eyed the discarded box and ribbon on the floor. He eyed the jabberwock tooth hanging from Alyss' necklace.

"The question is," he said, "what are *you two* doing?"

Neither Alyss nor Dodge answered.

"Playing mushy, mushy love with the princess, are we?" He laughed and approached Alyss, touched the jabberwock tooth hanging at her throat.

"Leave that alone," Dodge warned.

"Sweet Princess, when we're older and you're my wife, I'll

give you presents of diamonds and more diamonds, not the rotten teeth of stupid animals."

"Just go away," Alyss pleaded.

"Leave her alone," said Dodge. "I mean it."

Jack of Diamonds turned to face this son of a guardsman. He put a finger to his lips and pretended to be deep in thought. "Let me see now . . . ah, I've got it. Eenie meenie miney *moo*, I'm more important than *you*."

Dodge flung out his fists and knocked Jack to the floor, left him splayed there with his wig askew, looking not at all like a person of high rank. Dodge braced himself for a fight, but Jack scrambled to his feet and ran out of the room and down the corridor toward the royal gardens.

"We have to get out of here if we don't want to be in trouble," Alyss said. "He'll tell his father on you."

It wasn't at all the sort of thing a guardsman should do, but Dodge grabbed Alyss' hand and led her to a life-size sculpture of Queen Issa, Alyss' great-grandmother. He pressed on the ruby at the front of Issa's crown and a door in the wall appeared, opening on to one of the many servants' tunnels that ran under Heart Palace.

"Where're we going?" Alyss asked.

"You'll see."

Hand in hand they raced off down the tunnel, past guardsmen headed to their watch-posts, past servants carrying platters of jollyjellies, fried wondercrumpets, and tarty tarts.

CHAPTER 6

IF YOU'RE a queen, even the most lighthearted conversation on a festive day can lead to a discussion of troublesome topics. In the royal gardens, Genevieve found herself talking to the Lady of Clubs and the Lady of Spades about the unwelcome influence of Black Imagination societies on Wonderland's youth.

"I hear they drink jabberwocky blood," said the Lady of Spades.

"Well, I think it's disgusting that children today take for granted the peace and harmony that currently exist in the queendom," declared the Lady of Clubs. "It's as if they want to destroy the current state of things just for the sake of destroying it."

"We have members of the Millinery working undercover,

infiltrating many of the groups," Queen Genevieve informed them.

"Really?"

The Lady of Clubs encouraged any endeavor that might weaken Genevieve's grip on the throne. She smiled at the queen and decided, not without reluctance, to end her sponsorship of Black Imagination societies. It was as she came to this determination that Jack of Diamonds, running along a heart-shaped passage toward the gardens, suddenly found himself lifted off his feet, his wig again knocked askew. He wriggled to get free, his feet pedaling the air.

"What's the rush, little fellow?" asked Bibwit Harte. "What seems to be the trouble?"

"You're the little fellow!" Jack said.

"Hmm, well . . . in the grand scheme of the cosmos, I *am* a little fellow. We're all quite little, if you think about it that way. Good point, Jack."

Jack didn't know what the pale scholar was talking about and didn't care. "Unhand me, you tutor!"

With his feet once again on solid ground, trying to right his wig but succeeding only in turning it almost completely backward, Jack of Diamonds explained how he had been minding his own business when, all of a sudden, Dodge jumped out from behind a bookcase, knocked him to the ground and dirtied his pantaloons. Jack had only meant to rescue the princess, whom Dodge the commoner had been trying to kiss, and now he was on his way to tell his father and

Queen Genevieve so that they'd deport Dodge to the Crystal Mines, which surely wasn't too great a punishment for such serious crimes.

"Those *are* serious crimes," agreed Bibwit Harte. "But, Jack, don't you think it's time you started handling the responsibilities of your rank?"

The boy grew suspicious. "Maybe."

"At your age, you shouldn't need your father's help administering punishments. I will hunt out the culprit and bring him to you. Go and enjoy a nice bit of tarty tart and say nothing of this terrible incident to anyone until I return. You will surprise the queen with your judicious punishment of Dodge, I'm sure."

Bibwit watched the boy strut up the passageway, his round rear jiggling left, right, left, right, all the way to the royal gardens. With his ultra-sensitive ears, Bibwit Harte had heard everything that had happened in the Issa Room. Only when he was positive that Jack would say nothing of the trifling matter to the queen or the Lord of Diamonds, only when he heard the boy greedily munching on a tarty tart, did he set out after Alyss and Dodge. Cocking his head, as might a dog hearing a strange, high-pitched noise, he listened to far-off sounds. He heard a husband and wife discussing their upcoming safari in Outerwilderbeastia. He heard a shopkeeper totaling up his accounts three streets away. And then he heard a mishmash of humble voices. Using his hearing as a guide, he made his way out of the palace.

~

Alyss and Dodge ran through the servants' tunnels, Alyss yelping with laughter and quite enjoying herself, Dodge all business, until he shouldered open a door and they stepped out into the light of Wondertropolis. For the first time in her life, Alyss Heart was outside the grounds of the palace.

"Whoa."

It was a festive scene: Wonderlanders dancing, playing musical instruments, and acting out mini-theatricals. A shopkeeper spotted Alyss and, with respectful expressions of good wishes for her health, dropped to his knees. Seeing who was among them, Wonderlander after Wonderlander followed his example and, in less than half a minute, Alyss and Dodge were standing at the center of a bowing, reverent audience.

"Uh, yeah," Dodge said in a loud voice to no one in particular, "she looks a lot like Princess Alyss, doesn't she? But her name's Stella. She's nobody."

The Wonderlanders lifted their heads and turned to one another. How could this beautiful girl with her soft eyes and her black hair styled like the princess' *not* be Alyss Heart? Their confusion vanished with the appearance of Bibwit Harte. If the royal tutor was after her, then the girl had to be Princess Alyss.

At the sight of Bibwit, Alyss shouted, "Run!" But the scholarly albino was pretty fast and would have caught

up with them in no time if his robe hadn't sprouted the fluorescent feathers of a tuttle-bird, ballooned around him, and lifted him into the air.

"Alyss, noooo!"

Dodge glanced back. "What—?"

"I didn't exactly mean to do it," said Alyss. This was not how she should have been using her imagination and she knew it. "I just didn't want him to catch us." She'd had the faintest glimmer of an imagining to slow Bibwit down and then—bam!—it became a reality.

Bibwit dropped from the sky into mud-choked grass, slipping and sliding as he tried to get out of it, but Alyss and Dodge were already gone. They ran down brick lanes, cut through alleys, and crossed thoroughfares. Eventually, the polished shop fronts and glistening streets of the capital city gave way to a wood. The trees and flowers chirped in surprise at the sight of the princess, making sure to look as in-full-bloom as possible while moving their branches and petals out of her way as she and Dodge ran, jumping over rocks and creek beds until they came to a cliff and could go no farther. Alyss looked down from the vast height of the rock face. Below her stretched a body of water surrounded on all sides by a crystal barrier.

"What is it?" she whispered, partly in awe and partly because she didn't want Bibwit to track her with his hearing.

"It's called the Pool of Tears," Dodge answered, also

whispering. "They say that if you fall in, it takes you out of Wonderland, but no one knows for sure. People have gone in, but nobody's ever come back."

Alyss said nothing.

"People sometimes come here and wait for the return of those who've fallen in. They cry and let their tears drop into the water. That's how it got its name."

Alyss stared down at the water. It wasn't fair. How could the world be so sad on her birthday? She tried to imagine what she'd do if Dodge or one of her parents fell into the Pool of Tears. What would life be like without them? But she couldn't do it. Imagination failed her.

"We should go back," Dodge said.

"Yes, yes," said the trees and shrubs closest to them.

People would come looking for them, Alyss knew, maybe even Hatter himself. She could not escape being who and what she was.

"Maybe if we go back and act as though nothing has happened," she said, "it'll be like nothing *did*."

Dodge lent her his guardsman coat—no small gesture considering what it meant to him, Alyss knew. She wore it over her head like a shawl to avoid being recognized by Wonderlanders, part of a disguise that also included a caterpillar mask she imagined for herself.

To prevent Bibwit from tracking them, she and Dodge didn't speak during the journey back to the palace—a journey that seemed much shorter than their escape had been. Sooner than soon, they were making their way along the row of glorious fountains that led up to the front gate. Alyss could see the iridescent Heart Crystal beyond the locked entrance, giving off its white clouds of imaginative energy.

"Meow." A kitten with golden fur rubbed against her leg.

"Where did you come from?" She took the kitten in her arms. It wore a ribbon for a collar, and attached to the ribbon was a card with a simple greeting: HAPPY BIRTHDAY, ALYSS! "He knew me even through my disguise."

"Who's it from?"

"It doesn't say."

Dodge looked around to see who might have been so generous, but of the many Wonderlanders enjoying the festivities outside the palace, no one paid them any attention.

"It's smiling," he said. "I didn't know cats could smile."

"He's smiling because he's happy to be with me." Alyss wouldn't put her new pet down.

The guards at the front gate recognized Dodge Anders but said that they couldn't give entry to his friend without proper authority. Alyss took off her mask.

"Our humble apologies, Princess," said the guards, promptly unbolting the gate. "We didn't expect to see you. Beg your pardon."

"I will pardon you on one condition," Alyss announced. "You must tell no one that you saw me and Dodge outside the palace. Can I rely on you to say nothing?"

"Of course, Princess."

"Not a word."

The guards bowed. Alyss and Dodge entered the palace. Once the gate was locked behind them, the kitten jumped from the princess' arms and bounded down the hall.

"Kitty, no!"

But the kitten ran and ran, as if it knew exactly where it was going and had things to do, appointments to keep. Which, in fact, it did.

CHAPTER 7

QUEEN GENEVIEVE slipped away to her private rooms for a moment's rest, leaving the guests to occupy themselves. Without a word, Hatter Madigan followed and stood guard in the hall.

The queen's quarters consisted of three interconnected salons. One of these was filled with overstuffed couches and giant pillows to swaddle Her Highness in lazy comfort; another was a dressing room, storehouse for the queen's many royal outfits; and the third was a bathroom, outfitted with tasseled curtains made of a fabric more voluptuous than any found outside the queendom.

Genevieve studied her reflection in the bathroom looking glass. Her daughter's birthday always made her feel old. It wasn't very long ago that she herself had begun her training to become queen. She saw lines at the corners of her eyes and on both sides of her mouth that hadn't been there a year earlier. It was a shame that imagination had its limits, that it could affect the physical realm only so far and she couldn't imagine herself young again.

What was that smell? A familiar, spicy-sweet aroma. She saw a plume of blue smoke and followed it into the sitting room, where she found the blue caterpillar coiled dreamily around his hookah and puffing away. Ordinarily, Genevieve would have been angry to discover anyone, let alone a giant larva, in her private sanctuary without having been invited. But the caterpillar was no ordinary giant larva. There were eight caterpillars in Wonderland, each a different color. They were the great oracles of the region, already old at the dawn of the queendom. They served the Heart Crystal and didn't much care who occupied the throne so long as the crystal remained safe. It was said that they could see the future because they refused to judge it, but lately more and more members of the suit families were shrugging off the caterpillars' prophecies, claiming a reliance on them was nothing more than silly superstition, a remnant from more barbaric times. The caterpillars didn't actively interfere in the workings of the government or in the rivalries among the suit families, but they weren't above letting Genevieve glimpse the future if it concerned the safety of the Heart Crystal, so that she might take action to protect it.

"Thank you for coming today, Caterpillar," she said. "It's

an honor to play host to one so wise. We are all humbly grateful—especially Alyss."

"Ahem hum hum," grumbled the caterpillar, exhaling a cloud of smoke.

The smoke formed the shape of a butterfly with extended wings, then metamorphosed into a confusion of scenes. Genevieve saw a large cat grooming itself. She saw what looked like a lightning bolt. She saw Redd's face. Then the smoke again formed the shape of a butterfly. The butterfly folded its wings and Genevieve awoke on a couch with the smell of stale tobacco in her nostrils. The caterpillar was gone. Hatter Madigan and a walrus in a tuxedo jacket two sizes too small were standing over her.

"You must have fainted, madam," said the walrus-butler. "I will get you some water, madam."

The walrus hurried out of the room. The queen remained silent for several moments, then—

"The blue caterpillar was here."

Hatter Madigan frowned and put a hand to the brim of his top hat. His eyes scanned the room.

"I'm not quite sure *what* he showed me," Genevieve said.

"I will inform General Doppelgänger and the rest of the Millinery. We will prepare a defense for whatever's coming."

Just once, Queen Genevieve would have liked to relax the watchful vigilance she was forced to maintain every hour of every day to ensure Wonderland's safety. The caterpillars' prophecies were always so vague. Sometimes their visions

45

reflected only possibilities, the dark wishes of those who never planned to carry them out. But she couldn't take a chance, not when it concerned Redd.

"Make sure not to alarm our guests," she said.

"Of course." Hatter bowed and left the room.

Genevieve was lucky to have such a bodyguard. Hatter Madigan could swing a blade (or several at once) faster and more accurately than anyone alive. He was nimble, acrobatic. He could flip and tumble through the air without getting hit by a single cannonball spider in an onslaught of cannonball spiders. But even with all of his skills, he could not protect the queen forever. How could he have known that the precautionary measures he was about to take would prove useless, that it was already too late?

CHAPTER 8

*C*HE PARTY had moved to the South Dining Room for tea and most of the guests had returned home. The walrus made his way around the long table, at which sat Queen Genevieve and the suit families.

"Lump of sugar for your tea, madam? A drop of honey for your tea, sir?"

Genevieve smiled politely, not paying much attention to the goings-on. Because of the caterpillar's warning, because King Nolan should have returned hours ago and yet she had received no word from him, she couldn't concentrate. Ah, but here were Alyss and Dodge. What misadventures they'd been getting up to only the spirit of Issa knew.

"Well, well, if it isn't the girl of the hour," she said. "And where have you two been?"

"Nowhere."

Doing her best to look innocent, Alyss took her seat. She flashed Dodge a warning glance—*say nothing*—and he manned his guardsman's post as composedly as he could, across the room from his father. Jack of Diamonds, with tarty tart crumbs on his cheeks, down the front of his waistcoat, and in his wig, glowered at them. He opened his mouth to announce Dodge's punishment just as Bibwit entered, caked in mud and spotted with feathers.

"Bibwit!" gasped Queen Genevieve. "What happened to you?"

"Why, nothing ever so much, I'd say. My robe took on certain—how shall I put it?—*birdish* properties and I found myself floating in the air. Happily, I soon fell into some mud, from which it took a bit of ingenuity to free myself."

Queen Genevieve blinked a moment. "Alyss!"

"I didn't mean to," Alyss said. "Things just started happening—"

Jack of Diamonds leaped up on his chair and pointed a stubby finger at Dodge. "He dared strike my royal person and he kidnapped Princess Alyss, and you can see by the dirt on their shoes that they left the palace! I demand that the commoner be deported to the Crystal Mines!"

The suit families all started talking at once, grumbling their displeasure, guffawing in disbelief.

"Everyone, please calm down," said Queen Genevieve. "Bibwit, is this true?"

"Not precisely," answered Bibwit. "But I'm afraid the children did leave palace grounds momentarily."

"Dodge Anders!" bellowed Sir Justice. "You get over here right this minute!"

"Yes, sir."

"The Crystal Mines!" Jack insisted, biting into a tarty tart and spewing a mouthful of crumbs into the Lady of Spades' hair.

The Lord of Diamonds stood up, as if making an announcement in court. "Good and kind Queen, I expect an increase in lands and tithes as a result of this unfortunate occurrence. My family's name has been tarnished beyond recognition by my son's treatment at the hands of this . . . this . . . boy!" He gestured at Dodge.

The Lady of Clubs whispered into her husband's ear, "His family's name's suffered more harm from his own boy than any other."

The Lord of Clubs snorted with laughter.

"Hear, hear!" demanded the Lord of Spades, rising from his chair. "If the Diamonds receive more land and money, so do we!"

Queen Genevieve was getting a headache. "There will be no increase in lands or tithes for anybody."

The families protested, their voices rising in heated debate. Alyss' kitten trotted into the room.

"My cat!" Alyss cried.

The room went quiet.

"Your—?" Queen Genevieve said, but that was all she got out before a deep rumbling shook the palace, goblets and chandeliers trembled, and the kitten began a gruesome transformation, its limbs stretching and expanding until it stood on two muscled legs, its forelegs having become two lean and powerful arms and its front paws thick, with claws as sharp and long and wide as butcher's knives. Its face remained cat-like, with a flat pink nose, whiskers, and slobbery fangs. This was no adorable little kitten. This was The Cat—Redd's top assassin, part human, part feline.

Before General Doppelgänger or Sir Justice Anders had time to act, before even Hatter Madigan could tumble into blade-spinning action, there came shouts and an explosion from outside the dining room. The heavy double doors blew apart, a wall crumbled, and a horde of Redd's card soldiers charged through the blasted opening with swords raised.

Standing amid the crumbled stone and splinters of wood was a nightmare version of Genevieve, a woman Alyss had never seen before.

"Off with their heads!" the woman screamed. "Off with their stinking, boring heads!"

50

CHAPTER 9

TRAINING THE soldiers had taken time, effort. It disgusted Redd how many fools claimed to be practitioners of Black Imagination but didn't realize the amount of work needed to become halfway decent at it. Or they lacked the ambition, the spurs of vengeance and fuming hatred, that helped Black Imagination flower within them. But these had never been the most disciplined members of the queendom. Not only had Redd been banished from Wonderland years ago, forced to live in a grubby fortress on Mount Isolation in the middle of the Chessboard Desert—acres of icy snow alternating with acres of tar and black rock, forming what looked from the air like a giant chessboard—not only this, but she'd had to piece together a military force out of deserters, mercenaries, cutthroats. A good many of these had been

Twos and Threes in the Wonderland Deck, card soldiers who were little more than bodies to be thrown in front of incoming cannonball spiders and generator orbs, doomed to die. Luckily, Redd also had Fours, Fives, and Sixes at her disposal, and a ragtag group of ex-Wonderlanders who'd never been part of the Deck at all but who hadn't felt at home living in bright, happy Wonderland.

But how many times in the past fistful of years had she toured her training camps in the hope of witnessing the glory of a budding war machine with ranks of well-trained soldiers eager for bloodshed? 347. And how many times had she been disappointed, seeing only misfits engaged in sloppy, inefficient military maneuvers? 346. She once came upon a Six Card, a lieutenant, yelling at some idiot Two who was cradling a cute, fuzzy guinea pig.

"I tell you to think *black* thoughts and you come up with that!?" the lieutenant had screamed. "Is a guinea pig *bad*? Do you consider a guinea pig the representation of all that's evil?"

"Maybe . . . if it's an evil guinea pig?"

The lieutenant and Two Card had eyed the animal, which sat in the soldier's folded arm, twitching its nose, oblivious.

"That is not an evil guinea pig!" the lieutenant had shouted.

Even though she needed every able body she could get, Redd ordered the lieutenant to kill the soldier.

By the force of her vindictive will, as much as by the

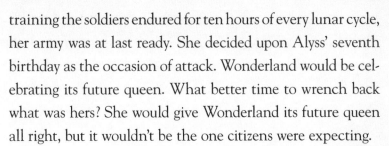

training the soldiers endured for ten hours of every lunar cycle, her army was at last ready. She decided upon Alyss' seventh birthday as the occasion of attack. Wonderland would be celebrating its future queen. What better time to wrench back what was hers? She would give Wonderland its future queen all right, but it wouldn't be the one citizens were expecting.

She sent out seekers—deadly creatures with vulture bodies and fly heads—for aerial reconnaissance. She had bred and trained them herself. Her troops suited up, sharpened blades, loaded crystal shooters and orbs. Redd stood before them on the jagged promontory of Mount Isolation. She spread out her arms as if to embrace all that was bad and threw her voice into the wind.

"Years ago I was told to leave the comforts of home by my own family. I was removed from the power to which I'd been born. All of *you* have had to leave your homes for one reason or another, and together we have suffered through our lives in this barren land. But all that's over now. Today we will return to our birthplace and remake it in our image—which is to say, *my* image. Today we will make history. But . . ." And here she scowled down at her troops massed before her at the foot of the mountain. "If there be any doubters among you, any who are unsure of their willingness to die for my cause, let them step forward now. They will be excused from this day's battle until they are ready to fight, and they can enjoy a nice cup of tea."

Redd then did an extraordinary thing: She smiled. But

her facial muscles weren't accustomed to being used in this way, and the soldiers thought they had never seen her look more fierce. They knew better than to step forward.

"To victory then!" Redd shouted.

~

She had to give her rogue soldiers credit: They might not have been the most imaginative, they might have been novices in Black Imagination, but every single one of them had learned well how to kill. Equally good with swords, knives, spiked clubs, spears, orbs, crystal shooters, they had little trouble getting past the guards that patrolled the edges of the Chessboard Desert, meant to contain her and her kind. And Redd herself made sure that no warning dispatch made it to the palace, rerouting it to oblivion by the power of her imagination. They had little trouble butchering the interior guards. They marched into Wondertropolis, hardly the worse for wear, trailing bloodred clouds and howling winds. At the sight of them, Wonderlanders, who had been celebrating only moments before, abandoned their games and ran off to what security their homes afforded. Every Wonderlander over the age of twelve remembered the devastation of the civil war between Redd and Genevieve. They knew why Redd had come.

The palace appeared in view, the Heart Crystal the only bright light in the gloom Redd had brought with her. She ordered her troops to surround the place. In her imagination's

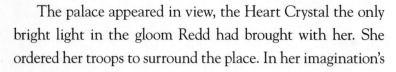

eye she saw her most formidable henchman, in the form of a kitten, padding silently along heart-shaped halls, past watch-posts where guardsmen said, "Hey, look at the cute cat," and, "Here, kitty, kitty." But the kitty was on a mission and didn't stop. He approached the Security Oversight Room and transformed himself from feline to assassin. The Cat smashed through the locked door, surprising the five guards lounging by the controls and monitoring crystals. With a few swings of his powerful arms, he flung them down like so many rag dolls, leaving them slumped and bleeding on the floor. He ripped the master key from the waistband of the highest-ranking guard and inserted it into the security console. He turned the key and flipped release switch after release switch; all over Heart Palace, bolts unlocked, doors and gates swung open, and Redd's troops stormed in. The Cat turned back into a kitten and bounded toward the South Dining Room, where the Hearts and their guests still had no idea what was happening.

Redd entered the palace for the first time since she was a girl—the palace in which she'd been born and spent most of her young life, *her* palace—and all the hurt and resentment she'd tried to keep in check for so many years started to boil over. With every step she took toward her sister, she grew angrier and angrier. So what if she'd been a "bad girl"? So what if she'd experimented with artificial crystal and imagination stimulants? So what if she'd never cared for justice, love, duty to the people, blah blah blah? She was her own person. Why couldn't her parents have respected that and left her alone instead of trying to turn her into the princess she could never be? Why couldn't they have loved her for who she was?

The time she was removed from succession to the throne came back to Redd with the full force of its heart-stopping gall . . .

The ever wise Queen Theodora announced that she could not allow such an unruly daughter to have queenly power. Genevieve was to be queen instead of *her*! Redd's features immediately began to change, to twist and sharpen, so potent was the fury within her. She had always been prone to jealousy, rage, and bitter hatred, but now she had fuel for all three to last a lifetime, and she cultivated them until—

Abandoning herself to her wrath, she slipped into her mother's dressing room.

"Even you cannot take away what is mine by birthright," she snarled and placed a deadly pink mushroom on her mother's tongue. Fed by the queen's saliva, the roots of the fungus worked their way down the sleeping sovereign's throat and strangled her heart. The mushroom cap poked out of her mouth to signify that the heart had stopped beating.

As for her father, she let him live—weak, useless man that he'd always been. After the murder of his beloved Theodora, Tyman went insane, chatting to his dead wife and shuffling aimlessly through the palace. And Redd would have been queen—she would have ruled with all the innate power she possessed—if not for the presumption of her sister. It was

almost laughable: Goody-Two-Shoes Genevieve actually believed that she should be queen. Redd armed her followers and Genevieve organized *hers*. They clashed. People died and homes were destroyed. Redd knew her imagination to be stronger than Genevieve's, but her forces were outnumbered and she didn't have anyone from the Millinery on her side, no one to rival Hatter Madigan. But now she had The Cat. And the seekers. Still, the sting of being roundly defeated and banished from Wonderland by her younger sister had been an embarrassment impossible to live down.

~

Seething with anger, Redd strode toward the South Dining Room, paying no attention to the explosions going off to the left and right of her, the palace guardsmen falling dead at the hands of her soldiers. An orb generator detonated directly in front of her but, without slowing her pace, she walked through the smoke and flames. She stood in the ruins, face-to-face with her sister at last, and screamed her head off.

She would kill them all.

CHAPTER 10

THE FORCE of the blast knocked Alyss over in her chair and she was still on the ground, coughing from dust and debris, when she saw innocent courtiers and civilians attacked by a mob of Redd's card soldiers and fierce ex-Wonderlanders.

"No!"

A hand clamped over Alyss' mouth. It was Dodge. He pulled her under the table with him.

"Keep quiet or they'll get you too. Stay here and don't move."

Alyss wasn't planning on moving, not out from under the table at any rate. Too much was happening and none of it good. But Dodge was with her. She had him. *As long as Dodge and I stay together . . .*

In the quarter-moment after the explosion, General Doppelgänger ran behind a thick curtain and pulled a lever attached to a crank half buried in the floor. The black floor tiles of the room flipped over to reveal an army of white chessmen—knights, rooks, bishops, pawns. The chessmen battled the invading card soldiers, blades swinging and bodies falling. General Doppelgänger split into the twin figures of Generals Doppel and Gänger, and each of *them* split in two, so that now there were two General Doppels and two General Gängers battling Redd's soldiers. Not that Alyss realized that the poisonous-looking woman who'd shouted "Off with their heads!" was her aunt Redd. She hadn't made the connection yet because . . . where was her mother? There, fending off Redd's soldiers two and three at a time. Alyss never knew her mother could fight. She flinched with each near hit Genevieve suffered, watching as the queen imagined new weapons for herself—swords, sabers, spiked clubs—whenever one was knocked from her grip. She was always armed with four weapons at once, her imagination swinging two of them, to fend off attacks from behind.

But why didn't she imagine the card soldiers dead? Alyss tried doing it herself; she closed her eyes and pictured the soldiers piled in a lifeless heap in the center of the room. Bibwit was not there to explain that, by the power of imagination alone, nobody could kill a creature that had the will to live. When Alyss opened her eyes, the room was still in chaos, white pawns and rooks and the occasional knight falling at the hands of the enemy. The cries of pain and defeat still filled her ears.

A body slammed against the tabletop. Dodge put his arm around her, as if that could keep her from harm.

"Don't move, don't move," he whispered.

She huddled against him. She didn't want to watch any more, wanted to bury her face in Dodge's shoulder and lift it up again to find the horrid scene over, everything as it used to be.

Hatter Madigan removed his top hat. Holding it by the brim, he flicked his wrist hard and fast; the hat flattened and divided into a series of S-shaped rotary blades held together at the center. He winged the weapon across the room, the blades spinning and slicing through the enemy before embedding themselves in the mortar of the far wall.

One of Redd's Four Cards pulled the weapon out of the wall. But throwing Hatter's top hat required a technique not easily mastered, and every time the soldier tried employing the quick wrist-flick he'd seen Hatter use, the weapon only clattered to the floor.

Hatter fought his way toward the top hat, flipping and tumbling through the air, his long Millinery coat flaring like a cape. His steel bracelets snapped open and became propeller-blades on the outward side of his wrists. His backpack sprouted blades and corkscrews of various lengths and thicknesses, like an open Swiss Army knife.

The Four Card was growing more desperate as Hatter

approached. The top hat clanged on the floor one last time. Hatter picked up the weapon, examining it to make sure it hadn't been damaged.

"One must learn how to use it," he said. "Here, let me show you the proper way."

These were the last words the soldier ever heard.

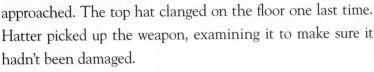

Redd strolled through the mayhem of the battle unharmed. Whenever a white pawn made the mistake of attacking her, she flicked him with a long, bony finger and sent him hurling into the stone walls or the pointed end of someone's spear. It gave her no small pride to see The Cat performing so well in combat, poking fatal holes in chessmen with his claws, easily taking out as many of them as Hatter did card soldiers. She was also pleased to note the speed with which the suit families had fallen into obedience. No sooner had she ordered the removal of everyone's head than the Lord of Diamonds bravely stepped forward, bowed, and said, "Your Majesty, we regret that we've been deprived of your presence for so long and rejoice that you've returned." The Spades and Clubs echoed him with bows and fond regards of their own. So she would let them live. For the moment. Besides, there was something intriguing about the young Diamond boy. He stood under the protective arm of his father, seeming more interested than scared, as if learning all he could from the violence around him. Who knew? He might grow up to be useful.

~

Sir Justice Anders cut and slashed at the invading card soldiers. He rescued several chessmen momentarily overpowered by a band of Two Cards, and when he spotted an opening toward The Cat, he made a run at the creature, sword poised to strike.

Dodge saw what was about to happen. "Watch this," he said to Alyss, proud of his father's skills and bravery.

But The Cat had no trouble dealing with the leader of the palace guard. With the back of his hand, he knocked Sir Justice to the ground, sent the man's sword skittering across the floor and out of reach. The Cat picked up Sir Justice and swiped him with a claw.

"Noooo!" Before Alyss could stop him, Dodge bolted out from under the table, snatched up his father's sword, and attacked The Cat. "Yaah!"

The assassin merely grinned, knocking him to the ground with a light blow. Six white chessmen converged on him and kept him from finishing off the boy.

His right cheek bleeding from the four parallel cuts left by The Cat's claws, Dodge hunched over his dead father, sobbing.

Alyss, alone under the table, also started to cry. Tears had been wetting her cheeks from the beginning, but they'd seemed to belong to somebody else, not a part of her, as if her body were responding to the horrific scene before her brain could comprehend it. Now she entered into grief, shaking with

the force of her sobs. *Sir Justice dead. Dodge abandoning me. Why did Father ever leave? And where's Mother? Where's—*

A face appeared before her: colorless, sunken eyes, ravaged and diseased-looking skin, matted hair.

"Hello, niece."

Alyss felt herself lifted out from under the table, held aloft by her long, black hair.

"So you were to be queen, were you?" the woman snorted, unimpressed.

"Aunt Redd?"

"None other."

"Let her go, Redd." It was Genevieve.

"Are you telling me what to do?" Redd sneered. "Look around. The time for giving orders is over."

"Please. Let her go."

Redd became impatient. "You know I won't. You brought this on yourself, *Queen* Genevieve. I can't afford to leave any Hearts alive—except myself, obviously."

"You can have me instead."

"Stupid sister. I already *have* you. And by the way, if you're still expecting your king, I regret to inform you that he won't be returning home. Ever."

Redd's scepter issued forth a cloud of red smoke, in the middle of which flickered a series of images: King Nolan and his men ambushed as they approached Heart Palace, Redd marching up to the king and killing him with her sharp, knobbly scepter.

"Father!" Alyss cried.

"Oh, my sweet king," Genevieve gasped and sent eighteen steel-tipped cones, each with a point as sharp as a dagger, zooming toward Redd, who lazily raised a hand; the cones froze in midair, then clumped on the floor. The heavy chandelier above Redd's head came loose and fell toward her. Redd made as if to brush a gnat from in front of her face and the chandelier crumbled to dust.

"Is that the best you can do, sister?" Redd scoffed.

A series of double-edged spears cartwheeled toward her. She knocked them aside one by one, bored with her own strength, tired of Genevieve's pestering.

"Playtime's over," she hissed.

Redd pressed her index finger against the ball of her thumb and Alyss started to choke; it felt as if her throat had swollen shut. It didn't matter that her mother had failed, she herself had to think of something, to *imagine* something. But she couldn't focus. A wheel of cheese rolled against Redd's foot. A pair of slippers danced in the air.

Redd laughed. "You were to be queen with an imagination like *that*?"

Alyss thought she was going to explode from lack of air. She fumbled with the jabberwock tooth hanging on her necklace and jabbed the pointed end into Redd's forearm as hard as she could. It stuck.

"Ah!"

Redd released her grip and Alyss dropped to the floor. Before she'd even sucked in one lungful of air, she and her mother were racing down a hall, their feet barely touching the ground. They charged into the queen's private rooms, past the couches and overstuffed chairs, past the royal outfits hanging in the wardrobe, and headed for the bathroom, where—

The Cat stepped in front of them, lunged. It looked like the end for both of them, but something whirred past the princess' head and—thomp!—into The Cat's chest. The Cat fell at their feet. Hatter stepped over the beast and removed his top hat from the fatal wound.

"Take Alyss and go," Queen Genevieve said, pointing at the looking glass. "As far away as possible."

"But, Your Majesty—"

"I'll follow you, if and when I can. You have to keep the princess safe until she's old enough to rule. She's the only chance Wonderland has to survive. Promise me."

Hatter bowed his head. His life's mission was to protect the queen. So long as Genevieve lived, he should remain and fight the enemy. But he understood that Wonderland's future depended on Alyss' survival. The queendom was more important than any single queen. He lifted his eyes to Genevieve's. "I promise," he said.

Genevieve knelt down in front of her daughter. "No matter what happens, I will always be near you, sweetheart. On the other side of the looking glass. And never ever forget who you are. Do you understand?"

"I want to stay with you."

"I know, Alyss. I love you."

"No! I'm staying!" Alyss threw her arms around her mother.

A wall crashed down and there stood Redd with a platoon of card soldiers behind her. "Aw, how sweet. Let's have a group hug," she said, moving toward them, hardly looking like the hugging type.

Hatter grabbed Alyss and jumped into the looking glass. Genevieve smashed the glass with her scepter and turned to face Redd, unable to believe it when, in her peripheral vision, she saw The Cat, on the floor with a gaping hole in his chest, open his eyes. His wound healed and he jumped at her. It all happened in an instant: Genevieve conjured a white bolt of energy from her imagination and thrust it into The Cat, killing him a second time. The card soldiers stepped forward to attack the queen, but Redd stopped them. She yanked the jagged bolt out of The Cat and twirled it like a baton. It turned red in her hand.

"Well, sister, what can I say? I'd be lying if I didn't say that I'm tickled to death to see you go."

She slammed the bolt into the floor. Dozens of black roses sprouted from the point of impact, their thorny stems wrapping themselves around Genevieve, pricking her skin and binding her fast. The rose petals opened and closed, toothy mouths eager for a bite of royal flesh.

"Off with your head," Redd ordered, pulling the energy bolt out of the floor.

"No!" Genevieve struggled against the stems of the roses. Her people would be abandoned to Redd. And Alyss . . . just a child.

Redd swung the bolt hard. Genevieve's head went one way, her body another, and her crown rolled along the floor like a dropped coin. Redd picked up the crown and put it on her own head.

"The queen is dead. Long live the queen . . . me."

The platoon of renegade soldiers cheered.

Redd kicked The Cat where he lay on the floor, tongue lolling in his mouth, the picture of death. "Get up! You still have seven more lives."

The Cat's eyes fluttered open.

"Find Alyss and kill her."

With a wave of her hand, the looking glass was once again whole. The Cat jumped through, in pursuit of the only living Heart besides Redd.

CHAPTER 11

CRYSTAL TRANSPORT, also known as looking glass transport, was not unusual in Wonderland. Most looking glasses served as portals to the Crystal Continuum, a network of byways that enabled any and every Wonderlander to enter through one looking glass and exit from another. Focused looking glasses led to specific destinations (like the corner of Wondertropolis Way and Tyman Street). Unfocused looking glasses allowed travelers to choose their own destinations, provided that there were looking glasses at those destinations out of which they could be reflected. *In Queendom Speramus* states: "As a body underwater tends to rise to the surface, a body entering a looking glass wants to be reflected out." It took practice to stay inside the Continuum and master basic navigational skills. An inexperienced traveler might enter a

looking glass in his own home, thinking to pay a visit to a friend across town, only to be reflected out of a looking glass at his next-door neighbor's house.

The traveler might then enter his next-door neighbor's looking glass, only to be reflected out at the house next door to his next-door neighbor, and so on and so on until he reached his friend across town. Given time and experience, he would be able to make the trip with fewer stops. Covering long distances in the Crystal Continuum was tough, nearly impossible for all but the most experienced traveler. But short trips were within the skill range of everyone.

The looking glass in the queen's private rooms, however, was not linked to the rest of the Continuum. It was a focused glass, to be used for emergencies by the royal family and their intimates. It deposited the traveler deep in a forest. The exit glass was well camouflaged by a tight-lipped shrub.

Having entered the Continuum, Alyss glanced back to see the wavering image of her mother growing progressively smaller among the brilliant, crystalline surfaces along which she and Hatter traveled. Her mother exploded into a thousand fragments, jagged bits of Genevieve fluttering separately—"Mother!"—and then there was nothing but blackness. It seemed like the end of everything. A black void rushed up behind them, as happened when a focused looking glass was destroyed, its path to a specific destination obliterated.

Where was she being taken? *Where, where, where?*

Closer and closer the void came, gaining on them, and then—

She awoke, still in Hatter's arms, her cheek bouncing against his shoulder. Portal Sleep was a side effect of looking-glass transport among the young and inexperienced. Alyss and Hatter were no longer in the Continuum; they raced through a pitch-dark wood. Alyss could see nothing ahead of her or behind, and she wouldn't even have known they were in a wood if she hadn't heard the whispering voices of the trees all around. It started to rain, to thunder and lightning. The wind picked up. How could Hatter see where he was going?

From overhead she heard the sound of screaming, pain-riddled banshees.

"Seekers," Hatter said, more to himself than to Alyss.

Yes, seekers alerting whoever was following them of their location. Because someone or some*thing* was definitely following them. Hatter could hear it speeding toward them through the underbrush, breaking branches and splashing through puddles in its headlong pursuit.

After what felt to Alyss like a lifetime, the Whispering Woods opened onto a wide expanse and they came to a precipice. It took her a second to realize where she was: the cliff overlooking the Pool of Tears, where she and Dodge had stood only a short time earlier. How she wished Dodge were with her now. The water was dark and roiling. All at once she understood.

"No one ever comes back," she said, looking forlornly into the pool.

"But *you* will," said Hatter. "You have to."

Which was when The Cat burst into the clearing and sprang at them, his arms extended. Hatter jumped. The Cat snagged the sleeve of the princess' birthday dress, tearing it off with his claws, but that was all he got. Alyss Heart, holding tight to Hatter Madigan, plummeted toward the surface of the water below.

CHAPTER 12

"POINT YOUR feet down!" Hatter shouted, holding himself as straight as he could. He knew that if he and Alyss didn't hit the water with as little impact as possible, it would be like landing on a sheet of diamond and they'd be killed.

Alyss barely had time to do as he instructed before they shot deep into the pool. She lost her grip on the Millinery man. He reached for her, but she panicked, flailing, and then she was out of reach. Falling deeper underwater, she opened her eyes, saw nothing but foam and a rush of bubbles, and shut them again, not wanting to face the unknown. Just when she thought that she couldn't hold her breath any longer and would drown in the depths, she stopped and reversed directions, heading up toward the surface with the same force and speed as her descent.

Whoosh!

She was out of the water and in the air, cannonballing out of a dirty puddle in the middle of a street where a parade was taking place. People dressed in various shades of dull, with strange, anonymous faces, were crowding the pavements and applauding her.

All these jumping and spinning and juggling people. And . . . are those soldiers? She had been mistaken for a member of a gypsy troupe tumbling and twirling and performing magic tricks alongside a marching regiment.

"Bravo! Bravo!" the crowd applauded.

Five bowler hats, an ivory-tipped cane, a pair of tortoise-shell eyeglasses, a rolled-up newspaper, a potato, and two plates of steak and kidney pie took to the air and circled overhead. The rolled-up newspaper smacked into a boy sitting on his father's shoulders. One woman ended up with pie in her face. Dazed, Alyss didn't even realize it was her imagination that had caused the objects to take flight. She was keeping her eye on the dirty puddle, hoping Hatter would appear. Then a gilded open carriage pulled by eight horses decked out in jeweled harnesses splashed through the puddle and she caught a glimpse of a woman—a queen, surely it was a queen!—inside, waving to the crowds.

"Mother?"

It was possible. Genevieve might have arrived in this world before her. *If anyone could do it . . .* And maybe being a queen in one world meant you were recognized as such

73

in another? Alyss forgot about the dirty puddle and chased after the carriage, at which point the bowler hats, eyeglasses, cane, potato, and steak and kidney pie dropped to the ground.

"Mother! *Mo-ther*, wait!"

She weaved her way through the parading soldiers toward the queen's carriage. The soldiers bumped and elbowed her.

"Get lost, brat."

"Away with you, dirty urchin."

She hardly noticed. She was gaining on the carriage. Her mother would see her, order her lifted up onto the equipage's plush cushion, and they would be reunited. It had been a test, Genevieve would say, Alyss' first test as future queen and nothing more.

She was within a hundred feet of the carriage when, having reached the end of the parade route, it abruptly turned into a side street and picked up speed, the entrance to the street blocked by a line of soldiers to prevent anyone from following. With as much pride as she could muster, armed with a firm belief in her own entitlement (she *was* a princess), Alyss approached the soldiers standing guard.

"Where is that carriage going?"

No answer. Maybe they hadn't heard her? She was about to ask again when one of the soldiers deigned to look in her direction and, judging by the look on his face (as if someone had shoved a smelly radish under his nose), he was not

74

impressed by Alyss' rough-and-tumble appearance. Alyss glanced down at her dress, torn by The Cat and wet from the Pool of Tears. She looked far from regal.

"To Buckingham Palace. Where d'ya think?" he said.

But Alyss wasn't thinking, events still following too closely and too quickly one after another for her to make much sense of them. Buckingham Palace was simply the place where her mother had gone.

"And where is the palace?" she asked.

"You don't know where Buckingham Palace is?"

"If you don't tell me, I can make life difficult for you."

This amused the soldier. "That right? And why should I tell you where the palace is? Like as not, you're after doing the queen some harm."

"I am Princess Alyss Heart. The queen is my mother and—"

"Your—? Well, well." The soldier turned to the fellow standing next to him, who had overheard everything. "Heh, George. This girl here says her mother's the queen."

"You don't say?" said George, turning to the soldier next to him. "Timothy, you hear that? This little girl's mother's the queen. You and me'd have to die protecting her, I suppose."

"All hail the royal lady," Timothy said, bowing.

The soldiers laughed.

Nothing was worse than imagination used in the service of anger, Alyss knew, but these soldiers were too disrespectful.

It may have been the distorting properties of her anger, or the muck of this alien city, but when she imagined the soldiers' mouths sewn shut, their coats and breeches tore at the seams instead.

Thinking they had split their uniforms from laughing so hard, the soldiers laughed even harder.

Alyss' anger drained out of her, leaving her sad and doubtful. Could it be that her mother hadn't been in the carriage? Hadn't she seen her mother burst into a thousand fragments, leaving only blackness, nothingness in her place? And why had her imagination failed her?

Without realizing it, she walked away from the soldiers. "Hatter?" she called.

But there were only strangers, clots of them conversing on the pavements, others hurrying on their way to who knew where. There was only the grime and soot and horse-dung stink of the streets.

"Hatter!"

She had to get back to the puddle that had landed her in this world. It could reunite her with Hatter, maybe even return her to Wonderland. She retraced her steps. But the street was mottled with so many puddles. What if she'd gone too far and passed it? Everything appeared equally unfamiliar. Could she have covered so much distance while chasing the carriage? What if she never found the puddle? What would happen when the sun broke through the clouds?

If she stopped to think about what she was going

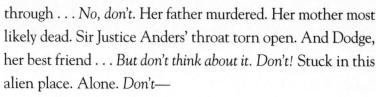

through . . . *No, don't.* Her father murdered. Her mother most likely dead. Sir Justice Anders' throat torn open. And Dodge, her best friend . . . *But don't think about it. Don't!* Stuck in this alien place. Alone. *Don't—*

She had to be strong. She was a princess, the future Queen of Wonderland. She shouldn't weep like a baby.

She took a running start toward the nearest puddle, jumped, and landed in the middle of it, splashing herself and a lady and gentleman walking past.

"Oaf! Good heavens!" the woman protested.

The man made as if to chase after Alyss, but she had already stamped out of the puddle and was sprinting toward another. She jumped into it and thoroughly soaked a dapper young chap who'd just come from a visit with his tailor.

"Ugh! This cravat alone is worth more than *you*, you beastly thing!"

Alyss splashed from puddle to puddle, squeezing shut her eyes as she took to the air and imagining hard that she was back in Wonderland, opening her eyes as she came down, sprays of water going every which way, only to find that she was still in this alien world.

I'll never find my way home. Never ever EVER!

All hope gone, she jumped up and down in a single puddle, yelling, "No! No! No!" until it was impossible to tell which were her tears and which splotches of street water.

"You taking a bath or what?" said a boy watching from a safe distance, out of splashing range.

She stopped jumping, sniffed. The boy wore gray breeches patched at the knees and thighs, a frock coat much too big for him, the tail of which reached down practically to his heels, and cracked leather boots with no laces.

"I'm Princess Alyss Heart of Wonderland," she said defiantly.

"Yeah, and I'm Prince Quigly Gaffer of Chelsea. That's one loony outfit you're wearing."

She looked down at her damp, dirty birthday dress: a flouncy thing, tight at the waist and poofing out below her knees in a cumbersomely wide circle, its collar high and floppy and ruffled. It was decorated with appliquéd hearts, in colors only available in Wonderland, and the dress was a rare sight even there, where it would be taken from the princess' wardrobe and aired only once a year, the royal tailors refitting it to accommodate Alyss' growing body.

"It's all I have," she said, which started her crying again.

Quigly considered her for a moment. Even smudged with dirt and scum, and with tears leaking out of her eyes, there was something about the girl that intrigued him. She seemed *brighter* than everything around her. It was as if she were lit from within by a lantern that shone faintly through the pores of her skin.

"Better come with me if you want dry clothes, Your Majesty," he said.

He started to walk off. Alyss hesitated. Half a block away, Quigly turned.

"Off we go!" he called, waving for her to follow.

She looked around one last time for Hatter, then abandoned her puddle. She couldn't afford *not* to have a friend.

CHAPTER 13

No AMOUNT of Millinery training could have prepared Hatter for getting sucked through the Pool of Tears.
Having somersaulted out of a puddle and landed on his feet
with the agility of . . . well, of a cat, he let his instinct for
self-protection take over. His backpack sprouted its usual
array of weaponry. His steel bracelets popped open and spun
in propeller-like action. He reached for his top hat but it
was gone, which was bad news. Really bad news. The top
hat was his signature weapon, the one he had worked the
hardest to master. And he was probably going to need it,
judging by the shocked and alarmed faces all around him. He
had emerged from the exit portal in Paris, France, 1859, and
found himself standing in the middle of a wide thoroughfare
known as the Champs-Elysées. Parisians spilled their café au

lait at the sight of him. His sudden appearance upset traffic, carriages veering left and right. One carriage knocked over a fruit stand, another crushed baskets of baguettes and loaves. Horses whinnied and neighed, edgy.

Who was this strangely attired man with knives and over-sized corkscrews jutting out of his backpack and rotary blades on his wrists?

Hatter kept an eye on the puddle, expecting The Cat or Redd's soldiers to spring from it at any moment.

"Alyss?"

But she was nowhere to be seen. This was worse than not having his top hat. In the Pool of Tears for hardly any time at all, with only one job to do, one simple job—to look after the future Queen of Wonderland—and he'd let her fall away from him. She must have been sucked through the portal to another location.

Men were coming toward him—men in uniforms and small, firm caps with brims, looking confused and more than a little frightened. He snapped his wrist-blades closed and ran, not because he was afraid of them, but because he was afraid of what he might do to them. Even here in another world he would abide by the codes of Wonderland's Millinery, which stated that combat skills were not to be used on a person until he was a proven enemy, and even then only to the extent that they were necessary. Plus, it was best to draw as little attention to himself as possible, to disappear into the underground in order to find Princess Alyss.

His Millinery coat swooped out behind him as he cut across the Champs-Elysées and down a residential street. He was faster and more agile than the Frenchmen and would have easily escaped their pursuit if he'd known his way around Paris. Time and again he thought he'd lost them, that they were no longer following him, only to discover that they must have taken a shortcut through an alley, because now they were in front of him.

He had to get rid of them for good. He stopped running and let them approach. When they were within ten paces of him, he flicked open his wrist-blades, feinted at them, and they scattered into cafés, brasseries, patisseries, and boulangeries, lunging for safety anywhere they could find it. Hatter snapped shut his wrist-blades and ran, and this time they didn't follow.

He hid under a bridge on the banks of the Seine until nightfall, when he could more easily move through the city undetected. He planned to canvass the streets, search every lane and alley for the princess before moving on to another town or city. He would get maps, systematically scour this entire world if necessary, familiarize himself with intercity routes, pass across borders like a phantom. His promise to Genevieve, the queen he'd left behind, demanded it.

Under the blanket of darkness, he made his way up and down streets, starting at one end of the city and working his way across it. And now that he had an opportunity to notice, Hatter saw that some people had a glow about them. Supposing them suffused with the luminescence of imagina-

tion, he followed one glowing man down the rue de Rivoli to a modest shop with a wooden sign in the shape of a top hat hanging over its door. It could have been a station for the Millinery men and women of the city. Perhaps he would find camaraderie and assistance here. He followed the man into the shop. It was filled with every variety of hat: derbies, bowlers, tams, fezzes, berets—an array of headware that impressed even Hatter. He picked up one of the top hats and flicked it, but it held its innocent shape.

A diminutive gentleman with a wispy mustache approached. *"Bonjour, monsieur. Est-ce-que je peux vous aider?"*

"I come from Wonderland," Hatter said. "I oversee the Millinery there." He waited, hoping the meaning, the import, of this would make itself felt to the shopkeeper.

"Cela est un bon chapeau," the man said, pointing to the top hat.

Hatter set down the item. "I am searching for Princess Alyss Heart of Wonderland. She has landed somewhere in this world, as I have, through a portal and . . ."

But the shopkeeper's eyes showed no recognition at Alyss' name, no understanding of what Hatter was saying. When the man tried to show Hatter the merits of a certain beret, Hatter left the shop. He would try others, however. He trusted those who dealt in headwear more than he trusted anyone else.

A few doors down, three men emerged from a café, tipsy with drink. They stopped in bleary-eyed surprise at the sight of Hatter, his odd-looking clothes.

"Je n'aime pas des étrangers," one of the men said.

Hatter didn't have to understand French to hear the hostility in his voice. The man pretended to punch Hatter and his companions laughed.

Hatter didn't flinch. "I don't want to fight you," he said.

"Non?"

"No."

The man shoved Hatter, who stood his ground, an exemplar of restraint. *"Qu'est-ce qu'il y dans le sac?"* the man asked, indicating Hatter's backpack. *"Donnez-moi le sac."* The man took a step toward Hatter, reached for the backpack.

Only an enemy would try to take Hatter's weapons. Activating his wrist-blades, the Milliner flipped backwards to give himself some space. He reached into his backpack and let fly with a handful of daggers. Thimp! Thimp! Thimp! The daggers pinned the men to a wooden cart by their shirt-sleeves: a feat of martial skill Hatter hoped would show that he could kill all three of them if he so desired.

More men appeared, spilling out of the nearby cafés, alarmed. They surrounded Hatter—fifteen of them. One of them aimed a pistol at his head.

Hatter vaguely recognized the pistol as something invented by a Wonderlander during his boyhood. To reacquaint himself with its capabilities, he eyed the man and said, "Boo!"

Panicked, the man fired.

A round steel bullet shot toward Hatter, but with the speed

of a jabberwock's tongue, he ducked and it whizzed past.

Hatter punched a button on his belt buckle and a series of curved saber blades flicked open along the surface of his belt. But before the blades sliced into action, the group scattered, each man running as far from Hatter as he could get, which didn't stop them from later reporting that they had witnessed the menacing figure kill upwards of twenty innocent civilians with his elaborate weaponry, themselves living to tell about it only by the grace of God.

The sabers on Hatter's belt retracted. He snapped his wrist-blades closed and allowed himself a brief smile, relieved that he hadn't had to kill anyone. He didn't see the large, elaborately decorated rug closing in on him, held up from behind by six of Paris' bravest carpet salesmen. The rug knocked him down and the men rolled him up tight in it. His backpack weaponry poked through the thick pile, but his arms were pinned to his sides; he was unable to reach his belt buckle or flick his wrists to activate his deadly bracelets.

Hoisting the rug-cocooned Hatter onto their shoulders, the men hauled him off to the Palais de Justice. But as he breathed in the rug's fibers, Hatter's concern wasn't for his own safety, but for that of Alyss Heart, a lost princess in a hostile world.

CHAPTER 14

THE CAT stood at the edge of the cliff and stared down at the foaming, rippling spot where Alyss and Hatter had splashed into the water. Lightning flashed, thunder broke overhead, and rain fell in sheets. If there was one thing The Cat didn't like, it was water. Rain, showers, baths, it didn't matter which; he hated getting wet. He turned and stalked back into the forest with the scrap of Alyss' dress in his fist.

"You let them get away," a voice said.

The Cat stopped, tense.

"They escaped," said another.

He spun round but saw no one. The forest was talking to him, the trees and plants and flowers.

"What's the matter?" asked a nearby lilac bush. "Afraid to take a dip in the water?"

The forest had a good laugh at that, but The Cat didn't appreciate the teasing. He bent down and tore the lilac up by its roots and threw it on the ground. The forest fell silent. The Cat walked up to a tree.

"Were you talking to me?"

The tree said nothing.

The Cat glanced to his left, then right. "I don't see anyone else here, so you must have been talking to me."

Still the tree said not a word. It didn't matter. The Cat raked his claws down its trunk, skinning off the bark.

"Aaaaahowwww!" the tree cried.

The Cat reentered the Crystal Continuum through the forest looking glass (its guard, the tight-lipped shrub, now more tight-lipped than ever) and reemerged in Genevieve's sitting room. He hulked through the destruction of the sitting area and down a heart-shaped passage to the South Dining Room, stepping over dead card soldiers and guardsmen as if they had never been alive at all, never beings who laughed, cried, rejoiced, or had loved ones waiting for them at home.

Notwithstanding the blast that had rocked the palace, the bodies splayed in all manner of death on the tables and floor, the South Dining Room was a scene of celebration. Redd's soldiers helped themselves to wondercrumpets, fried dormice, and whatever other delicacies they could find, and none too delicately shoved them into their mouths. Not being much interested in tea, they'd raided the palace's wine cellar, and now flooded their bellies with goblet after goblet of the queendom's finest wine.

"To the health of Queen Redd!"

"To the death of Queen Genevieve!"

These toasts were one and the same to Redd, who was lounging in a chair, wearing the bloody crown. "Well?" she said when she saw The Cat. "Where are their heads?"

One didn't admit failure to Redd and get away with it without suffering pain or worse. The Cat held up the shred of Alyss' dress. "This is all that's left of them. I'm sorry, Your Highness. I couldn't control myself."

"It's unwise to control yourself in a situation like that," Redd said. "Well done."

But a scheming, dishonest mind such as Redd's always suspects others of scheming and dishonesty. She tried to see Alyss in her imagination's eye, to discover the truth for herself: nothing. Imagination could not penetrate the Pool of Tears, which was lucky for The Cat.

"She's dead?" said a voice from behind a curtain. "Alyss is dead?"

Redd waved her hand and the curtain swung back to reveal Bibwit Harte. "If it isn't my wise and learned tutor," she said.

Bibwit Harte was a loyal fellow, and it was because of his loyalty to Genevieve and Alyss and White Imagination that he determined, then and there, to ensure his own survival by appeasing Redd. Though a scholar, he vowed to one day topple

this mistress of Black Imagination and return Wonderland to the glory of peace. He bowed his head. "At your service, Your . . . Imperial Viciousness."

Redd sneered. "'Your Imperial Viciousness'? Ha! Yes, that's perfect. From now on everyone will refer to me as 'Your Imperial Viciousness' or die. You there!"

"Yes, my quee—" a Two Card started, but was immediately pierced through the lung by one of The Cat's claws.

"You!" Redd said to a Three Card.

"Um, y-yes, Your . . . Your Imperial Viciousness?"

"I want a list of those considered sympathetic to the former queen who are not dead in this room. I am aware that General Doppelgänger is not among the bodies here. Begin the list with him. For the rest, ask *them*." She turned her gaze upon the suit families, who stood clustered together, trying to take up as little space as possible. "I'm sure they'll be helpful."

"Oh yes," declared the Lord of Diamonds, still with a hand on Jack of Diamonds' shoulder.

"Absolutely," said the Lady of Spades.

"Of course, by all means," said the Lady of Clubs and her husband.

Redd was not an idiot. She knew that she couldn't rule the queendom by fear and intimidation alone. The suit families had relationships with mayors of principalities and influential businessmen, with key members of what remained of the queendom's military force—relationships that would have to be exploited for her profit and exaltation.

"There are to be some changes in the queendom, which may prove beneficial to you all," Her Imperial Viciousness announced. "Not the least of which is that since I have no heirs of Heart descent, nor do I want any, I will choose my successor from one of the ranking families. Whoever among you serves me best can be assured of nothing, but you will at least have a better chance at the crown than the others." She ventured a smile, which the Lady of Spades, for one, found more gruesome than many of the lifeless bodies surrounding her, and which, if truth be told, it physically hurt Redd to accomplish. "I trust you don't mind my preying on your ambitions in this way?"

"Oh no," declared the Lord of Diamonds.

"Absolutely not," said the Lady of Spades.

"By all means no," said the Lady of Clubs and her husband.

The suit families struggled to remember who had escaped, mentioning pawns, a rook, a knight, numerous card soldiers.

"Dodge Anders has escaped!" Jack of Diamonds asserted, louder than the others.

"And who might Dodge Anders be?" asked Redd.

"He is in love with Princess Alyss but pretends not to be. He's a guardsman's son. That's his father, there." Jack pointed to Sir Justice, lying dead on the floor.

Redd approached the boy. The rogue soldiers paused in

the midst of their celebrations. The Cat stood motionless. No one knew what Redd might do.

"You're a helpful one, aren't you?" she said, squeezing his cheeks like a loving grandmother.

Jack couldn't answer because of her grip.

"Add Dodge Anders' name to the list," she commanded, and released Jack of Diamonds. Small bruises formed where her fingers had touched his cheeks. She removed the crown from her head and tossed it to Bibwit. "Prepare for my coronation at the Heart Crystal. *Now.* All members of ranking families must attend—unless, of course, they prefer the comfort of eternal sleep."

~

Surrounded by Bibwit Harte, The Cat, the suit families, those of her soldiers who were not too drunk to remain upright and some who were, Redd stood in the palace courtyard before the Heart Crystal and lifted her voice to the lightning-storm sky.

"I am prepared to forgive those who thrived during my exile and did little to support my return, with this exception: Anyone harboring or aiding a creature sympathetic to the former queen or White Imagination will be hunted down, imprisoned, made to suffer untold tortures, and then executed. Now put the crown on my head."

Bibwit Harte stepped forward to fulfill the request, but fast as he was, he proved not fast enough for Redd. With a curl of her finger, the crown leaped from his hands and landed on her head.

"I reclaim my queendom," she declared, placing both hands on the Heart Crystal.

A jolt of energy shook her. The crystal turned from white to red—a red so deep and piercing that Bibwit and the others had to turn away or close their eyes to prevent their pupils from scorching.

Redd had claimed the power of the Heart Crystal as her own.

CHAPTER 15

GENERALS DOPPEL and Gänger and the few who survived Redd's attack avoided the Crystal Continuum in case the invading force had already taken control of its shimmering byways. They made their way on foot to the Everlasting Forest, found refuge in a small clearing surrounded by trees that would alert them of approaching enemies. The healthy carried the wounded, but all suffered emotionally from their defeat and the loss of beloved left behind.

"We must organize quickly," General Doppel urged.

"Before Redd settles into her rule," agreed General Gänger.

The white knight nodded.

"Our only chance to amass an army is *now*," Doppel continued. "However ill-timed such recruitment may be."

The three turned their eyes toward the battle-numbed card soldiers dragging themselves into the sanctuary of the forest.

"My bishops and I are prepared to risk everything for the good of the queendom," said the knight. "We *will* find Wonderlanders to fight with us against Redd, you can rest assured."

The knight gathered his bishops and their pawns. "Spread out through the capital city," he ordered. "Find anyone willing to fight for White Imagination and tell them where we're camped. They must make their own, careful way to us. But be sure they're sincere in their wish to join our cause or you will give us away and we'll be doomed."

~

Among the soldiers gathering in the forest sat one who wasn't a soldier at all—just an inconsolable boy, slumped against the base of a tree, crying in fits and jags and not caring if Redd herself heard him. The generals would have known better how to subdue a raging jabberwock than a mourning child.

"You should never have brought me here," Dodge moaned. "I shouldn't have left them."

"There was nothing you could do, son," General Doppel said.

"You would have been killed," said General Gänger.

"At least I would have died alongside my father! I could have protected Alyss!"

"If Hatter couldn't—"

"Then no one could have provided protection enough, I'm afraid."

Dodge wiped his nose.

"We *are* sorry," generals Doppel and Gänger said as one.

"I've lost my father and . . . and Alyss!"

The Generals lowered their heads, took a moment to speak.

"We have all lost Princess Alyss—"

"And feel your suffering on that score."

Dodge doubted it. They couldn't possibly know how he felt—the pain, the sudden wretched loneliness. They might have lost their princess, but Alyss was so much more than that to him. Would he never more see lively, sweet-smelling Alyss Heart? Never again confide to her his dreams of soldier-fame? What good were dreams now? And then his father . . . he could hardly take it all in. He would never see his father again. Where the two greatest loves of his life had been, he was faced with nothing, blankness.

"We are sorry," the generals said again. But they had what remained of their army to comfort; they left him and strode among their soldiers, dispensing words of consolation to the wounded and commendations of bravery to all.

95

Dodge didn't remember falling asleep, wasn't aware that he'd even been sleeping until he woke the next morning with a sudden start, an idea blazing in his brain and the resolve to carry it through already firm. When the generals came upon him, he was ripping the fleur-de-lis badge off his guardsman coat, and they watched as he put his coat on inside out and rubbed handfuls of dirt over himself until it became virtually impossible to tell that he wore a guardsman's uniform.

"What are you up to?" General Doppel asked.

"If it's too late to do anything for Alyss, there's at least something I can still do for my father."

The generals exchanged a worried glance.

"I'm going to get his body," Dodge said. "The leader of the palace guard deserves a burial proper to his station and I'm going to give it to him."

"You can't go back there," General Gänger said.

"Why not?"

"Well," said General Doppel, "who's to say that Sir Justice's body is even still there, and—"

"And Redd's soldiers are everywhere," General Gänger finished. "You'll never make it."

"I'm going."

"But we forbid it!"

Dodge Anders had always shown respect for chains of command, for the discipline required of military men, but he suddenly barked, "Who are you to forbid it? Do you have Anders blood in your veins?"

"I'll go with him if it'll make you feel better, Generals."

The white rook. Dodge felt his heart thumping in his throat. He was breathing short and fast. The chessman came and stood next to him. It was all right. Dodge didn't know the rook well, but it was all right. It would be good to have company.

The generals shook their heads, couldn't help being impressed by the boy's character despite the foolishness of the proposed errand. In silent agreement, they removed the exact same crystal and gemstone quadruple-heart medal from their uniforms and presented them to Dodge.

"With utmost respect for your father," General Doppel said.

"Please give him these," said General Gänger.

Dodge took the medals in his hand and pocketed them carefully. He could feel his bottom lip quivering. He turned and hurried into the woods.

"Take care of him," the generals told the chessman.

~

The rook knew he would be easy to spot in the capital city, so as he left the encampment, he grabbed a blanket and draped it over his battlements to give himself the appearance of an anonymous pauper. Silent, alert, he and Dodge made their way to Heart Palace.

They found Wondertropolis practically deserted. Small clans of Redd's soldiers lolled outside abandoned cafés, drunk on wine and harassing the few Wonderlanders who braved the streets, hurrying to their destinations with lowered heads, intent on keeping to their own business.

Dodge and the rook cut this way and that through the city, avoiding the soldiers. They made it to the palace without incident, surprised to find it unguarded, unmanned.

"Where's the Heart Crystal?" the rook asked.

Dodge paused to study the courtyard. How gloomy it was—forsaken and without the light of the powerful crystal. Suddenly, a figure scurried out of the palace. Dodge and the rook reached for their swords, but there was no need. The figure—a male—didn't seem to notice them; arms laden with goblets and dishes, he ran past and was gone. Another Wonderlander trotted out of the palace and through the courtyard, carrying a music box and several pillows.

Dodge looked at the rook. What was going on?

In the palace's darkened halls they discovered looters moving about in silent hurry, helping themselves to souvenirs of the former ruling family. A Wonderlander ran past with one of Alyss' old toys in his arms: a set of glow-gwormmies. Dodge made a move to trip the thief, but the rook put a hand on his arm and shook his head: Dodge had to focus on what he'd come to do.

As flitting as the looters, Dodge and the rook drifted through banquet rooms and salons. They saw a great many of Redd's soldiers passed out on the floors and tables. But no sign of Redd or The Cat. They drew closer to the South

Dining Room, stepped over dead card soldiers and guardsmen.

"That smell." Dodge clamped a hand over his nose.

"It'll be worse inside," the rook said.

They found the dining room deserted, the stench too much for the looters. The rook paused just inside the room, shaking his battlement-topped head at the carnage. But as ghastly as the scene was, Dodge saw only his father's body. He stood over Sir Justice and cried silent tears.

"We should hurry," the rook said gently.

Dodge wiped his face and nodded—more to himself than to the rook, a nod to convince himself that he had the strength to do this.

They carried Sir Justice out to the garden and, using broken chair backs as shovels, began to dig. It wasn't easy going. They sweated; their muscles ached. But the hole was at last large enough. Once Sir Justice was lying in the ground, Dodge removed from his pocket the medals the generals had given him and he laid them on his father's chest. With timid, unsteady hands, he began to shovel soil into the grave.

No! It was impossible! Worse than anything he'd ever experienced, to see the soil fall on his father, the man who had given him life! A cry burst from him, he threw his makeshift shovel to the ground, ran and hid in a corner of the garden. How could he live? *Why* should he live when those he had held most dear did not? He became quiet, subdued. How and why should he live? These were questions to be answered. The *only* questions.

When he finally stepped out from his hiding place, Sir Justice was buried. The rook had taken care of everything . . . almost.

"Would you like to do this?" the rook asked, holding a seed out to Dodge: the Hereafter Seed.

Dodge took the seed and dropped it on his father's grave. Instantly the seed took root and up grew a large, beautiful bouquet of flowers, the arrangement of which formed Sir Justice's likeness; a living memorial.

"Thank you," Dodge murmured.

The rook accepted the thanks in silence, detected no sign of tears on the boy's cheeks. Dodge's tight, squinting expression looked more angry than sad.

They stood together over the grave in final tribute.

"He was a good man," the rook said, "a brave and honorable man."

Dodge snorted, bitter. "Yeah, and this was his reward."

CHAPTER 16

ALYSS THOUGHT Quigly Gaffer the nicest in the band of homeless orphans and runaways of which he was a part, and not just because he was so attentive to her. He was attentive to everybody. He was the least sullen, the least prone to depression, the one who, with his lively, confident attitude, kept everyone's spirits up when there weren't enough crusts to go around, when it was cold and wet and they'd been chased out of too many sheltered doorways to count. In other words, Quigly Gaffer gave them hope when life seemed particularly hopeless. And he had suffered as much as anybody.

Walking alongside Alyss that first day in London, he said, "So, Princess, tell us about yourself," and she voiced her woeful condition with a viciousness that surprised her.

"I saw my father, the King of Wonderland, murdered. My

mother, the queen, is dead. Both of them were killed by my aunt. But it wouldn't matter even if they were alive, because I'll never make it home."

"I saw my folks murdered, same as you," said Quigly. "We were driving along in our coach when a couple of thieves decided they didn't like the look of us and killed my father with a club to the head. I watched my mother get beaten to death with that selfsame club, all the while begging for mercy. And I would've been greeted with the club too if I hadn't run into the dark and hidden while the thieves were trying to take the rings off Mother's fingers. So I suppose you and me have something in common, what with our parents being dead, right enough."

Alyss could think of other things she would have rather had in common with him. She didn't know it, and this certainly wasn't how Bibwit Harte would have taught her, but in the person of Quigly Gaffer, Alyss was learning something that would one day serve her well as a queen.

Lesson number 1b in Bibwit's carefully planned curriculum: For most of the universe's inhabitants, life is not all gummy wads and tarty tarts; it is a struggle against hardship, unfairness, corruption, abuse, and adversity in all its guises, where even to survive—let alone survive with dignity— is heroic. To soldier through the days in the wake of failure is the courageous act of many. To rule benevolently, a queen should be able to enter into the feelings of those less fortunate than herself.

"Never mind that dress, I knew from your gab that you ain't from anywhere round here," Quigly said. "You don't have any accent I recognize. I don't know just what it is."

"It's Wonderlandian, I suppose."

"Right, right. You're from Wonderland, you say?" Quigly laughed. "Why don't you tell us about the place, Princess?"

So she did, and the more she talked, the more she felt the cold, impersonal tone she'd used to describe her parents' deaths fall away till she was almost overcome with sadness and longing for what, so quickly and suddenly, so unexpectedly, had become part of her past. She was sure the Inventors' Parade wouldn't seem so boring to her now, if she could only get back to the royal balcony to watch it.

"You see that light?" she said, pointing at one of the gas lamps lining the street. "That was invented in Wonderland, but instead of an open flame it had a glass bulb inside and you only had to flick a switch to turn it on."

She described Heart Palace, the singing flowers in the royal gardens, the Crystal Continuum.

"And I don't mean to brag," she said, "but I have a powerful imagination."

"I'll say."

"You think I'm making everything up?"

Quigly didn't answer. Alyss saw a lone dandelion poking out of some mud. She stared hard at the flower and imagined it singing. It seemed to require more effort than it would have done in Wonderland, and it took longer. But then the dandelion's petals moved and from the bud at its center came a thin little voice.

"La la la la, la la la la, la la la la, laaaaaaah."

That was all Alyss could manage, but Quigly was impressed. He'd heard about magicians who could "throw" their voices, making it sound as if a person or object across a room were talking when it would be the magician himself standing right next to you.

"Nice trick."

"It's not a trick." And then, sadly, just remembering, the exiled princess added, "It's my birthday."

"Happy birthday, ma'am."

Alyss felt her eyes water, sorrow weighing her down.

"Aw, no crying on birthdays," Quigly said. "You oughta meet some of my friends. They'll cheer you right up."

So they walked to a blind alley in the shadow of London Bridge, where a ragtag group of children ranging in age from five to twelve lounged around on old crates.

"Hear ye, hear ye," Quigly announced. "I bring a new-comer into our ranks."

The children looked at Alyss, uninterested. They had seen newcomers before. Fact was, the makeup of the group was always changing, some boy or girl entering into it one day, sharing their bread for weeks or months and then going off, never to be seen again, no one ever knowing if they'd been arrested for stealing, stuck in a home, murdered, or what.

Quigly introduced everyone to Alyss. "The big one's

Charlie Turnbull. The one next to him with the mole on his nose is Andrew MacLean—he's an orphan too. That one there is Otis Oglethorpe—a runaway, but his mother's dead. And in the ladies, we've got Francine Forge, Esther Wilkes, and Margaret Blemin—all of them orphans. Everyone, may I present you with Princess Alice of Wonderland. She's come to us through a puddle of water, and I suggest you be on your best behavior in front of royalty."

"Puddle of water?" Charlie Turnbull guffawed. "Princess of Wonderland?"

Quigly didn't bother to explain. He dug in a heap of what looked like rags and held up a pair of trousers, a blouse, and a man's coat for Alyss' approval. "These should fit you right enough."

Where was she supposed to change out of her wet things?

"Sorry, Princess," said Quigly. "No private rooms for you here in the alleys of London."

She stripped, trying to act as if taking off her clothes in front of everybody wasn't unusual. The blouse fit her well enough, but the trousers and coat were too large. She added her birthday dress to the pile of clothes and blankets for anyone who might want it once it was dry. She slipped her feet into a pair of boots Quigly had rummaged up for her, discarding her Wonderland birthday shoes.

"Righty right, let's see what we've got," Quigly said to the others.

They pulled various coins and foodstuffs out of their pockets—a few pence, a mostly empty wallet, cheese, sausages, a chicken leg. Otis Oglethorpe produced a loaf of bread he'd been hiding under his coat and Charlie Turnbull brought out half a meat pie from under his hat.

"What about you?" Otis asked Quigly. "What've you brought?"

"I brought the princess right enough."

"We can't eat *her*," said Charlie Turnbull. "And that's another mouth eating what could've been going into *our* bellies."

"I'll make it up tomorrow, when me and the princess'll bring plenty for all of you, don't worry."

Charlie glared at Alyss. Meeting Quigly's friends wasn't in the least cheering.

The food was divided evenly into eight portions. The cheese and sausage did not taste like their counterparts in Wonderland, the cheese somehow soggy, the sausage flavorless. The meat pie, Alyss thought, tasted like a stuffed old stocking.

After eating, Andrew, Francine, and Margaret—the youngest of the orphans—crowded together on the clothes heap and snuggled down to sleep. Charlie made a bed for himself by pushing three crates together and covering them with an old quilt. Otis simply went to bed on the hard ground, using his coat as a blanket. Esther Wilkes dozed off sitting up, leaning back against a wall, her legs sticking out straight in front of her into the alley.

Alyss couldn't sleep. She tried counting gwynooks. *One gwynook, two gwynook, three gwynook.* It didn't help.

"Restless, Princess?" Quigly asked, and offered to keep her company for a bit. "We scatter about during the day," he explained, "to beg, borrow, or steal, as the case may be. Francine, Andrew, and Margaret work as a team. Two of them get a bloke's attention while the third picks his pockets. Some days one or another of us'll make the rounds of the shops, looking for stale food they might want to throw away. But every night we meet here and share what we've got. I don't know if it's easier on us to make our way together, and Charlie doesn't always give up everything he gets in a day—he doesn't know I know, so don't tell him—but it feels better to most of them to be in a group. It can get lonely with no proper family."

"I'm sure it can," said Alyss.

"Well now." Quigly curled up on the ground, using his hands as a pillow. "Gotta get some sleep. I made a promise to the others and tomorrow's gonna be something big, I can tell you. I got plans for us—you and me. G'night, Princess."

"Good night, Quigly Gaffer."

It wasn't long before Alyss was alone with the steady, rhythmic breathing of the slumbering street urchins. Francine mumbled in her sleep and buried her face in the crook of Andrew's arm. Charlie started to snore. Alyss turned her face to the sky, to the limitless expanse that, ever since she could remember, had served as a reminder of the wondrous possibilities open to her. *Four gwynook, five gwynook, six.* Now, starless and close, the sky just seemed empty. *Seven gwynook, eight gwynook, nine gwynook, ten . . .*

~

The last to fall asleep, Alyss was the last to wake, still rubbing the crust from her eyes when Quigly presented her with a white flower whose roots were tangled in a mud ball he cupped in his hands.

"You think you can do that trick again?"

It took her a second to understand: the singing flower. "It's not a trick."

"Yeah, but you think you can do it again?"

"I don't know . . . I suppose."

"Do it."

It took longer than it did the previous day, required even more effort and concentration, but at last the flower chirped into song.

"Yeay-hoo!" Quigly celebrated, prancing around the alley.

"Where are the others?" Alyss asked.

"Already gone about their daily business, Princess. And it's time we went about ours."

He chose a busy corner. All Alyss had to do, he said, was sit on an upturned crate and make the flower sing when he gave her the wink.

"What's this, ladies and gents?" he cried, raising his voice to the Londoners hurrying past. "Why, the world's only singing flower, that's what it is! The lass of the flower here has come all the way from Africa with as rare a flower as ever you saw! Oh, it looks like any common flower, I'll grant you that! But it is by no means common, I tell you! It sings! Who's for a bit of singing? Come on now!"

When enough curious people had gathered to watch, Quigly gave Alyss the wink and she made the flower sing. It wasn't for more than a few bars, but it was enough. The crowd thought it a wonderful feat of magic. Quigly made the rounds of the audience, convincing each and every person to drop a few pennies into his hat.

"Spare a few, ladies and gents, for it's not everyone that's witnessed the amazing singing flower from Africa. Come now, the passage from Africa ain't cheap."

Alyss managed four more performances, one every hour, each draining her more than the last. She had to stop for the day. But by then, they had earned more money than Quigly had ever seen in one place. They headed back to the alley to meet up with the others, who emptied their pockets—a tinkling of pennies, a broken watch, cheese, a salami, a few boiled potatoes.

"And what've you two brought us?" Charlie asked.

"Not much, I'd say," said Quigly, dumping the coins from his pockets.

The others couldn't believe it. Where had Quigly and

Alyss gotten so much money? Quigly wouldn't say; he wanted to keep Alyss' talent to himself.

"But tomorrow'll bring us the same," he said. "Me and the princess got us a workable scheme now, that's all any of you need to know. Charlie, Otis—you come with me. Let's buy a feast we won't soon forget. Who wants what now?"

~

When the others had gone to bed, Alyss told Quigly that they didn't have to stand on a street corner all day to earn money.

"I'll imagine however much we need," she said.

"I'll be happy to spend whatever money you come by, Princess, no matter how you come by it."

So Alyss tried to imagine a pile of the different coins she'd seen that day. She tried to imagine them weighing down the pockets of her coat. But she was still fatigued from her exertions with the flower, and before she could bring a single coin into existence, Quigly started laughing at her.

"Your face!" he said. He tried to imitate her expression, her face scrunched in dogged effort.

Alyss wasn't amused. "Never mind then," she said. "I'm not imagining a pile of money for you, ever."

"Aw, Princess, c'mon now. I wasn't teasing you. We all look funny sometimes. Some of us look funny *all* the time. You go ahead and imagine what you will."

But Quigly couldn't stop himself from laughing, so Alyss

didn't attempt to imagine a pile of money again that night or any night thereafter. *We'll do things the hard way since that's how he wants it.*

~

They spent their days on street corners, she making the flower sing while he collected money from the audience. But every new day seemed to weaken her ability with the flower and her performances became less frequent. The more time Alyss spent in this wet dreary city, the less she believed in her imagination.

It's not as strong as Mother thought. Probably never was.

At least twice a day, between flower performances, she tried to imagine Hatter's whereabouts. Inevitably, she saw nothing. Imagination's eye? She hadn't had enough training. Eventually, she had the strength and will to bring about only one flower performance a day, so Quigly made sure it'd be when they could attract the largest audience—at dusk, the streets especially crowded with people on their way home from work.

Every night, after the meals afforded by Alyss' performances, Andrew, Margaret, and Francine would ask her to tell them about Wonderland.

"Please, please, please," they'd say.

Imagining themselves in the bright, crystal world Alyss described, with heart palaces, walrus-butlers, frog-messengers, and giant, pipe-smoking caterpillars, they were able to escape for a short while from the poverty and squalor and daily scrounging of their own lives. Otis, Quigly, and Esther didn't enter into Alyss' tales of Wonderland as fully as the younger orphans, but they enjoyed her stories enough to listen to them in wistful silence. Charlie Turnbull, on the other hand, made it clear he didn't believe a word she said.

"Nothing but bleeding nonsense," he'd say.

She told Andrew, Francine, and Margaret all about Hatter Madigan and how awful it was to have lost her bodyguard because he was so accomplished at fighting. If she'd had the Milliner by her side, she said, she would never have met Quigly or any of them. To show what a man like Hatter could do, she described the injured card soldiers writhing on the floor of Heart Palace, hands pressed against their wounds and blood pulsing out between worrying fingers.

"Do you really know a man who can fight so many people?" Margaret asked.

"I do."

"It's a lie," said Charlie.

"But it's Dodge Anders who's going to be the greatest guardsman Wonderland's ever had," Alyss went on. "He's handsome and brave and kind and intelligent. He'll grow up to be almost as good a fighter as Hatter. I help him practice his swordsman drills sometimes. I hold shields with different colors on them and when I call out a color he has to jab his sword at it while I shake and move the shield and make it as hard as I can for him. He's my best friend and . . .

no . . . I mean, was." With a look around the alley: "He *was* my best friend."

"Go on, Alyss," Andrew said after she'd been silent for a time.

"No," said Alyss, her voice hushed. "I don't want to talk about Wonderland anymore."

~

Then came the day her imagination failed altogether. It was dusk, the usual time when Quigly, ever the showman, rounded up a crowd of Londoners curious to see the singing African flower. Quigly gave Alyss the wink and she envisioned the flower petals opening and closing like lips, the bud gathering its voice and singing a few bars, a lullaby maybe, or—

But nothing happened. She strained, groaned. Some of the onlookers thought she was going to be sick.

Sing, flower!

Seconds passed. A full minute. Alyss began to sweat through her dirty, ragged clothes.

Sing, flower, sing!

With grumblings and curses, the crowd started to disperse.

"She needs encouragement is all!" Quigly cried, upending his hat and begging for money. "Two pennies apiece and I guarantee that African flower'll sing like you never heard!"

No one threw money into the hat. One gentleman threatened to call for a policeman. That was all Quigly had to hear; he grabbed Alyss' hand and they ran off, leaving the flower and crate behind.

"I'm sorry," Alyss said, once they were safe and had stopped to catch their breath.

"What happened?"

"I don't know," she said. It scared her. It was like losing her hearing or her sight. "Maybe the longer I'm away from Wonderland . . . maybe the less my imagination works."

"Hmm," Quigly said, unbelieving.

"I'm sorry, Quigly."

"I'm sorry too, Princess."

It was the first time she'd ever seen him angry. She had failed him. She had failed Francine, Margaret, Andrew, Esther, Otis, and Charlie. She had never before failed anyone who was counting on her, and she didn't like the way it made her feel.

In silence, she and Quigly walked back to the alley to meet up with the other orphans. Along the way, they stopped in at the Kettle o' Fish and the Grizzled Seaman pubs, hoping for a little charity. All they got was a bag of crusts.

"We was thinking of having duck tonight," Andrew said, running up to her as she and Quigly turned into the alley. "With orange sauce and stuffing. Me and Francine and Margaret and Otis never had duck before."

Having reached the end of the alley, Quigly flashed Alyss a look, summoned a lighthearted tone, and declared duck to be perfectly awful. "You ain't missing much, I can tell you. It ain't a coincidence 'duck' rhymes with 'yuck.' But I suppose this is as good a time as any to tell you . . . looks like we're back to the old ways for a time, each of us having to get what we can get during the day and bringing it here to share."

"What're you saying?" Charlie asked.

By way of answer, Quigly turned out his empty pockets, pale linen tongues of poverty. "So . . . what we got?"

"I've got nothing!" Charlie said. "What I stole I ate for breakfast and I got nothing else 'cause I thought we'd eat just like we been doing."

It was the same with the others.

"Well, at least we have these crusts," Alyss said.

"A hearty food if ever there was one," replied Quigly, trying not to sound too disheartened. He divided the crusts into eight portions, claiming he was full before he finished eating his share. But Alyss could see that his bright, cheerful manner was forced, even a little sarcastic.

She stayed awake after the others had gone to bed. *I have to think of something. Why can't I make the flower sing? Because my imagination was nothing special after all, that's why. So think of something. I will. I will I will I will I will.*

~

"I know how we can get as much food as we're used to having," she told Quigly in the morning, "but we need Charlie, Otis, and Esther to help."

"Whatever you say, Princess."

He wasn't very enthusiastic, didn't seem as though he much wanted to talk to her. *He'll be happy afterwards, once our stomachs are full.*

She dressed in the finest coat she could dig out of the alley's heap of clothes and blankets, and she used her own saliva to wash the dirt from her face and hands. With the stub of a pencil, she wrote out a list of meats on a small square of paper, then she led the others to a butcher's shop that she and Quigly had often passed.

"Stay hidden behind the carriage here and wait for my signal," she told them, and entered the shop.

"And what can I do for you today, young lady?" The butcher was a large, beefy man with a ruddy face. He wore a bloodstained apron.

"I'm supposed to get these for my mother." She handed him the list of meats.

"Hmm. Seems like a lot for you to carry."

"Our carriage is outside but the driver is off on another errand."

She gave him her biggest smile and he couldn't help but believe her. Mere circumstances could not disguise the warm look of a princess.

"Let's see. It says here, one eight-pound rump joint . . ."

He walked through an opening into the back of the shop and she waved for Quigly and the others to hurry inside. They grabbed the chickens hanging in the window, the sausages

116

and hams, Alyss helping load them up when their arms were too full to reach for more.

"Hey!"

The butcher dropped the joint and scrambled from behind the counter. The orphans bolted out of the shop, scattering in different directions.

"There y'are!"

A passing bobby caught Alyss by the collar of her coat. She slipped out of it, her dirty street urchin's clothes visible for all to see, but she only got a few steps farther before he caught her again.

"Let me go!" she said, imagining a tuttle-bird flying in the man's face or biting the hand that held her, neither of which happened.

Quigly had paused at the end of the street and was looking at her, a chicken under each arm, his pockets stuffed with sausages. Maybe he'd come to her rescue? Maybe he'd risk his own safety and do something clever to free her and they'd both get away?

But no. He turned and sprinted around the corner, out of sight.

Alyss never found out if she was the only one of the orphans who'd been caught that day (she was), but even before she'd been roughly escorted to the Charing Cross Foundling Hospital, where she would live until she was adopted by the Liddells, and even before she realized that she would never see Quigly Gaffer again, she had started to think that maybe

it wasn't worthwhile getting attached to people. All they ever did was betray you. They betrayed you by leaving.

Alyss tried not to hear when a warden at Charing Cross opened the door to a large room with cots lined up in two rows against the walls, children screaming and yelling and fighting, and said, "Welcome to your new home."

CHAPTER 17

FOLLOWED BY an angry mob, the Frenchmen brought their prisoner to the Court of First Instance in the Palais de Justice. People pushed and shoved one another, trying to get a better view of the proceedings. The air in the room quickly became hot and stale from so many bodies packed into such a modest enclosure. The men placed the rug upright in the middle of the court, before the magistrate.

A chuckle passed among the prosecutors, advocates, and court reporters.

"Quel est ceci?" asked the magistrate, not amused.

The public prosecutor, a gowned and whiskered gentleman, stood up and said a number of things in French, which, muffled though the unintelligible words were, Hatter could hear from within the confines of the rug.

"*Où est le prisonnier?*" the magistrate asked.

The public prosecutor pointed to the rug. Again, the court regulars laughed. With a heavy sigh, the magistrate warned the gentleman not to make a mockery of the court. The prosecutor apologized and explained that he had no intention of doing any such thing, but that the prisoner was *très dangereux* and the carpet the only means that had been found to subdue him.

A man stepped forward and declared that the prisoner possessed violent, other-worldly powers. The gallery of onlookers, none of whom had witnessed the fight on the rue de Rivoli, came alive with loud assertions of "*C'est vrai! C'est vrai!*"

The magistrate, however, had seen quite the parade of motley life from his perch in court and merely wondered if he might not treat himself to a little fried mutton along with his usual wedge of brie and bottle of bordeaux at his favorite café, Le Chien Dyspeptique.

"*Je voudrais voir le prisonnier,*" he said.

The prosecutor cleared his throat several times and said that, with all due respect, he did not think releasing Hatter from the rug was a good idea. The magistrate huffed and ordered the prosecutor to remove Hatter from the rug or he would find himself in prison for contempt of court. The rug was laid on the floor. The gallery of onlookers surged, people squeezing forward, sensing that something dramatic was about to happen.

They were not mistaken. No sooner was Hatter unrolled from his confinement than he jumped up and—

Thwink!

His wrist-blades sliced the air, blurry with speed. He grabbed a dagger from his backpack and threw it, skewering a painting on the wall next to the magistrate's head—an action that caused the wise man to hunker down beneath his bench for safety.

Before the court police gathered their courage to attempt recapture, Hatter corkscrewed out the nearest window and landed on the sidewalk at a run. The onlookers crowded at the window, hoping to catch a last glimpse of the mysterious man. The magistrate peeked up over his bench to see if his life was still in danger. After surviving such a day, he decided, a plate of fried mutton was well-deserved.

~

Rumors began to spread about a man with spinning knives on his wrists who appeared out of puddles. With the passing months, and after numerous sightings of Hatter had been reported but never officially proved, the rumors fossilized into legend. Civilians claimed that he could defeat an entire regiment on his own. Military men wondered aloud what more Napoleon might have accomplished if he'd had the man in his ranks. Young boys imagined themselves in his shoes, playing the part of a superhero. In drawing rooms, wealthy, educated ladies and gentlemen put aside their usually reserved manners and attempted to imitate his acrobatic spins and twirls, and even, on occasion, his somersaults. Maidservants all over

France gathered in dim kitchens and told one another romantic stories about the legendary figure, with whom they'd fallen in love. A woman must have broken his heart, they imagined, because surely no man would behave as he did for any reason but the suffering of unrequited love? Upon turning in for bed, these lovesick servants left candles burning in their windows, and had Hatter been able to fly over Paris in the middle of the night, he would have seen a sleeping city dotted with these flickering lights of longing—pinpricks of warmth in the cold dark, illuminating the way to women's hearts. But Hatter would have felt anything but deserving, for he was wrestling with an unfamiliar emotion: inadequacy. He had failed to keep his promise to Queen Genevieve.

CHAPTER 18

ALYSS DIDN'T get along with the other children living at the foundling hospital—children who had seen their share of heartache and sorrow, as she had, but who were no less eager to lose themselves in games like jacks, hopscotch, and hide-and-seek. *All so silly and immature.* Thoughts of Redd, about what might have become of Dodge, clouded Alyss' head. She couldn't for the life of her muster up any enthusiasm for games.

The wardens of Charing Cross took a special interest in her and this only served to further alienate her from the rest of the orphans. Anyone could see that she was going to grow into a beautiful woman. It was thought that her beauty might gain her entry into ranks of society rarely attained by orphans, which could bode well for Charing Cross, leading to donations from wealthy families on the hunt for unearthly beauties of their own. Whenever Alyss mentioned Wonderland, she was shushed more harshly than she would have been if the wardens hadn't taken an interest in her.

"That's all in your head, little miss, and no one will want a daughter who talks rubbish all the time. Unless you want to live here forever, you'll clear your mind of that ridiculous, fantastical stuff."

Dr. Williford, the doctor on the staff at Charing Cross, listened patiently to Alyss' ridiculous, fantastical stuff.

"I'm sure you've had to face things that no young girl should ever have to face," he said. "But you cannot hide in fantasy, Alice. Accept what has happened to you and know that you are not alone in misfortune. Try to focus on the sights and sounds around you, because they are reality. There is still a chance for you to lead a normal, fruitful life."

She stopped confiding in Dr. Williford and spent her days staring out a window at a dirty, leaf-strewn courtyard, which was where one of the wardens found her on an afternoon that would (yet again) change everything.

"Alice, I'd like you to say hello to the Reverend and Mrs. Liddell."

 Alyss turned from the greasy window to look at the couple—the woman with the hard eyes and uneasy smile, the doughy man in overcoat and gloves. All strangers were the same to her: strange, far removed, unable to reach her.

"She *is* pretty," Mrs. Liddell said, "but a haircut and a thorough scrubbing are in order, I think."

"Quite," said the reverend.

~

The Liddells lived in Oxford, where the reverend was dean of Christ Church College. Nothing happened, it seemed, that didn't bring with it an element of misfortune. No sooner had Alyss left Charing Cross than she found herself in circumstances hardly more pleasing.

"Not another word!" Mrs. Liddell scolded when Alyss described the Inventors' Parade to her new siblings.

"Animals can't talk because they're dumb beasts," she rebuked when Alyss claimed otherwise.

"Flowers can't sing because they don't have larynxes," she insisted when Alyss told of flowers with beautiful voices. "Keep talking nonsense and I'll wash your mouth out with soap."

"I'm a princess and I'm waiting for Hatter to come and rescue me," Alyss said. "You'll see."

"Alice, if you want to amount to anything in society," Mrs. Liddell warned, "or at the very least show appreciation for what we've done by welcoming you into our home, you'll stop embarrassing this family and live with your head firmly in this world and do as others do."

As punishment, Mrs. Liddell would send Alyss to her room, where she had to stay for days, sometimes a whole week, at a time; meals would be brought to her. That suited her perfectly well. It meant she wouldn't have to see *them*. Wrong! Though she couldn't go out, her new sisters weren't forbidden from visiting, and the second afternoon of one of her confinements Edith and Lorina marched into the room and sat on Alyss' bed, studying her. She tried to ignore them, working hard to remember every gemstone of Heart Palace, every turn of every heart-shaped passage. Numerous drawings of the palace were tacked to her walls. *Fourteen steps leading from the lower courtyard into the ballroom, seventeen bathrooms in total, and—*

"Why don't you draw something else for a change?" Lorina asked her.

"Because I don't want to forget where I came from."

"Better draw the orphanage then!" Edith shrieked, and she and Lorina ran off, laughing.

Alyss sat with pencil poised above her drawing. *I shouldn't care what they think. I don't.* But their mocking laughter had caused a twinge of . . . what? Embarrassment? Shame? Princesses didn't like to be made fun of any more than ordinary people. Alyss pushed the drawing away from her. It would remain forever unfinished.

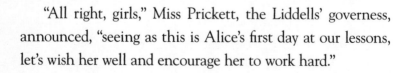

"All right, girls," Miss Prickett, the Liddells' governess, announced, "seeing as this is Alice's first day at our lessons, let's wish her well and encourage her to work hard."

Alyss sat at the dining-room table with Edith, Lorina, and Rhoda, paper and pencil neatly arrayed in front of her. A blackboard rested atop the sideboard. The words "Welcome Alice Liddell" were written on it.

"That's not how you spell my name," Alyss blurted.

Miss Prickett looked at the blackboard, then at Alyss. "No? Perhaps you'll be kind enough to come up here and show me how to spell it. I'll let it pass this time, Alice, but in the future, you are not to speak out. You raise your hand and wait to be called upon."

Alyss held her head high and stared straight ahead as she walked to the sideboard. At the blackboard, she erased *ice* from her name and wrote *yss* in its place. Edith, Lorina, and Rhoda erupted with laughter.

"That *is* enough!" scolded Miss Prickett. "Alice, you will write your name one hundred times on the blackboard. A-L- I- C- E. Now begin."

So she was stuck there, in front of them, while Miss Prickett began the lesson. Edith, Lorina, and Rhoda peeked around their books at her, threw one another giggling glances. Alyss wanted their hair to fill with gwormmies, their eyes to seal shut, their laughing tongues to tie into knots.

Nothing happened.

Useless. White Imagination or Black, it doesn't matter, because I can't conjure. She'd written A- L- I- C- E ninety-nine times. Miss Prickett wasn't looking. She spelled out A- L- Y- S- S on the blackboard and started toward her seat.

127

Miss Prickett turned to the board. "Just a moment, please! I'm sure you think you're clever, Miss Liddell. But let's see what such cleverness gets you. Wipe the board and start again. Another hundred times. A- L-I- C- E. Begin."

Alyss did as she was told, no longer wanting to stand on exhibition.

"Maybe now you'll remember how to spell your name correctly," Miss Prickett scolded when she'd finished.

As she returned to her seat, Lorina whispered, "Odd Alice," and the label stuck. It probably didn't help that whenever the children of family friends thought they'd take a chance and chat with her, Alyss filled their ears with talk of Wonderland.

"She must think she's better than all of us, calling herself a princess," the children huffed.

Alyss got into fights and traded insults with her tormentors, often returning home scraped, bruised, and humiliated. She tried to shut her ears to it all, but doubts began to plague her. *Can everyone be wrong?* She grew tired of persisting in her convictions against the Liddells, their friends, everyone. *Is it really possible that every single person I meet is wrong and I'm right? A whole lot easier if I could just forget.* Might she have imagined that she'd been a princess in another world? *What if I dreamed it up while sick in bed?*

Then the simplest and yet most miraculous thing happened. She found a friendly ear—or rather, two. They belonged to the Reverend Charles Lutwidge Dodgson, the mathematics

lecturer of Christ Church. He was a gentle, shrinking-violet type of fellow who lived at the college and sometimes came to the Liddells' for tea. An amateur photographer, he took pictures of the girls. Alyss posed for him in a corner of the garden, wearing a light-colored dress with flared sleeves, white socks, and patent-leather shoes. She faced to the right of the camera and smirked at him, shy but proud, as if the two of them shared a secret. But it wasn't until a boating trip to Godstow that she told him about Wonderland. They had stopped for a rest, were lounging on the grass while Edith and Lorina played in the shallows of the river Isis, as that particular stretch of the Thames was called.

"Don't you want to join your sisters?" the Reverend Dodgson asked.

Alyss no longer bothered explaining to people that she didn't have any sisters. "No," she replied.

Dodgson thought this a charming answer. "But why not?"

"After you've been a princess and had your queendom taken from you, as I have, it's hard to get excited about a mess of fish and weeds in a river."

The Reverend Dodgson laughed. "Alice, whatever are you talking about?"

Should I? Will he believe? He does seem different from the others. Should I, one last time? The restraint she'd been under gave way. Memories poured out of her as if they had to be spoken aloud, and quickly, to convince her of their truth or be forever forgotten. When she mentioned Dodge, Charles Lutwidge Dodgson started to take notes. Dodge. Dodgson. *He* was the boy. The reverend was flattered to be part of Alyss' dream world.

"You have the most amazing imagination of anyone I've ever met," he told her.

Alyss knew better. She hadn't conjured anything in a long time.

"Let me see if I understand you correctly," Dodgson said. "People can travel through looking glasses, enter through one and exit from another?"

"Yes. I've tried it here but none of the glasses work."

She watched him jot something in his notebook. "Are you really going to write a book about Wonderland, Mr. Dodgson?"

"I think I might. It'll be *our* book, Alice. Yours and mine."

The book would prove that she was telling the truth. She would not give up on herself. Not yet.

PART TWO

CHAPTER 19

IN A region somewhere between the Everlasting Forest and Outerwilderbeastia, remarkable only for its desolation, Wonderlanders who not long before had been law-abiding, family-loving folk slaved away in Redd's most notorious labor camp, Blaxik. Having fallen into the queen's ill favor, they worked in unventilated factory rooms for seventeen hours a day on nothing more than water and infla-rice—a food favored by the poor because each grain inflated in the stomach, making the recipient feel full.

It had been decreed that every Wonderlander was to have a three-foot-high porcelain and crystal statue of Redd in his residence, the set piece in a shrine to the queendom's ruler. Surprise spot checks by Redd's soldiers were not uncommon. Those in violation of the decree, anyone whose statue was not in pristine condition, found themselves hauled off to Blaxik, where—in a bit of irony Redd found pleasing—they were forced to make the statues until death descended upon them.

But tonight something was wrong. Production of the statues had been interrupted by a rebel attack. Periodic explosions rattled camp dormitories. Flares zoomed through the night, illuminating figures engaged in hand-to-hand combat. Card soldiers from Redd's technologically advanced, ultramodern army, known as The Cut, were trying to fend off the attack, which shouldn't have been so difficult considering that the rebels were nothing more than a hodgepodge of ex-Heart soldiers and Wonderland civilians. But the rebels had righteous anger working for them, which could be a better weapon than mere combat skills, and among them was one who suddenly split in two so as to lend an extra body to the fight: Generals Doppel and Gänger, battling alongside a white knight, a white rook, and several pawns. The rebels called themselves Alyssians, in honor of the young princess who'd been killed before her time, never able to ascend to the throne. Princess Alyss Heart: not alive in flesh and blood, but very much alive as a symbol of more innocent (though still imperfect) times, an icon of hope for peace's return.

Among the Alyssians, one particular soldier was making a name for himself with his growing military prowess and suicidal bravery. If this renegade didn't always mix with his rebel brethren, if he kept to himself when not engaged in battle, at least he was on *their* side. Better to have him as a friend than an enemy, as anyone who'd seen him fight well knew. It was this renegade who broke away from the cover of the other rebels at the Battle of Blaxik. Without concern for his own well-being, and with sword glinting, he slashed his way through Redd's soldiers, who looked like ordinary playing cards (albeit larger) when unengaged, but who now fanned out as if the hand of a giant poker player was spreading them across the green baize of a gaming table. Each card flipped open to form a soldier almost twice the height of an average Wonderland male, with limbs of steel and a brain that understood little more than how to follow orders in combat. One by one, the renegade aimed the point of his blade at the soldiers' upper chests, their single vulnerable spot (a medallion-sized area above the breastplate, at the base of the steel-tendoned neck); a direct hit cut through vital inner workings and sent sparks flying, killing them. He fired a cannonball spider at the doors of the factory; in midair it mutated from ball to massive black spider and tore through the doors. As the renegade slashed and hacked at Redd's soldiers, the slave workers were able to flee across the plain into the Everlasting Forest.

A burning dormitory illuminated the renegade's face: handsome and rugged, with four parallel scars visible on his right cheek. Dodge Anders. Only fourteen years old but fighting like a grown man.

~

A handful of years had passed since Redd's initial invasion of Heart Palace, and the chaos that resulted from her takeover of the queendom had settled into a new order. Upon hearing of Redd's coup and fearing the kind of ruler she'd be, many citizens had immediately packed their bags and tried to emigrate to Boarderland, that independent country separated from Wonderland by the tangled expanse of Outerwilderbeastia and overseen by King Arch. But whether these would-be emigrants didn't bribe Boarderland's border officials generously enough, or Redd had anticipated an exodus among the cowards of the population and made an agreement with King Arch, no one was able to leave. All were stuck in Wonderland, forced to endure the teeth of Redd's anger. Entire families were shipped off to labor camps or, worse, exterminated. Others, who hadn't attempted to flee the country but nonetheless had issues with Redd being queen, heard about the Alyssians and fled what they knew of normal life to join the resistance.

Redd chose to rule the queendom from her fortress on Mount Isolation. The fortress served as a constant reminder of her years in exile and unjust banishment at the hands of her dear departed sister, and thus was a spur to her ruthless methods. Soon after her coronation, and very hush-hush, Redd had the Heart Crystal moved to the fortress, and she could feel it now, shimmering in its secret chamber as she paced back and forth, listening to Bibwit Harte recite pages of *In Queendom Speramus*, which she was rewriting, the tutor acting as her secretary.

"... *the queendom had always been a naïve, optimistic place*," Bibwit read. "*It was as if Wonderland were run by girls and boys—*"

"By children," Redd corrected.

"*—by children who had yet to put away their childish toys and face the harsh realities of the universe.*"

"Good," Redd said. "Now continue: *A universe in which only the cruelest survive, a jabberwock-eat-jabberwock universe, so to speak.*"

The pointed tip of Bibwit's quill scurried against the royal papyrus. The Cat entered the room.

"Yes?" Redd asked.

The Cat hissed, "Blaxik has fallen and the slaves escaped. The Alyssians were responsible."

Redd clenched her fists. Items around the room began to quiver. The Alyssians: a boil on the face of her reign, a thorn in the fist of her rule. Why hadn't The Cut done away with them already? Weapons and furnishings, anything not bolted down, shook with her mounting fury. Knowing her intolerance for failure, Bibwit Harte and The Cat hurried from the room.

"Yaaaaaaaaah!" Redd yelled, standing at the center of whirling chairs, lamps, swords, spears, platters, and books, a tornado brought forth from the bottomless well of her hateful imagination.

Blaxik attacked? Slaves freed? Heads were going to roll.

~

In the aftermath of the Blaxik battle, their adrenaline still pumping, Dodge and the white rook braved a walk through the teeming urban slum Wonderland had become to remind themselves why they fought. The rook camouflaged himself in a hooded coat, but Dodge refused to do likewise. He would not hide who he was from his enemies.

"I remember when Wonderlanders actually cared for this city," the rook said as they picked their way along a sidewalk choked with litter. "Streets were clean, roads swept. The curb-side shrubs and flowers were always humming bouncy tunes." He glanced at the curb: nothing but weeds and long-dead growth; all vegetation silent, killed by Naturcide, a chemical Redd had concocted specifically for that purpose. "And you could get a hot, fresh tarty tart on every corner. I miss tarty tarts."

Dodge nodded. He had his own memories: the glittering, quartz-like buildings of Genevieve's time, the twinkling colors of towers and spires regularly cleaned and polished. Wonderland had been a gleaming, incandescent place, filled for the most part with hardworking, law-respecting citizens. Now everything was covered with grime and soot. Poverty and crime had oozed out of the back alleys and taken over the main streets, and anything bright and luminescent had to hide itself away in the nooks and crannies of the city.

"Let's cross the street," the rook suggested.

Dodge saw why: Ahead of them, a fight had broken out—two emaciated Wonderlanders attacking a third. Probably an imagination-stimulant deal gone bad. Dodge and the rook could never walk more than a few streets without witnessing a brawl. It was best not to approach, to not draw attention to themselves.

They crossed the street and came to a corner crowded with smoky gwormmy-kabob grills and crystal smugglers hawking contraband. Dodge tried to call to his senses the aroma of freshly baked tarty tarts. Hadn't his father bought him one on this very corner? His sense-memory failed him. Impossible to enter into the past. Underneath the shouts and horns that echoed through the streets, he heard a disembodied voice speaking "Reddisms" from loudspeakers mounted overhead. *The Redd way is the right way. As in the beginning, there was Redd, so in the end Redd shall be.* Three-dimensional faces on holographic billboards told of the latest crackdowns and taxations. Piped in from who knew where played the background music of Wondertropolis' free fall into decay. It seemed to come from every crack in the pavement, every pothole in the street, every crevice in the time-battered buildings: a composition on infinite repeat, featuring lyrics Redd had written herself, which sang her praises as Wonderland's savior.

"I'd like to hear silence again," Dodge said. "A whole day's worth of quiet. Do you remember what that was like?"

"Yes. But you know how it is." The rook did his best imitation of Redd. "'Silence is hereby outlawed. Silence breeds independent thought, which in turn breeds dissent.'"

Not that there were many true dissenters, as they both knew. Those disloyal to Redd were quickly rooted out of the general population, never to be heard from again.

The Blaxik battle was growing more distant in their minds, their blood cooling. They had their choice of places to visit, provided they were careful.

"How about a jabberwocky match?" suggested the rook. At the amphitheater, they could watch the huge, ferocious beasts go at each other with a teeth-gnashing hatred rivaled only by that which audience members felt for one another.

Dodge shook his head. "Fights always break out and I don't like the feeling I get when we slip away without at least injuring a few of Redd's soldiers."

"The statue then?"

Again, Dodge shook his head. The Queen Redd statue stood at the city's western edge, where, from the observation deck, Dodge could gaze out through the eyes of this enormous agate replica at the city spread below. It sometimes helped his vengeance to imagine himself inside the queen's skull. But not today. "Let's just walk," he said.

They passed the boarded-up shop fronts in Redd Plaza, the pawnshops and moneylenders in Redd Square, and the mammoth complex of Redd Towers Apartments, whose advertising slogan, "If you lived here, you'd be home by now," did little to fill vacancies. They stopped in at Redd's Hotel & Casino where, in addition to gambling with crystal,

Wonderlanders could bet their lives on a single roll of the dice. Dodge picked up his pace when they passed Heart Palace—now fallen into disrepair and occupied by stimulant-addled squatters—on their way to the Five Spires of Redd construction site. Her Imperial Viciousness had promised that the Five Spires of Redd would be the tallest structure ever erected in the universe—a vertical column of steel sheathed in spiked and mottled crystal, rising magnificently into the sky and topped with five pointed spires like the fingers and thumb of the queen herself.

"Do you think she'll finish it?" the rook asked.

Dodge tensed. "I don't think we should give her the chance."

Everywhere they went, they saw signs urging Wonderlanders to attend meetings of the numberless Black Imagination societies that now flourished in every banqueting hall, while the few White Imagination societies were forced to gather in stealth and secret. Anyone exposed as a practitioner of White Imagination was sentenced to a slow, work-slogged death—shipped off to the Crystal Mines, just as practitioners of Black Imagination had been in Genevieve's time, but whereas then the emphasis had been on hard work and repentance with a chance for freedom, prisoners were now purposely worked past all endurance.

"What sort of world is this," the rook asked, angry, "where neighbors and friends inform on one another? Where children, mad at their parents because they didn't get a Black

Imagination starter's kit for their birthday, can complain to the nearest lieutenant from The Cut, saying they've heard their parents claim Redd isn't the rightful ruler of the queendom, and then their parents are hauled off to face unmentionable tortures? And I'm sure Redd doesn't care if they tell the truth."

"She probably prefers it if they don't," Dodge said.

The rook nodded, again imitated Redd: "'Because it's much more Black Imagination. My reign thrives on deceit and violence.'"

"And uncertainty."

The rook sniffed in disgust. "Different laws for different people. A member of the Spades or Clubs, he avoids being shipped to the mines with a generous donation to the queen's personal crystal account; whereas for the average Wonderlander, there's no hope: It's off to the mines he goes."

They turned their footsteps in the direction of the Everlasting Forest. They had seen enough.

"I'll tell you what sort of world this is," the rook said, answering his own question. "It's one that can't last."

"No," Dodge said. But he was no longer thinking of the rise and fall of queens, the corruption of general populations. He was thinking of something more personal, his motivation for getting up in the morning: assassination of The Cat.

CHAPTER 20

HATTER MADIGAN left Paris within thirty-two hours of escaping the Palais de Justice and scoured the country in search of Alyss. After weeks of fruitless searching, he arrived in the principality of Monaco on the Mediterranean coast. It was mid-August, the peak of summer. He hadn't yet visited a single hat shop when he was walking down a side street near the beach and heard a passing gentleman exclaim to a companion, "Ah, *regardes cela! Pauvre petit chapeau haut-de-forme!*"

Hatter had picked up enough French to know that *chapeau* meant "hat." As the men continued on their way, he turned for a glimpse of the headwear in question and saw a top hat floating in the middle of a puddle. He knew in a moment; it was *his* hat. How had it gotten there? Hatter examined the puddle. It should have been evaporating in the heat, but he could tell by its edges that it wasn't. An evaporating puddle would have had a ring of damp around it, indicating its original size before the effects of the sun.

Hatter had studied his share of puddles during his time in this world, wondering which of them, if any, might take him back to Wonderland once he was reunited with Princess Alyss. There had been nothing telltale about any of them, nothing signifying their use as a return portal. But this one . . . careful not to step in it, he bent down and picked up the hat. It was soaked but it looked all right. He flicked his wrist. There they were, the S-shaped blades. So the weapon still worked. With another wrist-flick, the blades morphed back into a dripping top hat, which Hatter put on his head, tapping the crown as might a dandy adding the final touch to his wardrobe before heading out for a night of frolic and fun. As a test, Hatter picked up a stone and dropped it into the puddle.

Ker-whoosh!

The water sucked it down and out of sight.

Could this be a return portal? Might the Pool of Tears, the only means out of Wonderland, have many return portals, various portal routes connecting to it like tentacles to the head of an octopus? And what if Alyss had discovered one of them—a puddle situated where no water should naturally have been—and traveled back to Wonderland? It was unlikely, since no one who'd entered the Pool of Tears had ever yet

146

returned. But Alyss was not your average Pool of Tears traveler. She wasn't average in anything. If she had returned, she
would not survive long. She didn't have the training, her
imaginative muscle unexercised, and Redd wouldn't stand
for it.

Hatter flattened his top hat into blades, aligning them in
a stack to make them as compact as possible. He tucked the
weapon into a secure, thick-lined pocket inside his coat; he
had no intention of losing it again.

But what if his theory was wrong? What if this puddle led
to some unknown destination instead of back to Wonderland?
Stepping into it was a serious risk. For Alyss' sake, and for that
of the queendom, it was one he had to take.

CHAPTER 21

AFTER THE temper subsides and one has a moment to calmly reflect, it isn't uncommon for declarations shouted in a fit of rage to strike one as untrue, and because they may have been hurtful to family, friends, lovers, husbands, or wives, one wishes them unsaid. But this was not the case with eleven-year-old Alyss Heart, who had waited with impatience for the Reverend Charles Dodgson to complete the book describing her life in Wonderland, all the while entertaining visions of comeuppance for those who'd doubted her. When Dodgson at last presented her with a copy of the book during a picnic of cold chicken and salad along the river Cherwell, and she discovered that it had little to do with her and that he'd purposely twisted everything she'd told him into nonsense—*How could he?*

A *vicious joke!*—anger filled her to the tips of her fingers. If her talk of Wonderland wasn't fantasy, it might as well have been, for all the hurt and trouble it had caused her.

She meant exactly what she said and never once, in all the years afterward, regretted it.

"You're the cruelest man I've ever met, Mr. Dodgson, and if you had believed a single word I told you, you'd know how very cruel that is! I never want to see you again! Never, never, never!"

She left Dodgson on the riverbank, perplexed, and ran the entire way home. She stomped into the hall and slammed the door behind her, surprising Mrs. Liddell.

"What, back already?"

But Alyss—her face twisted with grief and rage—didn't stop. *A cruel, vicious man! What am I supposed to do now? Can't live as Odd Alice.* She took the stairs two at a time up to her room and locked the door.

"Alice?" Mrs. Liddell called, following her. "Where are Edith and Lorina? Where's Mr. Dodgson? What's happened?"

But Alyss wouldn't say, nor would she come out of her room. She didn't hear Mrs. Liddell knocking at the door, the annoyed but futile turning of the doorknob, or the imperious demand: "Alice, open this door. Open it this minute." The blood roared in her veins and suddenly she was ripping the drawings of Heart Palace off her walls a fistful at a time, tearing them into confetti. *No more. Erase it all. I will no longer be Odd Alice. Odd Alice must die.* Yes, it was a solution: Give up her so-called ridiculous, fantastical delusions and enter wholeheartedly into the world around her. Become just like everyone else.

Listen.

Mrs. Liddell was no longer accosting the door to her room. She heard voices downstairs. Dodgson and her sisters must have returned. *The beastly man!*

"Alice, come downstairs!" Mrs. Liddell called. "Mr. Dodgson is here!"

"I won't see him!"

Thinking afresh on what he'd done, remembering the feel of his idiotic book in her hands, she became enraged all over again—*He tricked me! A man with a heart of ice!*—and kicked at the heaps of confetti lying on the floor. *What was—?* Something had moved in the looking glass: not a reflection of herself, of anything in the room. *No!* It was Genevieve, dressed as Alyss last remembered her, but without her crown.

"Never forget who you are, Alyss," Genevieve said.

"Shut up!" Alyss cried, and threw a pillow at the looking glass.

Her mother—or whoever the woman in the mirror was—had never been through what she'd had to deal with these last four years. The mirror was suddenly empty, reflecting only the room. But of course nobody had been in the mirror. How stupid! Her imagination had been playing tricks on her.

Exhausted, Alyss dropped to the floor, sobbing. Before long, she fell asleep amidst the scraps of paper palaces. When

she emerged from her room the next morning—a room perfectly clean, no confetti on the floor, no sign of the violence
done to it hours earlier—the Liddells were at breakfast in the
dining room. They immediately noticed a change in Alyss
without being able to pinpoint what it was. Edith and Lorina
fell still, mid-chew, their open mouths revealing a mash of
scrambled egg. Dean Liddell paused in the midst of buttering
his scone, and Mrs. Liddell continued pouring tea into her
cup even after it spilled over onto the saucer. Not until the
servant started to clean it up did she notice what she'd done.

"You're wearing the dress," Mrs. Liddell said. The dress
she had purchased months before but which Alyss had always
refused to wear because she feared it would make her appear
common.

"Yes, Mother."

But that wasn't it, didn't account for the change.

"You look . . . rather lovely," said Dean Liddell.

"Thank you, Father."

The change was in subtler things—the tilt of Alyss' head,
the particular sweep of her arms, her careful steps forward.
The Liddells were so taken with her appearance that they
failed to realize it was the first time she had ever called them
by those most intimate of endearments: Mother and Father.

CHAPTER 22

HATTER PUT one foot in the puddle, but the sole of his shoe never touched the bottom. He tumbled down, falling deeper and deeper until he stopped and floated in the depths, only to shoot up again as fast as his descent had been. When he broke the surface, he was in the Pool of Tears.

The clouds above swirled violently and the water was rough and choppy. He swam to the crystal shore, his senses alive to any sign of Redd or her hordes. He climbed out of the water and stealthily approached the nearest tree—a beaten old thing with a scarred trunk and leafless, craggy branches.

"Has Princess Alyss returned to Wonderland? Have you seen her come out of the pool?"

"Princess Alyss is dead!" the tree said loudly, as if for the

benefit of an unseen but all-hearing force liable to inflict great hurt at the slightest provocation.

"I have no evidence of her death."

"Princess Alyss Heart is dead!" the tree said louder than ever, but added in a whisper, "Redd's Glass Eyes are everywhere. It's dangerous to talk. The princess has not returned."

Hatter didn't know what the Glass Eyes were—Redd had only recently unleashed them on the queendom—but he wasn't going to stick around to find out. As long as he had strength in him, his duty dictated that he return to the other world and search for the princess. He would find her, train her in the ways of a warrior queen, as he had her mother; then they could both come home to face plenty of trouble, the Glass Eyes being only part of it.

He dived back into the Pool of Tears, the gravity of the portal—already growing more familiar to him—pulling him down. Likewise more familiar to him was the pause in the deep, the momentary suspension, followed by the heart-in-mouth feeling as he rocketed up and out of a puddle behind a milking shed on the outskirts of Budapest, Hungary. Three unimpressed goats were the only earthly creatures to see the figure twirl out of a sun-scorched puddle and land confidently on his feet.

Hatter wondered whether he could learn to navigate the Pool of Tears as he did the Crystal Continuum, so that he might be able to choose his earthly destination. Control would be more difficult to attain than it was in the

Continuum. Water was a heavy medium; to maneuver in it would require skill, balance, endurance, strength of body and mind. But these were considerations for another day, another year, because Hatter's worldwide search for Alyss now began in earnest.

He trailed people alight with the glow of imagination, believing that one of them would lead him to Wonderland's princess, who couldn't fail to glow in this world.

He visited hat shops in the towns and cities of Spain, Portugal, Belgium, Switzerland, Austria, Bavaria, Italy, Prussia, Greece, Poland (to name but several). In 1864, five years into his search, having twice circled the European continent, he took the Calais ferry to Dover, England. Had *Alice's Adventures in Wonderland* been published by the time he arrived, any one of the salespeople in the hat shops and haberdasheries he visited would have been stung with recognition upon hearing the name Princess Alyss Heart of Wonderland issue from his lips, though they might have thought him mad—a man in search of a fictional character. As it was, they only tried to sell him hats he didn't need while complimenting him on the one he wore. Hatter would be far from England a year later when Charles Dodgson's book was first published.

As he roamed the world in search of Wonderland's princess, maps sticking out of every available pocket, worn from use and much scribbled on with notes of where he'd been and what routes he'd taken, Hatter's legend grew. Though the

languages in which it was told varied as widely as the terrain he covered—ranging from Afrikaans to Hindi to Japanese to Welsh—and the details of the story often changed, its basic premise was the same: A solitary man blessed with fearsome physical abilities and armed with a curious assemblage of weaponry crossed continents on a mysterious quest that led him to headwear merchants the world over—whether a peddler of knitted caps operating from a tent in a North African Bedouin encampment or an exclusive hat shop in the heart of Prague.

Hatter sightings were reported in America, which was nearing the end of a civil war—glimpses of him stalking streets in New York and Massachusetts, tramping the snow-covered hills of Vermont, the icy roads of Delaware, Rhode Island, New Hampshire, and Maine. He traveled down through Mexico and South America, skirted the Antarctic Peninsula, and circled back up to California and Oregon. He passed into Canada and eventually made his way to the Asian countries and the Far East.

Then, in the third week of April 1872, thirteen years after he lost Alyss, Hatter entered a shop in a crowded bazaar in Egypt, in the shadow of the Great Pyramid of Giza.

"I'm looking for Princess Alyss Heart of Wonderland," he said to the shopkeeper. "I'm a member of Wonderland's Millinery. Any information you have pertaining to Princess Alyss will be highly appreciated and, in due time, rewarded."

He had uttered these exact words so many times, and not

once met with success, that a normal man would have given up on their power to provoke a meaningful response. The truth was, he didn't expect the shopkeeper to have any information, so he was surprised when the man beckoned him toward a high shelf, where a book was leaning between a miniature sphinx carved out of sandstone and a basket of dried camel tongues. The man dusted it with his sleeve and handed it to Hatter. It was an English edition of *Alice's Adventures in Wonderland*.

Her name was misspelled, but . . . Wonderland? Surely, it was his Alyss. How could it be anyone else? The girl in the illustrations looked nothing like her, and yet it could not be coincidence. Hatter's future path had become clear: To find Alyss, he would first have to find the book's author, Lewis Carroll.

CHAPTER 23

BULLET-LIKE, DODGE raced headlong through the kaleidoscopic glitter of the Crystal Continuum. "Yeah-ha! Wooooo!"

Wonderlanders, struggling to get out of his way, were sucked up through crystal byways and reflected out of looking glasses into seedy restaurants or the homes of strangers—looking glasses out of which they had never meant to be reflected, on their way to other destinations.

"Yeah, yeah, yeah!" Dodge shouted. "Come on!"

Four Glass Eyes were chasing him. They looked like ordinary Wonderlanders except for the implants of reflective colorless crystal in their eye sockets. An artificial race with enhanced sight, strength, and speed, Glass Eyes were built for hand-to-hand combat, and they patrolled the

Crystal Continuum with orders to annihilate anyone suspected of being an Alyssian. Their patrols had effectively
limited rebel mobility, all but choked off a major channel
for rebel communications. Handheld looking glass com-
municators had never been viable for anything but short,
cryptic intelligence reports, as dispatches could be inter-
cepted by anyone at any time. The most effective means
of sending and retrieving sensitive Alyssian intelligence
had been to use portal runners to traverse the Crystal
Continuum. But that was before the Glass Eyes. Now being
a portal runner meant dying sooner rather than later. Portal
runs were one step removed from suicide missions. Dodge
Anders had made more portal runs than any Alyssian and
he always volunteered to deliver the most important mes-
sages, warnings, and intel updates. The occasion for this
run: Redd's troops had been active and General Doppelgänger
suspected an impending attack on an Alyssian outpost situated in the Snark Mountain foothills. The outpost had to
be warned.

Shoooooooomph!

Dodge flew through the Continuum, the Glass Eyes gaining on him. These contests of navigational skill and strength
were the only times he felt anything even approaching
happiness.

It didn't matter that he might be killed. He was being useful
and it made him feel that much closer to exacting his revenge.

In front of him, the Continuum splintered in many

directions. He threw his body weight to the left and made a sharp turn at the last minute. He looked behind him: One of the Glass Eyes hadn't made the turn. Three more to go. And he had to lose them quick, before others joined the chase.

Spinning to avoid the Glass Eyes' gunfire, Dodge removed his sword from its scabbard and held it firmly with both hands. With a great effort of will, he came to a sudden stop. The Glass Eyes weren't expecting it, came rushing upon him, and the frontrunner impaled himself on Dodge's sword. Before the two remaining Glass Eyes could regain their equilibrium, Dodge relaxed, surrendered his body to the pull of the nearest looking glass, and was sucked up out of the Continuum, reflected out of a glass in the lobby of an apartment building. In less time than it took a galloping spirit-dane to make a single stride, he pressed himself flat against the wall next to the looking glass. The Glass Eyes flew out of it and past him. He smashed the glass with the handle of his sword. As fragments of mirror scattered and fell, Dodge squeezed his entire body back into the Continuum through a reflective sliver no larger than a jabberwock's toe—a feat the Glass Eyes hadn't mastered, for when they tried, they couldn't get their entire bodies into the Continuum, only those parts that had been reflected in the fragment. Zooming through the looking glass' fast-disappearing crystalline byway, the void racing up behind him, Dodge looked back a final time and saw one Glass Eye with half a face, a shoulder, and little else, the other with a head and torso but no arms. The Glass Eyes had no strength and were swallowed by the void. He too would have become part of the nothingness if he hadn't hooked up with the Continuum's main artery when he did.

Dodge continued on his way, heading for a certain looking glass not far from Snark Mountain. He emerged from the Continuum and made the rest of the journey on foot. But the joy he'd felt during the chase quickly vanished. He had reverted to his usual tightly contained self by the time he arrived to warn the leader of the Alyssian outpost of a possible attack from Redd.

Mission completed. What now? He could head back to the Everlasting Forest, but all he'd probably find there would be General Doppelgänger and the others sitting around talking strategy. Anything was better than just sitting around.

So he risked an extra portal run, emerged near the Whispering Woods, and passed through them to the Pool of Tears. He came here every once in a while, stood on the cliff overlooking the pool, thinking about the life that had happened to him. Like his father, he had once believed in the principles of White Imagination—love, justice, and duty to others. But he knew better now: An adherence to higher principles got one nowhere in this world. It was not, as his father had preached, its own reward. What sort of reward allowed others to conquer and murder and do away with all you held dear?

He had been reckless to come to the pool. Shouldn't have taken the unnecessary risk. He had to stay alive. His vengeance required it.

CHAPTER 24

ALICE WORKED hard to enter into the world in which she found herself and refused to see Dodgson whenever he came to the house. Pained by her refusals, he came with less and less frequency until he ceased coming altogether. The book he'd written for her was published for the public's enjoyment under the title *Alice's Adventures in Wonderland*. It was widely known that Alice's fantastic stories had served as its inspiration—fodder for poking fun at her, if ever there was—but so well had she adapted to the customs and beliefs of the time, so well had she adopted the inclinations of other girls her age, that she'd befriended those who used to tease her mercilessly. And although Mrs. Liddell never discovered the cause for Alice's tantrum that fateful afternoon at the river Cherwell, she was more than

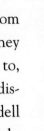

pleased with her daughter's behavior ever since. Far from being flattered by Dodgson's silly scribblings, it was as if they had brought home to Alice, as nothing else had been able to, just how inane all her Wonderland talk had been. She distanced herself from the book and its author, and Mrs. Liddell took this to mean that she was finally growing up—which, indeed, she was.

Beginning in her sixteenth year, while on Sunday strolls along High Street with her mother and sisters, it was as the wardens of Charing Cross had predicted: Young men of rank paused in appreciation as Alice passed, took pains to learn who she was, invited her to parties where they did their best to impress her with their wit and knowledge of worldly affairs. They did not find Miss Liddell lacking in intelligence. Some perhaps even found her a bit too intelligent. She was a thoughtful, well-read young woman, with opinions on a variety of topics such as the responsibility that came with Britain's military power, the nature of commerce and industry under a monarchy, how to care for the poor and neglected, the sensationalist tendencies of the Fleet Street papers, and the convolutions of the legal system as exposed by the eminent author Charles Dickens.

Many well-to-do dandies—even those uncomfortable with any woman who appeared smarter than themselves— thought it unfortunate that she'd been adopted. It meant that they could never marry her. Of course, these fellows took it for granted that Miss Liddell would have considered herself lucky to marry any one of them. But she was not easily impressed, nor prone to fall in love. The vicissitudes of her life had caused her to keep her feelings for others in check: It was dangerous to care for people; inevitably, you got hurt. She talked with young men, accepted their invitations to parties and galas, but more because it pleased her mother than because of any affection for the men themselves.

The Reverend Dodgson published a sequel to *Alice's Adventures in Wonderland* entitled *Through the Looking-Glass*. Again, his scribblings met with popular success. Alice herself did not read the book, but not long before its publication, and against her wishes, she found herself in the same room with its author. Oxford was not a big town and she'd often seen Dodgson in the street, or crossing the college grounds, but she had taken care not to get caught in conversation with him; she would offer a word of greeting as good manners required, but that was all. Alice's eighteenth birthday having passed, Mrs. Liddell thought it time to document for posterity the young woman her daughter had become. She wanted Alice to sit for a photographic portrait and she asked Dodgson to be the photographer.

"Mother, please. You know I don't wish to see him," Alice said.

"A lady might not like a man," Mrs. Liddell said, "but she shouldn't show it so explicitly as you do."

So Alice agreed to sit for the portrait. On the appointed day, she heard Dodgson enter the house and begin setting up his equipment in the parlor.

164

Detestable man, how can you not understand what you did to me? Should I forgive? I can't, I can't. Must be polite. But be quick about it. Get in and get out.

Alice could not completely hide her feelings, and when Mrs. Liddell called her down, she moved with the briskness of one overburdened with appointments.

"Good afternoon, Mr. Dodgson," she said, and fell into a chair.

She slumped there, hands in her lap, head tilted toward her right shoulder as she eyed Dodgson from under her darkened brow until—as fast as he could: her behavior made him uncomfortable—he took the picture. Then she heaved herself up out of the chair.

"Thank you, sir," she said, looking not at him but over his head as she left the room.

By Alice's twentieth year, Mrs. Liddell was becoming anxious for her to choose a husband from among her many suitors.

"But I don't feel anything for a single one of them," Alice complained, shaking her head to fling out the unwanted memory of a boy left behind long ago. *Don't think of him! I mustn't!*

Then, one Saturday, the Liddell family attended an outdoor concert by a quartet at Christ Church Meadow. They were about to take their seats when a young gentleman, under the pretense of introducing himself to Dean Liddell, approached. He was Prince Leopold, Queen Victoria's youngest son, and he had been sent to Christ Church so that Dean Liddell might oversee his education. This was his first time meeting the family.

Mrs. Liddell became fidgety and excited as she was introduced.

"And these ladies," said Dean Liddell, presenting his daughters, "are Edith, Lorina, and Alice. Girls, say hello to Prince Leopold."

Alice held out her hand for the prince to kiss. He seemed reluctant to let it go.

"I'm afraid you can't keep it, Your Highness," she said. And when he didn't understand: "My hand. I may have use for it still."

"Ah. Well, if I must return it to you, then I must, though if it ever needs safekeeping . . ."

"I shall think of you, Your Highness."

Prince Leopold insisted that the Liddells sit with him. He placed himself between Alice and Mrs. Liddell, and when the concert began with a Mozart medley, he leaned over and whispered in Alice's ear, "I don't fancy medleys. They skip lightly over so many works without delving thoroughly into any one of them."

"There are quite a few people like that as well," Alice whispered in return.

Mrs. Liddell, not hearing this exchange, flashed her daughter a look, which Alice was at a loss to interpret. The prince talked to her through the entire concert, discussing

everything from art to politics. He found Miss Liddell unlike other young women, who spoke of nothing but velvet draperies, wallpaper patterns, and the latest fashions, women who batted their eyelashes and expected him to swoon. Miss Liddell didn't try to impress him—indeed, she gave the impression that she didn't much care what he thought of her and he rather admired that. And her beauty . . . yes, her beauty was undeniable. All in all, he thought her a delectable puzzle of a creature.

No sooner was the concert over and Leopold gone than Mrs. Liddell voiced what she'd been trying to communicate to Alice with her eyes.

"He's a prince! A prince! And he's taken a fancy to you, I'm certain!"

"We were only talking, Mother. I talked to him as I would have talked to anyone."

But her mother's awe and enthusiasm were difficult to ignore, and she started running into Leopold all over town. If she strolled through the Christ Church Picture Gallery, she found him gazing intently at an oil painting by one of the old masters. If she visited the Bodleian Library, she found him thumbing through a volume of Gibbon's *The History of the Decline and Fall of the Roman Empire* (which she had read in its entirety).

He's handsome enough, I suppose. And obviously well bred.

Yes, but so were many of the men who vied for her attention. At least he didn't stroke his mustache with impatience as she talked of the need to provide for Britain's poor.

"A nation should be judged on how it looks after its more unfortunate children," she explained. "If Great Britain is truly to be the greatest kingdom in the world, it is not enough to flaunt our military power and our dominance in industry. We must lead by example and be more charitable to and protective of our own."

Prince Leopold always listened to her judiciously, weighing her arguments and reasonings with seriousness. He never agreed or disagreed with her.

Mother may be right. I could certainly do worse than marry a prince. But although Alice tried to feel something for the man, her heart remained unconvinced.

~

Three months after the concert at Christ Church Meadow, while taking a ride in his carriage to Boar's Hill, Prince Leopold said, "Your father tells me that you'll be visiting the Banbury Orphanage tomorrow afternoon. I'd like to come along, if you'll have me. One never knows what sort of troubles might beset a young woman there."

"If you think it best, Your Highness."

He offered to take her in the carriage, but Alice said that she'd prefer to walk.

"You see so much more of the town when you walk—a little curiosity shop or a snatch of garden where you wouldn't think it possible to have a garden, choked as it is by city

things. In a carriage, you hurry past these treasures without noticing them."

She didn't take the slightest quirk of mankind for granted, but viewed it as a small miracle and cause for celebration, and the prince had begun to love her for this.

At Banbury, the orphans crowded around Alice, hugging her skirts, all shouting at once. Alice laughed, held four conversations simultaneously and, to Leopold's eye, set off against the soot-stained walls, the drab and loose-hanging clothes of the orphans, and the pale, bloodless faces of the wardens, she looked more radiant than he'd ever seen her. On a tour of the orphanage, a train of children following at their heels, one young boy refused to let go of Alice's left thumb.

Alice requested a thorough accounting of the troubles facing the Banbury Orphanage. The wardens pointed out floors rotten from overflowing sewage, the sagging infirmary roof, the time-worn mattresses as thin as wafers. They showed her the pantry, empty save for sacks of dried kidney beans and uncooked rice.

"The children have had nothing but beans and rice for two weeks," one of the women told her. "We were supposed to be getting a supply of beef ribs, but so far . . . nothing. This sort of thing happens rather frequently, I'm afraid."

Prince Leopold had been silent for some time. He cleared his throat. "What of the warden responsible for ensuring that Banbury receives the food and clothes the children need?"

"The chief warden is very selective as to who gets what

and how much of it, Your Highness," the warden explained. "He says we take in too many children and that perhaps they are not so deserving. For example, that one there"—the warden pointed at the boy holding on to Alice's thumb— "he has a real talent for thieving, though often as not what he steals is food because of how hungry he is. They all are." She gestured at the surrounding orphans.

Alice looked at the boy clutching her thumb, suddenly reminded of Quigly Gaffer. *What's become of him and the others? Andrew, Margaret, and Francine were hardly old enough to dress themselves, never mind living on the streets without the love and support of family.*

The mournful, faraway look on Alice's face had a profound effect on the prince. "I shall talk with the queen," he said after several moments. "I think we might establish a Commission of Inquiry into the matter and, in the meantime, arrange for an increase in food rations. How does that sound?"

"It sounds like generosity rarely met with among the living," said the woman.

"Well, no one here shall soon discover if it's to be met with among the *dead* either, if I can help it."

The orphans blinked and said nothing, hardly believing what they had heard: Queen Victoria and Prince Leopold were going to work on their behalf! The wardens offered the prince their thanks many times over, while Alice looked on and smiled, which was all the thanks he desired.

On the walk home, they stopped to rest in the university's botanic garden, where Alice found herself sitting on a bench with Leopold suddenly kneeling in front of her.

"No matter what you decide, Alice," he was saying, "I want you to know that in the coming years I will be only too glad to assist you in your charitable endeavors. But I hope with all my heart that you'll allow me to do so as your husband."

Alice didn't understand.

"I'm asking for your hand in marriage," Leopold explained.

"But . . . Your Highness, are you sure?"

"That is not exactly the answer for which I was hoping. Alice, you are a most uncommon commoner, to say the least, and I would be proud to call myself your husband. Of course, you realize that you will not have the title of princess, nor be entitled to ownership of the royal estates?"

"Of course." *Marriage?* Again, she felt the tug of a long-buried affection for one who . . . She would not allow herself to think of him. She had to be realistic. The marriage would please her mother. She would do it for her mother, for her family's sake. "I accept, Leopold."

She let herself be kissed, feeling the coolness of dusk settle in around her.

"I have already spoken with the queen and I have asked for, and received, your father's blessing," the prince said. "We shall host a party to announce the engagement."

If she'd had time to think about it, Alice might have stopped herself, considering the idea too whimsical. But the words had a force of their own, and only after she said them aloud did she realize just how appropriate the idea was.

"Let's have a masquerade."

Yes, it felt right: a masquerade to celebrate the orphan girl's impending marriage to Prince Leopold of Great Britain.

CHAPTER 25

THE LONG, tortuous trail of publishers and translators led Hatter to Christ Church College in Oxford, England. He stood outside the door of a bachelor's apartment in Tom Quad. The time was 12:30 P.M. He was closer to finding Alyss Heart than he had been in thirteen years. On the other side of the door: Charles Dogson, aka Lewis Carroll. He knocked.

"Who's there?" a voice called.

"My name is Hatter Madigan. I am a member of Wonderland's Millinery and I've come to find Princess Alyss Heart."

There was a long pause from the other side of the door, then, "I-I don't know who s-sent you, but th-this isn't fu-funny. It is Sunday, sir, and n-n-not a day f-for whimsy."

Hatter stood outside the door long enough to realize that Dodgson was not going to open it.

Shwink!

The blades of his left bracelet began slicing the air and he pushed them into the door. It splintered apart and Hatter stepped through the opening into a small, warm room where a fire burned in the hearth. Dodgson jumped up, spilling tea onto the rug and dropping his fountain pen, which dripped ink onto the pages of his journal.

"I beg y-your—" Dodgson started, backing into a corner of the room.

Hatter snapped shut his wrist-blades. The man before him had the brightest glow of anyone he'd ever seen. "Where is Princess Alyss?"

"Wh-wh-who?"

"Princess Alyss of Wonderland. I know you've been in contact with her. I'm in possession of your book."

As Hatter reached into a pocket of his Millinery coat, Dodgson whimpered.

"Please, n-n-no!"

But Hatter was only reaching for the copy of *Alice's Adventures in Wonderland*. He returned the book to his pocket, strode to the writing desk, and flipped through the pages of Dodgson's journal.

"Do you know who I am?"

"I . . . I th-think I know who y-you're s-s-supposed to b-be. But I can't s-say that I f-find . . . find this a-at all amusing. Did

A-Alice send you t-to make fun of m-me?"

"I've searched many years for the princess—more than half her life—and made little progress. But now I've found *you*—"

"Y-you c-can't be s-s-serious?"

"Oh, I'm very serious. And I will find her whether or not you tell me where she is. But it will be better for your health if you help me."

"But I've hardly s-seen her in n-n-nine years. She re-re-refuses t-to have anything t-to do w-w-with m-me."

Hatter considered the sadness, the mournful reminiscence, in the reverend's tone. The man was telling the truth. "Where do I find her?"

"Sh-she l-l-lives at . . . at the d-deanery here at Christ Ch-Ch-Church."

Hatter was about to ask where the deanery was, but his eye alighted on a newspaper spread open on the tea table. One of the headlines caught his attention:

ALICE IN WONDERLAND WEDS
Lewis Carroll's Muse Alice Liddell to marry
Prince Leopold

Alice *Liddell?*

"She goes by a different name?" he asked aloud, but more to himself than to Dodgson, who said nothing. There was urgency in his voice when he asked this time, "Where is the deanery?"

"In . . . in the n-next quad. The b-b-blue door, but . . ."

"But what?"

"She is currently at K-K-K-Kensington Palace, prep-p-p-paring for—"

Hatter snatched up the newspaper and bolted from the apartment, scanning the article as he sprinted in the direction of London. Why had the princess taken a different name? How could she pretend to be an ordinary, soon-to-be-married young lady of Earth? He hadn't known what to expect when he found the princess: perhaps a young woman not quite ready to fulfil her destiny, a woman who would need convincing of her own powers, in whom the bravery of a warrior queen was not yet second nature, but he hadn't expected *this*.

~

Kensington Palace. Hatter ran toward the front gate, showed no sign of stopping.

"Halt!" one of the guards ordered.

Hatter leaped, somersaulted over the gate, and dropped to a crouch, startling a young, baby-faced guard patrolling the grounds. The guard tripped, his rifle went off, and—

Hatter spun with the force of the bullet. He'd never been shot before. Incredulous, he touched the bloody wound. The guard stared at Hatter, paralyzed, unsure what to do.

Whistles were blown. The clap and patter of running feet all around. The wild, angry barking of guard dogs set loose.

Hatter had little choice but to run. The bullet had hit him in the shoulder, severing tendons and ligaments, shattering bone. He couldn't move his right arm. It hung limp, banging against his side, trailing blood. With his free hand, he put constant pressure on the wound to slow the bleeding. With difficulty, he jumped over the palace wall and hurried into a darkened street, got two-thirds of the way down it before he discovered that it was a dead end.

The pack of dogs had already closed in when three guards appeared at the street's entrance, came forward with drawn rifles and bayonets, squinting into the shadows where Hatter stood, trapped. No doubt a dagger or corkscrew would have whistled out of the darkness into their vitals if Hatter had had no other choice. But when the guards reached the end of the drive, it was empty, deserted. They saw only a puddle on the ground where no puddle should naturally have been, the dogs growling at it until, with a few tentative sniffs, they began to lap up the dirty water.

CHAPTER 26

AFTER THIRTEEN years, morale among the Alyssians was low. They languished in conditions hardly fit for mud-grubbing gwormmies. Every day brought defections and security breaches. The unspoken consensus was that a meaningful victory like the one at Blaxik would never be theirs again. Driving Redd out of Wonderland had once been a realistic vision, but the Alyssians were now reduced to a handful of splinter groups striking at insignificant targets in remote regions—an outpost monitoring jabberwocky movement in the Volcanic Plains or a weighing station for corpse-laden smail-transports at the edge of the Chessboard Desert.

Redd had made it known that she would reward those who turned traitor to the Alyssian cause. One and two at a time, Alyssians surrendered to members of The Cut and divulged the location of Alyssian camps. The camps would be bombarded with cannonball spiders and glowing orb generators, or flattened to dust by Redd's rose rollers—onyx tank-like vehicles with treads of black, toothy roses. Defectors were never heard from again, but Alyssians with their own thoughts of defecting chose to believe that their former comrades were too drunk on the pleasures of Redd's reward to send word. The truth was, surrendering Alyssians were bound hand and foot, their limbs and chests slashed to spur the appetites of the flesh-eating roses, and thrown into pits where the roses ate them alive.

At the oldest of all Alyssian camps, deep within the Everlasting Forest, General Doppelgänger had called together a meeting of advisers. The camp was protected by a Stonehenge of massive, intricately balanced mirrors reflecting the sky and forest, an unending vista of foliage and clouds to confuse the not-quite-all-seeing eye of Redd's imagination, as well as any of The Cut who happened to be dealt through the forest. The mirrors were not connected to the Crystal Continuum and had been scavenged from labor camps raided in the first year of Alyssian activity. Guards patrolled the perimeter, and a mirror keeper was responsible for maintaining the mirrors' delicate balance, shifting them here and there according to changes in light, cloud movement, and the bloom and rot of the seasons. To the untrained eye, and unless you were directly in front of a mirror and glimpsed your own reflection—a thing not so likely, considering the complicated overlap of mirrors at myriad angles, the fragmented nature of their reflections—the camp was invisible.

"She's offering a small portion of Wonderland, probably in Outerwilderbeastia but still to be decided, in exchange for a cessation of all rebel activity," said a plump fellow wedged into a chair and wearing the long mantle common among young men of suit families. "We will be free to govern ourselves unmolested, but we must give up the name of Alyssians. We won't have to swear our loyalty to Redd or the ways of Black Imagination, but we won't be able to practice White Imagination either. She has proposed a summit to work out the details of the agreement."

"Why'd she pick you to deliver the message?" asked the rook. If *he'd* been face-to-face with Redd, he would have known how to take advantage of it. Redd would have found the Alyssian response to her offer at the point of his sword.

The plump gentleman adjusted his white powdered wig. He was none other than Jack of Diamonds, now grown into this flabby, overfed man. His prominent rear ballooned out from both sides of his chair, tussocks of flesh swelling from between the armrests and seat cushion.

"I don't know," he said. "I was powdering my wig when her image appeared in my looking glass. She must have thought I'd know sense when I heard it, since I come from a ranking family."

"It sounds suspicious," the knight said. "Are you sure one of Redd's seekers didn't follow you here?"

"Please. I'm not new to the ways of subterfuge and secrecy, you know."

The rook grunted. "It's a trick, in any case."

Jack of Diamonds had doubled his family's fortune since Redd's accession to the throne. His powers of observation had served him well in a society where only the shrewdest, most opportunistic, most selfish, and least loyal to friends flourished. As a boy, he had frequently accompanied the Lady of Diamonds to Redd's fortress on Mount Isolation. It was the best education he could have received: watching his mother flatter the queen and paying rare crystals to get whatever small concessions she wanted; studying Redd's negotiations with arms dealers and entertainment impresarios who wanted licenses to poach jabberwocky from the Volcanic Plains and pit them against one another in Wondertroplis' amphitheater.

Strictly speaking, he was not an Alyssian—more a "Jackian," only concerned with his own well-being and profit. With Redd's permission, he procured food for the Alyssians; in exchange, he provided her with intelligence on their military maneuvers—intelligence from which he left out important details, for if the Alyssians were decimated, he would not be quite so rich. His methods were indirect and labyrinthine, but they brought him twice the profit of simpler business arrangements. He would learn when a shipment of cannonball spiders was leaving a factory, and then, using a reprogrammed Glass Eye as intermediary to protect his identity, he would sell this information to certain unsavory individuals. Once the theft had been carried out, his Glass Eye would inform on the criminals to Redd's authorities, but by the time the authorities interrogated the criminals and discovered where the cache of cannonball spiders was hidden, Jack would have already removed it and sold it to the Alyssians.

"You think we should agree to the summit?" General Doppelgänger asked him.

"I don't see what choice we have."

"Knight, what do you say?"

"She is not to be trusted. But I will follow your orders, whatever they may be."

General Doppelgänger sighed and—much as a drop of water might divide in half to form two identical droplets—split in two. Generals Doppel and Gänger paced the floor.

There were others who should have been at this meeting. The royal secretary, Bibwit Harte, had been unable to attend; it wasn't often that he could safely get away from Redd. And Dodge Anders . . . nobody knew where he was. He frequently went off by himself, no one knew where and no one had ever felt it right to ask. He was such a brooding, private man.

"General Doppel?"

"Yes, General Gänger?"

The generals stood looking at each other for a moment,

nodded; they had reached a conclusion. General Doppel spoke.

"Obviously, we don't trust Redd either, but we agree with Jack of Diamonds. Our forces are weakening. Before long, Redd won't have to bother with the pretense of making any deal with us."

"Then I'll arrange it," said Jack of Diamonds, attempting to wrench himself free of his chair. "I look forward to the day when I can sit with you all on some decent furniture. Now if someone . . . would . . . help me."

The generals didn't mention their contingency plan, to smuggle key Alyssians into Boarderland and make an under-the-table agreement with King Arch to overthrow Redd: receiving soldiers and weapons in exchange for the promise of a male ruler. For now, they decided to keep this plan a secret even from their advisers, hoping necessity wouldn't demand its implementation.

CHAPTER 27

DODGE STOOD on the cliff above the Pool of Tears. The water sloshed and lapped in the breeze. Whether it was the wind that caused it or something else, he wouldn't have admitted, but a tear fell from his cheek into the water below. How he missed his father. How he wished he could still believe in the queendom of Genevieve's time, the one he had lived in a lifetime ago, when he and Alyss used the palace as their playground. But those years of innocence and indulgence belonged to someone else, another Dodge, not the man standing here.

He turned to leave, saw something on the surface of the pool: a male figure swimming with difficulty toward the crystal-barrier shore. The trees and shrubs and flowers began to chatter and Dodge charged down a steep, rocky path to the edge of

the pool, stumbling, not caring if he fell. The Wonderlander swam using only one arm; no wonder he was having trouble. But even after so many years, Dodge recognized him.

"You're Hatter Madigan."

"Yes."

He helped Hatter out of the water and saw that the Milliner was injured. Hatter's shirt was torn, his right shoulder sopped with blood. Through a ragged hole of tissue and muscle, Dodge could see crumbs of bone. He pulled off his coat and made a tourniquet out of it, to slow Hatter's loss of blood.

"I'm Dodge Anders. The son of Sir Justice, who used to command the royal guardsmen."

"I remember you."

"We were told you were dead, that The Cat—"

"It makes no difference if I'm alive or dead except as it concerns the princess. I will not completely fail to fulfil my promise to Queen Genevieve. Princess Alyss Heart is alive. She's grown into a woman, old enough to return and claim her place as the rightful queen."

Dodge had long ceased to be surprised by negative twists of fate. But Princess Alyss alive? Hatter Madigan returned to Wonderland through the Pool of Tears?

"It's been a long time since anything good happened," he said, staring at Hatter until it occurred to him that he ought to get the man out of the open, to where his shoulder could be examined in safety.

Dodge decided not to risk a portal run. The Millinery man leaned on him for support as they traveled by that most archaic of Wonderland means: They walked through the Whispering Woods and into the slum of Wondertropolis.

"You won't recognize this place," Dodge said.

Hatter did recognize some of the buildings, as dilapidated as they were, but he couldn't afford to feel sorrow for the changes wrought in the capital city since Redd's coup. He was exhausted, wanted sleep. He had to stop several times to rest. He could no longer feel his right arm.

"Not much farther," Dodge said, when they entered the Everlasting Forest.

They came upon Alyssian guards patrolling what looked to Hatter like more forest, indistinguishable from the rest. The guards stopped in disbelief when they saw him, glances roving from Hatter's face to his bracelets and back. They bowed and stepped aside.

"You've turned into a legend," Dodge explained. "You and Princess Alyss."

They entered the Alyssian camp through an opening between two mirrors. Alyssian soldiers fell silent at the sight of Hatter. Whispers of the Milliner's return spread rapidly through the camp. Dodge led Hatter into the tent, where the knight, rook, and General Gänger watched General Doppel hold a chair steady as Jack of Diamonds tried to yank himself out of it.

"Yah! Hi-yumph!"

At the sight of Hatter, a mixture of shock, wonder, joy,

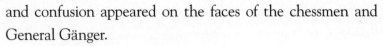

and confusion appeared on the faces of the chessmen and General Gänger.

General Doppel spotted him just as—

"Hooah!" Jack of Diamonds lurched out of the chair, massaging his bruised buttocks and cursing the detestable piece of furniture that had held him captive. "You'd have to be the size of a gwynook to fit in that thing!"

Then he too saw the mythic man.

"Hatter Madigan," Generals Doppel and Gänger said simultaneously.

"Get the surgeon," said Dodge.

The knight hurried from the tent, returned in half a moment with the surgeon, who, although in awe of Hatter like everyone else, did a commendable job of hiding it and going about her business. She touched at Hatter's wound with a glowing rod to clean it and stop the bleeding, then slipped a U-shaped sleeve of interconnected NRG nodes and fusing cores over his shoulder, giving it time to repair his broken bone, torn ligaments, muscles, veins, and tendons. She removed the sleeve and cauterized a patch of lab-grown skin over the open wound.

Hatter tested his shoulder, moving his right arm in circles. With his strength slowly returning, he explained what had happened after he and Alyss had plunged into the Pool of Tears.

"So Alyss Heart is alive?" Generals Doppel and Gänger breathed.

"This is absurd," Jack of Diamonds sputtered, having listened to Hatter's account with growing concern. "Mr. Madigan, I am Jack of Diamonds. Doubtless you remember me. I was a boy before your untimely exit from Wonderland. I mean no offense when I say that I mourn for Princess Alyss as much as anybody, but things have reached a crisis here. We have no time to go chasing after phantoms."

"I'm supposed to be dead and yet here I am," said Hatter. "I'm telling you that Alyss Heart is alive and she's old enough to return and claim her rightful place as queen." He stood. "I'm going back to get her."

"No. Let me go," Dodge said.

"My duty is to protect the princess."

"So as to ensure a future worth having for Wonderland, if I remember rightly. But look at you. You're not exactly at your physical peak."

Hatter said nothing, only swiveled his arm in its new socket.

"With your skills and experience, you're more valuable to the Alyssians than I am," Dodge said. "Stay and help the generals. Preparations have to be made. Alyss will need an army behind her."

"Isn't everyone forgetting?" Jack of Diamonds whined. "We've agreed to stop all Alyssian activity."

"If we have Alyss, there may be other options," Generals Doppel and Gänger said.

Hatter considered: The surgeon's handiwork aside, it would

take at least a day or two for his shoulder to feel normal. A little strategizing and a bit of meditation might do him some good, and the queendom even more so. He handed Dodge the soggy newspaper detailing Alyss' upcoming engagement party.

"To find the return portal, look for water where no water should be."

Dodge nodded, paused as he was leaving the tent. "A lot's happened around here and none of it good. There are things you should know. Ask the generals to brief you."

There were indeed things Hatter needed to know: The Millinery dissolved, its studies illegal. The Millinery had always been a staunch supporter of White Imagination and it had been too much of a risk for Redd to leave it functioning. Students and graduates of the place—Caps, Brims, Cobblers, Girdlers—had been ambushed in the night by Glass Eyes and unceremoniously slaughtered. Among them a woman of ordinary birth who, though not herself a member of the Millinery, had overseen its administrative necessities, and for whom Hatter had cared more than any other.

CHAPTER 28

TWENTY-YEAR-OLD ALICE Liddell flitted gracefully from one group of well-wishers to another, her long silk gown trailing on the ballroom's parquet floor, her black hair rippling down past her shoulders, her skin like smooth, unblemished ivory in the light of the crystal chandeliers. The most prominent members of British society were on hand for her engagement party—dukes, duchesses, knights, earls, counts, viscounts, and country squires—and all of them hid their faces behind masks, as did Alice. In the morning, newspapers would print detailed accounts of the masquerade for the benefit of the city's washerwomen, footmen, tavern keepers, cooks, and maidservants, the lower-class folk who struggled day after day to make ends meet and liked to gossip about a world in which they could hardly believe, a world of such rare privilege and comfort as Alice Liddell's had become.

"Why, Miss Liddell." The Duchess of Devonshire stopped Alice on her tour across the ballroom. "Your dress is as stunning as one would expect of you. And your mask too—only, what are you supposed to be, dear?"

Alice's mask was as featureless as could be: wax paper on a wire frame, with holes punched in it for eyes, nose, and mouth.

"I'm everywoman," Alice replied. "Neither ugly nor beautiful. Neither rich nor poor. I could be any woman, any woman at all."

Leopold approached for a dance. He wore a mask similar to Alice's in simplicity, although not as perplexing to guests. It was a mask of his own face, rendered in oils by a local artist.

"My dear," he said, offering his hand.

The orchestra struck up a waltz, and the couple danced around the room, the guests leaning against the walls to watch. Along with the many pairs of eyes cast on them, there was yet another—a stranger watching through the window. Prince Leopold was not a good dancer, neither light on his feet nor easy with his turns. Alice was almost thankful; it somehow lessened her guilt for not loving him. Dancing was the only activity in which he appeared less than perfect.

The waltz drew to a close and the prince noticed the queen frowning in a corner of the room.

"I think I'd better pay my compliments to Mother," he said, kissing Alice's hand.

Leopold took off his mask and set it on a table. The stranger who'd been watching through the window entered the ballroom and, unnoticed, scooped up the mask.

Alice had barely finished refreshing herself with a few sips of wine when she felt a tap on the shoulder. She turned and saw her intended husband wearing his mask, holding out his hand in request of another dance.

"Already?" she said. "But what about the queen?"

The man in the mask remained silent. The orchestra swelled into another tune and he led her out to the dance floor. With an arm around her waist and a hand at the small of her back, he moved her easily this way and that, twirling her here, dipping her there. They were in perfect step with each other, as if they had been dancing together all their lives. The guests couldn't fail to notice; they cleared a space for the couple and applauded.

Alice realized that whoever she was dancing with, it certainly wasn't her fiancé. "You're not Leopold," she laughed. "Halleck, is that you?" she asked, naming the prince's friend.

The stranger said nothing.

"Who is hiding behind that mask?"

Still, the stranger remained silent. Alice reached up and removed his mask, revealing the face of a handsome young man with almond-shaped eyes, a nose that had probably been broken more than once, and dusty, disheveled hair.

"Do I know you?"

"You knew me once," the stranger said. He turned his

192

right cheek to her, showing the four parallel scars that shone pink and ragged against his pale skin.

She stopped dancing, startled. "But . . . ?"

She felt a commotion among the guests behind her. Mrs. Liddell and Prince Leopold appeared at her side. She turned, but the stranger had vanished.

"Who was that man?" Leopold demanded.

"So rude. I'm sure he's nobody," Mrs. Liddell fretted. She'd never seen the prince so upset. "Tell him, Alice. Tell him that man was nobody."

"I . . . I don't know," said Alice. "I don't know who he was. Please excuse me. I need some air."

She hurried out to the balcony. *It couldn't have been him.* The man with the scars. *It couldn't have.* He didn't exist.

CHAPTER 29

$\mathcal{T}$HE CAT swatted at a length of rope hanging from the ceiling of the Invention Hall. All around him early prototypes of Redd's numerous inventions were on display in spotlit alcoves: a seeker with the body of a tuttle-bird and the head of a gwormmy; a dry, withered shrub that had been Naturcide's first kill; a Two Card from The Cut, half steel and half flesh, more vulnerable and not as mobile as the card soldiers that eventually made it to production; a preliminary model of the rose roller; a Glass Eye with one long horizontal crystal for vision-intake instead of the more humanoid orbs in two sockets; even an early version of The Cat himself, with smaller claws and (as The Cat himself liked to think) not as good-looking as the completed assassin had turned out.

He could play with the rope for hours—catching it on a claw, releasing it, snagging it again. He had begun to purr when Redd's voice reverberated through the hall.

"Cat, come to the Observation Dome at once."

Usually, a summons from Redd meant bearing a heap of verbal abuse, having his shortcomings shouted into his ear. But this time Redd had sounded different, almost pleasant, as if to surprise him with a treat. And it was about time. He deserved praise and spoils, since he was the one responsible for maintaining discipline among Wonderland's masses.

The Observation Dome occupied the top level of the Mount Isolation fortress—slick, polished stone flooring with walls of telescopic glass panels that provided a 360-degree view of Wonderland. The Cat bounded into the dome with a meow, but quick as a tail flick his mood darkened. The walrus-butler and Jack of Diamonds were in the room. Why Redd insisted on tolerating Jack of Diamonds, The Cat would never understand.

"I've been taking a stroll down memory lane," Redd said, "and Cat, I'd like you to tell me again how you tore Alyss Heart into little fleshy bits and hurled them into the Pool of Tears all those years ago."

Something was wrong. The Cat could smell it. Jack of Diamonds' grin was more self-satisfied than usual and the walrus hadn't looked at him once since he'd stepped into the dome, too busy dusting the crystal-sticks at the center of a long table, sprinkling dust on objects and surfaces as they needed. The walrus had been dusting the same crystal-stick ever since The Cat's entrance, a mound of dust rising on the table.

"I followed the princess and Hatter Madigan through the Crystal Continuum," The Cat started. "I tracked them to a cliff—"

A volume of *In Queendom Speramus* flew at him from the side of the room and conked him on the head.

"—ugh! So . . . I tracked them through woods to a cliff above the Pool of—"

The walrus's pouch of dust shot toward him. He saw it coming, moved at the last second, and it exploded on the glass panel behind him.

"—above the Pool of Tears. And Hatter—"

A chair skidded toward him. He stepped out of its path.

"—he tried to jump off the cliff into . . . the water—"

Chunks of volcanic rock materialized and came hurtling toward him. He ducked out of the way of one rock only to be hit by another coming from a different direction.

"—ow! I knocked Hatter back onto—ah!—the ground, and then—ow!—I tore him and Alyss into little fleshy bits and—ow!—hurled them into the Pool of Tears."

He fell to the floor, tired and hurt. Redd came and stood over him.

"You lie, Cat. You have allowed me to believe your lie for thirteen years. I have been informed that Hatter Madigan is in Wonderland and Alyss Heart alive."

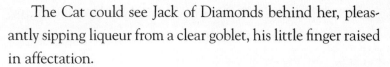

The Cat could see Jack of Diamonds behind her, pleasantly sipping liqueur from a clear goblet, his little finger raised in affectation.

"It is of course all right for you to lie," Redd continued, "so long as you don't lie to *me*. It appears that if one is clever enough to figure it out, there is a way to return to Wonderland through the Pool of Tears."

Her left hand formed into a cat's paw. She speared him through the stomach with the claws of her index and middle fingers. The Cat gurgled and convulsed, blood trickled from his mouth, and he died.

The walrus did his best to ignore what was happening and nervously spread dust over the entire table with both flippers. Jack of Diamonds chuckled, but he stopped abruptly when his goblet leaped from his hand and spilled its contents onto The Cat's face.

The Cat sputtered, coughed. His eyelids stuttered open.

"Don't be so dramatic," Redd told him. "You still have six lives left. Lie to me again and you will have none. Now get up and wipe your chin."

The Cat stood, licked his paw and rubbed it over his chin and whiskers, cleaning off his blood.

"Here's what's going to happen," Redd said. "You and a platoon of card assassins of my choosing will pass through the Pool of Tears. You will find my niece and you will rip, chop, or twist off her head—I don't care which so long as her head comes *off*. You will bring this head to me. If you return without it, I will assume that Alyss is alive and you have failed, and that will be the end of you. If you don't return to Wonderland because you fear what I will do to you, rest assured that I will send others after you and you will die six more deaths."

The Cat bowed. "I thank you for being merciful, Your Imperial Viciousness. I will not fail you this time."

"No, I don't suppose you will."

Briefed on Alyss' whereabouts by a smug Jack of Diamonds, The Cat led his card assassins to the cliff overlooking the Pool of Tears. With no fanfare save for the wind in the mute trees and the beating of their illicit hearts, they jumped, succumbed to the extended downward tug of the portal, the upward velocity, and sprang from a puddle *inside* the Houses of Parliament. They flew up out of it and smashed through the windows, landing on the sidewalk in a shower of shattered glass.

CHAPTER 30

DRESSED IN her wedding gown, Alice stood before a full-length mirror in the vestry of Westminster Abbey. In less than half an hour she would be married to a prince, raised to the highest ranks of society's esteem without giving her heart to a man she neither disliked nor loved. But her future seemed as uncertain as her past had once been.

The room began to vibrate with the strains of the organ, but she hardly noticed. She reached out toward the mirror. Her fingers touched the cold reflective surface and she stood fingertip to fingertip with her mirrored image. What more had she expected? For her hand to pass into the mirror? Ridiculous. A knock came at the door. Mrs. Liddell bustled in, holding the skirts of her gown to prevent them from dragging on the floor, and Alice was glad to be rescued from her solitude.

"It's time, dear. It's time. I can hardly believe it!"

"Nor I," Alice said, feigning breathless excitement.

She kissed her mother on the cheek and together they walked to the abbey's atrium, where bridesmaids and grooms-men waited to make their entrance, along with Dean Liddell, who would escort his daughter down the aisle.

"To think that the next time we speak, you'll be married to a prince," Mrs. Liddell sighed.

"And you'll be a mother-in-law to one."

"It tickles me to be reminded of it! You've made me terribly happy, Alice."

With a last hug, Mrs. Liddell left to take her seat next to the rest of the family at the front of the abbey.

The wedding march began, and bridesmaids and grooms-men started down the aisle a pair at a time. Alice peeked out at the guests. Queen Victoria and her entourage occupied the first few pews on the right side of the church. A buffer of soldiers separated the queen from the rest of the guests, who completely filled the abbey. In the rear of the church, news-paper reporters jotted notes. All were turned in their seats, waiting with anticipation for Alice to make her entrance. But she had wanted to take this opportunity to spy on her guests. Why? Because she was looking for somebody, one face in particular. She'd been wondering if he would show up today as mysteriously as he had at her engagement party. Wasn't that him, standing in the shadows underneath the left balcony? She couldn't see his face clearly, but—

Dean Liddell held out his arm for her. She was being such
a fool. Why torture herself over a stranger just because he had
a few scars on his face? Lots of men probably had similar scars.
It signified nothing. Likely, the man at the engagement party
had just been a rival of Leopold's and wanted to show him up
with his dancing. She took hold of her father's elbow.

"Alice, my love," said the dean, "if it were anybody else
marrying into such a public family, I should worry whether
they were up to it. But not so with you. I suspect that not only
will you continue to make Prince Leopold proud, and hold
his love fast, but that you will teach him more about acting
as a force for good in the world than I, merely as dean of his
college, could have ever hoped to accomplish. He is lucky to
have you."

"Thank you, Father."

With measured steps, father and daughter started down
the aisle. Alice's face showed no sign of concern, no hint of
the consternation that had been plaguing her since the masquerade. One might have assumed that all her thoughts were
on the momentous occasion at hand, which was certainly
what Prince Leopold believed. Dressed in full military uniform, ancestral sword at his hip, he stood before the high altar
with the archbishop. Dean Liddell kissed Alice lightly on the
cheek and deposited her at Leopold's side, then padded to his
seat next to his wife.

Leopold smiled at his bride. It was such a shy, awed,
pleased, and overwhelmed smile that it fairly overwhelmed

her. Alice feared he was making more of her than he ought, that not loving him wouldn't be the hardest part of their coming years together; it would be living up to his estimation of her. She turned to face the archbishop. Behind her, pews creaked, throats cleared. The archbishop began to speak, but Alice hardly heard a word he said.

"If there is anyone here who objects to this union, let him speak now or forever hold his peace," the archbishop intoned.

Alice had a strong desire to glance toward the left balcony, to where she imagined the scarred man was standing, a man whose name she had with great effort tried to erase from her memory and which she didn't dare say to herself even now, as if to do so would be to conjure a figure whose nonexistence meant everything to her present and future happiness in England.

She heard herself repeating the archbishop's words without comprehending their meaning. *The vows. I've taken my vows. And now it's Leopold's turn.* She stood listening to the alternating timbres and resonances of the men's voices.

Then something strange happened. It was as if a gathering storm, moments from breaking, had sucked up all the oxygen from the enormous room, only to unleash itself with that much more vengeance. Alice would later swear that she had felt it coming beforehand, had felt *something* before the stained-glass windows on both sides of the abbey imploded as the strangest-looking creatures broke through them and

landed amid the shards and crumbs of colored glass. Guests ran screaming toward the exits, trampling one another in their haste. Others fell to their knees and prayed to be delivered safely from harm.

In the seconds between the shattering of glass and the first casualty, soldiers surrounded Queen Victoria and hustled her through a door normally reserved for the archbishop, who hurried after her with breathless prayers. Prince Leopold put a protective arm around his fiancée, but she shrugged it off, unthinking, and now stood watching the cat-like beast fight his way toward her, swatting soldiers and policemen out of his way, raking their flesh with his claws. She recognized him, as one suddenly remembers a dream hours after waking, and the recognition brought her a troubling relief, for if this *thing* was real . . .

She stood defenseless and unmoving amid the mayhem. These were not the card soldiers she remembered. *Can't remember what isn't supposed to exist.*

Leopold and Halleck were battling four of the tall, steel-limbed creatures whose backsides were protective shields engraved with card suits: clubs, spades, and diamonds. Both of the men had studied swordplay, but Alice could see that they'd be lucky to survive. *Please let Leopold be all right. Whatever else is to happen, may he—*

The Cat took to the air, lunging toward her. Still she didn't move. She extended her arm, reached out to feel once and for all if this beast was real, when—

I knew it!

The man with the scars came sprinting toward her from the periphery, pushing her out of the way just as The Cat landed and smashed the altar with a downward swing of his thigh-sized arms. And she was running now, her hand in his, the man whose name she would still not voice to herself. He pulled her out through one of the broken stained-glass windows and onto the street. The Cat and card assassins jumped out of the abbey after them. The London street was a blur, a confusion of shouting, screaming people. A card assassin fell onto the train of Alice's gown, bringing her up short. With a single swipe of his sword, the scarred man cut the train from the gown, spun around, and severed the leather harness ties that held a rearing horse to its carriage.

"Hey!" the carriage driver protested.

But the scarred man was already astride the horse, pulling Alice up behind him even as he spurred the animal at a gallop through the streets. The Cat chased after them on foot, his powerful legs making him as fast as any of Earth's four-legged creatures.

The card assassins had come armed with glowing orb generators and, as the scarred man urged the horse this way and that, from streets to sidewalks and back again, zigzagging to make a more difficult target, explosions shook the surrounding buildings. Dizzy with all of this action as she was, it seemed to Alice that her companion had a destination in mind, for if the horse skidded past a certain street, he would steer the

204

animal back to it and they would race along its course, past befuddled pedestrians and cursing carriage drivers.

The man *did* know where he was going. He had memorized the route he'd taken from his exit portal to Westminster Abbey and was traveling it in reverse. And they were getting close. A few streets still to go when an orb generator rocketed into an empty police wagon not twenty yards away, turning it into a fireball. Their horse reared, bucking them off its back, and they landed on a pile of cabbage in a street seller's cart. They jumped to the ground and ran, the scarred man pulling Alice, gripping her by the arm.

"Where are we going?" she breathed.

"You'll see!"

He pointed: a puddle. She was embarrassed by what she said next, the first thing that occurred to her as she and this man took a running jump into the puddle, their hands clasped. "I'll ruin my dress," she said, and then—

Shoosh!

They were rushing down, deeper and deeper. She lost hold of the man's hand. This couldn't be happening, it couldn't be . . . yet it was. And as she torpedoed up toward the surface, having worked impossibly hard to convince herself that the place about to be seen by her disbelieving eyes didn't exist, she said the man's name—Dodge Anders—and water filled her lungs.

PART THREE

CHAPTER 31

BIBWIT HARTE, blue-green veins pulsing anxiously beneath the translucent skin of his learned head, waited on the shore of the Pool of Tears with two spirit-danes hobbled at his side. It hadn't been easy for him to get here. Since learning of Hatter Madigan's return, Redd had become more of a tyrant than ever and demanded that he spend hours every day rewriting *In Queendom Speramus*, glaring over his shoulder to make sure he scribbled down her venomous words exactly as she spat them at him. He had been forced to cross out entire pages of the ancient text and replace them with Reddisms, as if Her Imperial Viciousness believed that, by excising passages in which Queen Genevieve had once found strength and comfort, she might be able to destroy Princess Alyss herself.

"You don't feel well?" Redd had screeched, hearing his excuse to forgo his secretarial duties that day. "What do I care if you don't feel well? I'll show you what it means not to feel well!"

"But my hand is terribly cramped and would welcome a small respite from its daily exertions," Bibwit had corrected. "With utmost respect, I suggest . . . couldn't Her Imperial Viciousness *imagine* the newly written pages instead of having me write them for her?"

Redd had laughed, showing her black, pointy teeth. "Bibwit Harte, you are not as cowardly as I thought. If I didn't let you live on the off chance of benefiting from all that lore you've crammed inside that pale, bald head of yours, I would almost be sorry to see you die. You have until the Redd Moon rises to meet me in the Observation Dome."

And so he had hurried to the Pool of Tears, knowing the risks: all Redd had to do was envision him in a flash of imagination's eye and that'd be it. But this was too important; he had to come.

Ripples appeared on the surface of the pool: a disturbance down below.

"For the sake of White Imagination, let's hope that Dodge has met with success," said the learned tutor, and one of the spirit-danes whinnied in response.

The ripples on the pool grew in size and number, expanding outward from a bubbling center. Dodge burst through, gasping for air. He was alone, looked wildly about him.

210

"Is she here?"

"No. I thought—"

Something bobbed to the surface: the body of Princess Alyss, limp and lifeless. The tutor rushed to the water's edge and helped Dodge carry the princess onto land, laying her out on the shore.

"What's wrong with her?" Dodge asked.

Bibwit put a large, sensitive ear to Alyss' slack mouth. "She's swallowed some water. I can hear it sloshing inside her."

As befitted a royal tutor, Bibwit kept many instruments of learning hidden in the folds of his robe. From an inner pocket he removed a soft flex tube, placed one end of it a short way down Alyss' throat, and sucked mightily from the other end. Four times he filled the straw with water and spat it onto the ground. Alyss convulsed, breathed, vomited water, and coughed her way back into full consciousness. Seeing her eyes open, a bed of nearby lilies broke into a giddy song of welcome. Dazed and bewildered, Alyss sat up, chest muscles aching from her rib-cage-rattling coughs.

"Bibwit Harte," she whispered.

The tutor's ears twitched with pleasure. "At your service, Princess."

She turned to her childhood friend and a faint, wary smile played about her eyes and lips. "Dodge Anders."

Dodge stiffened. Hearing Alyss say his name . . . it was like being reminded of a forgotten wound.

"Where is the music coming from?" she asked. The lilies sang louder and she saw them, swaying happily on their stems, petals opening and closing in song. "But flowers have no larynxes."

"What's a larynx?" the flowers said, and laughed.

It was as if she'd entered a comforting dream and for another moment she luxuriated in it, but then her features hardened with determination and she braced herself against the rich, almost palpable colors around her. "This isn't real," she said. "I shouldn't remember so vividly what's not supposed to exist. And you—all of this—*can't* exist."

Bibwit crinkled his brow in concern. "Why not?"

"Because." Not a very good answer, she knew. "No one can possibly understa—"

"We have to hurry," Dodge said.

Someone was coming; fresh ripples had appeared on the surface of the pool.

Dodge and Bibwit quickly lifted Alyss to her feet and onto a spirit-dane—a little too quickly perhaps, because she almost fell off, half-tumbled over the animal's flank. She regained her balance and settled on its back, facing in the wrong direction.

Dodge and Bibwit exchanged a look: *This is supposed to be our warrior queen?*

"You want to face the other way," Dodge said.

The ripples in the pool were larger now, foaming. Dodge and Bibwit helped Alyss turn around properly on the spirit-dane. Dodge hopped up in front of her and took the reins

while Bibwit climbed onto the other animal, and just as the sound of breaking water echoed off the cliff, they galloped into the woods. Alyss glanced back to see The Cat and his assassin force chasing after them. Perhaps she could still return to London and marry Leopold, to be the loving daughter of Dean and Mrs. Liddell and lose herself in that orderly and controlled life she had worked so hard to establish. Here, things were obviously in a bit of a tumult. But who was she trying to convince? It was pure fantasy, the idea that she could return to relatively innocent days in England. The Pool of Tears, Redd, and The Cat: She would be hunted down no matter where she was.

The whispers of the surrounding trees and shrubs became fainter, the sound of cracking branches and paw-crushed leaves closer, louder, even over the heavy footfalls of the spirit-danes. They would not be able to outrun The Cat. Alyss was sure of it and gripped Dodge tighter around the waist.

"They're faster than we are," she said.

"Good! Then we'll have to fight!" Dodge spun the animal around and hardly had time to raise his sword before he was locked in combat with two of the card assassins.

Alyss lost her balance and fell to the ground.

"Alyss!" cried Bibwit.

But The Cat was upon her. "How you've grown," he hissed. "The last time I saw you, you were only this high." He held a paw level with his waist and grinned, baring his fangs.

She tried to run, but he batted her back in front of him.

His tail puffed up and he spat. Again, she tried to run and again he swatted her back, toying with her as a kitten toys with a cockroach before killing it. She knew what she should do—imagine something, conjure a defense, but it had been so long since she'd been able to use her imaginative muscle that . . . *Try anyway. Have to* . . . She did try, shaking and frowning with the effort. But it was no use. Nothing happened.

The Cat raised his paw to strike. Alyss took in what she supposed would be the last things she ever saw: Dodge jabbing his sword into a card assassin, which folded to the ground, dead; the remaining assassins attacking him with increased fury; Bibwit hurrying toward her, saying, "I'm a scholar, not a warrior. In a battle of wits perhaps I could . . ." as he thrust himself between her and The Cat.

"Redd will not like such behavior from her secretary," The Cat hissed, claws glinting.

Bibwit squeezed his eyes shut. "A nano orb at rest tends to stay at rest and a nano orb in motion tends to stay in motion so long as neither is acted upon by an external force," he whispered, as if he might indeed combat The Cat's physical strength with the superior strength of his mind. He went on to recite a host of learned titbits that he was amazed he had time to utter considering the usual efficiency and speed of The Cat when piercing some poor soul to the quick.

Alyss was just as amazed as Bibwit, though for different reasons. Her eyes were wide open and, just as The Cat was

bringing his paw down on the tutor, five white pawns dropped from the trees, two of them taking the blow meant for Bibwit. A battery of white chessmen jumped from the brush, and a camouflaged pack of Redd's Cut dealt themselves out with the sound of rapidly opening and closing scissor blades. The Skirmish of the Whispering Woods was in full blood.

Alyss tugged at Bibwit's sleeve.

"Oh," he said, opening his eyes to the scene.

"Leave here!" a rook shouted at them. "We'll keep them at bay! But go! Now!" Though engaged in a deadly contest with a Three Card, the rook managed a bow to Alyss. "Princess," he said.

Dodge came galloping up on a spirit-dane, lifted Alyss into the saddle behind him. Bibwit clambered up after her, and the three of them sped off as the clashings of steel on steel, the guttural grunts and hoarse cries of combat faded into the distance. Alyss turned for a last look at the raging Cat, at the brave chessmen who had put themselves in mortal danger for her sake.

"Most of them won't make it," Dodge said, urging their spirit-dane toward Wondertropolis, where they would skirt major thoroughfares on their way to The Everlasting Forest. "But you're safe. For now."

CHAPTER 32

"THEY SHOULD have returned by now."

"I warned you," said Jack of Diamonds, nonchalantly popping dried dormice feet into his mouth. "Hope for the best, but expect the worst."

"They should have returned," General Doppelgänger said again, pacing back and forth in the tent, an activity that apparently fell short of soothing his anxiety, for he split into the twin figures of Generals Doppel and Gänger and *they* paced; but this did not ease their minds either, and the generals melded back into one.

"It will come as no surprise to me if Dodge fails," said Jack of Diamonds. "We should be planning for a future we still have the power to shape."

He glanced uneasily at Hatter Madigan, who'd been sit-

ting silent and still in a corner of the tent, a pocket-sized holographic crystal in his hand, ever since General Doppelgänger told him of the Millinery's bloody demise. Every so often, Hatter pressed his thumb against the back of the crystal and its image came to life, a female Wonderlander laughing and saying something in a teasing tone. Hatter made Jack uncomfortable. What was going on in that hatted head of his? What if he had gone slowly insane from his thirteen years of exile with its mysterious traumas and challenges? An insane fellow with such deadly skills . . . To lessen his fears, Jack tried to engage the Milliner in a little chitchat.

"Tell me, Hatter. On your travels, did you have much time to explore what the fruit pies were like?"

Ever so slowly, Hatter turned to face Jack and blinked several times, as if adjusting his eyes to the sight of the wigged gentleman.

Jack laughed uneasily. "Just trying to break the monotony of all this waiting." He held a handful of dormice feet out to Hatter. "Dormouse foot?"

Hatter looked away, said nothing. A cheer sounded from outside. Hatter stood, pocketed his holographic crystal, and walked quickly out of the tent. General Doppelgänger and Jack of Diamonds hurried after him, and if ever there was a welcome sight to a mourning Milliner, this must have been it: Princess Alyss, safe and apparently healthy, surrounded by happy Alyssians, gwynooks, and tuttle-birds, the forest trees adding their voices to the chorus celebrating her return. A

welcome sight, to be sure, yet Hatter showed little emotion—
a slight upward flicker at the corners of his mouth. Dodge
caught his eye and the two nodded to each other in mutual
respect.

"Is it . . . Hatter?" Alyss asked, spying his top hat in the
crowd.

The Alyssians parted to let him through.

"I am pleased to find you well, Princess."

Alyss looked at her surroundings. "Am I well? I shouldn't
say so."

Hatter lowered his head. "Yes, there is no excuse for my
losing you and I accept full responsibility. If you choose to
demote me to an inferior post as a result of my failure, I hope
I may accept it with grace. But Princess, there is much to do
if you are to be successful against Redd."

Alyss sighed, and when she spoke next she sounded more
like a monarch than she would have thought possible. "It's not
surprising, Hatter, that you blame yourself for this 'failure,' as
you call it. But I do not blame you. Who's to say it wasn't I who
lost you so many years ago? I just meant that all of this"—with
a gesture she indicated the Alyssian headquarters—"is a bit of
a shock to me after so long a time away."

Hatter stepped aside as General Doppelgänger bustled
up to her, bowing repeatedly, then splitting in two. "Princess
Alyss!" Generals Doppel and Gänger simultaneously cried.
"We are ecstatic to find you safely returned to us! Welcome,
Welcome!"

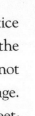

The assembled throng was too busy celebrating to notice the cloud that had darkened Jack of Diamonds' brow at the sight of the long-lost princess. But Jack was nothing if not willing to turn an unforeseen circumstance to his advantage. He worked his lips into a smile and, sensing a lull in the greetings, butted his way through the crowd.

"Ranking fellow coming through," he said. "Out of the way, out of the way."

His prodigious rear knocked people left and right with every stride. He presented himself to Alyss.

"Ah, Princess! Surely, you remember your favorite childhood playmate, Jack of Diamonds?"

Alyss glanced at Dodge, who fell to picking at the edge of his sword with great intensity.

Jack took her hand and kissed it. "I have been pining after you for ages, my princess. I'm sure you recall that we were to be married? I have not taken a wife in honor of your memory, and I flatter myself that you will still have me, provided you are as pleased as I am with my manly figure." He turned this way and that, modeling his physique for her.

Whether it was the unappetizing figure of Jack of Diamonds twirling around like a fairy, the expectant, joyous faces crowding around her, or both, Alyss herself couldn't say. But she suddenly felt that it was all too much.

"I think . . . if I could just lie down for a short while," she said.

"The princess wants a bed!" a nearby gwynook shouted.

"Princess wants a bed!" echoed a Two Card and, as the white knight and his pawn bustled off to make a bed for Alyss, Alyssian after Alyssian repeated this fact as if it were cause for celebration in itself, yet another remarkable happening for which they hadn't dared hope.

CHAPTER 33

WITH ALYSS resting in his tent, General Doppelgänger organized a meeting to discuss tactics. Bibwit Harte, the white knight, Jack of Diamonds, Dodge, and Hatter Madigan assembled in the Alyssian War Room, which wasn't so much a room as a patch of ground in the thickest part of the forest headquarters, furnished with a crystal-topped Hovering Table™ and matching chairs, as well as four EZ-Erase® gemstone writing boards that served as walls, on which every Alyssian military campaign of the last several years had been drawn up, hashed out, organized.

"But can she lead us?" General Doppelgänger was asking.

"She must," said Hatter.

"What lunacy!" boomed Jack of Diamonds. But after

seeing Hatter's expressionless stare, he added, "I mean . . . what lunacy, with all disrespect, sir."

"There is no doubt she will need as much training and education as can be had in the short time we have," said Bibwit Harte.

"All I see is a young woman unprepared to conjure even a jollyjelly with her imagination, let alone battle Redd for control of the queendom," said Jack of Diamonds.

The general nodded, thoughtful. "Knight, what do you say?"

"She is the princess. The line of succession rightfully ends with her. If she is willing to lead us—"

"If she's able, you mean," muttered Jack.

"—then we must let her, if we are truly to be called Alyssians."

Dodge, when present at these meetings, usually kept silent and listened to the exchange of strategies, disagreements over protocol, and interpretations of intel reports with stifled exasperation and anger: They were the self-proclaimed saviors of the queendom; they should have been engaging Redd in battle, not talking about it.

"I'm wondering," he said, gazing at nothing in particular, and the mere fact that he had volunteered to speak caused a sudden hush, "how Redd knew where Alyss was." He fixed his look on Jack of Diamonds.

"Are you accusing me of something?"

"Suppose I am."

"Gentlemen!" the general started.

"Then I need not *suppose* you're a simpleton," said Jack of Diamonds, "because I'll have it for a certainty."

Dodge stood, hand at his sword.

"We have enough trouble fighting Redd," interposed Bibwit Harte. "It won't help our chances if we are fighting among ourselves."

Jack of Diamonds chortled, smug and dismissive. "Gentlemen, I don't wish to fight. I have great respect for Mr. Anders' accomplishments on the field of battle, but he knows nothing about politics. He is, as I'm sure you'll agree, too apt to use his sword when he might better employ his tongue."

"And you are too apt to powder that wig instead of fighting alongside us when it counts."

Jack waved him off. "Let Mr. Anders believe what he wants. My only concern is Alyss. There's no doubt in my mind that she is our lost princess, but I don't think her mentally or physically capable of leading a charge against Redd."

"It *will* take time," Bibwit concurred.

"It will take the Looking Glass Maze," said Hatter.

"And that," Bibwit agreed.

Jack of Diamonds slapped his forehead in disbelief. "Not that old bunk. The Looking Glass Maze was proven pointless long ago. Redd herself never went through any maze."

"All the more reason why she can be defeated," said Bibwit.

"General, I urge you . . . let us agree to the summit and

stop this idiocy before it goes any further. An opportunity such as the one Redd is offering won't come again."

"No queen can reach her full strength and power without passing through the maze," said Bibwit.

Jack of Diamonds lost all patience. "Yes, by all means, let's run along to the maze! Hurry, hurry, to the all-important Looking Glass Maze while our future survival hangs in the balance!"

"We can't simply 'run along,' as you say," instructed Bibwit Harte. "Only the caterpillars know the location of the maze. Alyss must meet with the caterpillars."

"But they haven't left the Valley of Mushrooms since Redd became queen," said the white knight.

"Then she will have to go to them."

"She'll need a military escort," Dodge said.

Jack of Diamonds pulled his wig down over his face and spoke into its thick, powdered curls. Though muffled, his voice was audible: "If you want to force her into a confrontation she's ill-equipped to handle, all I can say is, May the spirit of Issa help anyone who should fall under your people's care. You'd march them off to their deaths."

"Why are you so eager for us to compromise with Redd, I wonder?"

The question came from Dodge. But Jack only buried his face deeper into his wig and groaned.

"Bibwit," the general said, "shouldn't you be getting back to Mount Isolation in case Redd suspects something?"

"I'm not going back. The Cat has seen me with Alyss. My place is here now, with her."

It would have been nice to maintain a spy in Redd's court, but the general understood. "Well, we're glad to have full use of you, at any rate."

Bibwit's ears twitched and a moment later they all heard it: someone quickly approaching. Hatter stood, hand at the brim of his top hat, and Dodge jumped up, ready to fight. But it was only the rook, battered and bruised from his skirmish with The Cat in the Whispering Woods.

"You made it," he said, smiling at Dodge.

"*You* made it. I'll get the surgeon."

The rook shrugged him off. "I'm all right. Surface wounds only. We lost four-fifths of our men, though. Didn't even take one of The Cat's lives. But the princess is safe?"

Dodge nodded.

"That counts for something." The rook lowered himself into a vacant chair. "So what'd I miss?"

"Well," said General Doppelgänger, "most here believe that Alyss must pass through the Looking Glass Maze if she is to successfully challenge Redd. But I haven't yet voiced my opinion."

Jack of Diamonds peeked out from his wig, hopeful.

"I think we should give Alyss the opportunity of meeting with the caterpillars in the Valley of Mushrooms," said General Doppelgänger. "Let her try the maze, if she is able."

"Nooo," Jack said and again buried his face in his wig.

"But in the meantime . . ." The general yanked Jack of Diamonds' wig off his face. "Inform Redd that we'd be pleased to attend her summit, if she's still willing to have it in light of Alyss' return." To the others, he said, "Responsibility to the cause requires we have alternate plans should the princess fail."

"She won't fail," Dodge said. "I won't let her."

CHAPTER 34

REDD MOON had risen. Its bloody light burned down on the Chessboard Desert through a cloud-clotted sky, toxic vapors burping continuously out of the factory engaged in manufacturing Redd's war machines.

The Cat skulked through the halls of the Mount Isolation fortress, his own unease dwarfed by the violence of the sky over the steaming desert—a sky that became visible to him only as he entered the spiral-shaped hall leading to the Observation Dome, where Redd waited for proof that her niece was no longer among the living.

This was not a briefing The Cat longed to make. He entered the Observation Dome and found his queen staring out of a telescopic panel at Wondertropolis, the walrus-butler busy polishing the other panels with a cloth.

Redd's back was to him. Without turning around, she said, "I see you but I don't see my niece's head," and before he could utter a syllable, her scepter speared him.

The walrus gave a little jump and started for the exit. "Oh! I'd better check on—"

"Stay where you are!" Redd shouted.

"Yes, I still have plenty of work to do here, Your Imperial Viciousness." Back to polishing the telescopic panels went the walrus-butler.

The Cat stood unsteadily on two legs, Redd's scepter jutting out of him. In theory, he was fortunate to have had nine lives. But each death was painful. The Cat sometimes wished for only one life.

He fell to the floor, dead.

Redd stalked back and forth next to his lifeless body. She took hold of her scepter. The Cat's eyes flickered open and the wound in his chest healed. He slowly got to his feet, licking himself clean.

"Tell me how you managed to fail this time," Redd demanded.

"The Alyssians reached her first. We chased them back through the Pool of Tears but—"

"Alyss in Wonderland? Unacceptable!" Redd screeched, and again The Cat felt the stinging, mortal blow of her scepter.

The walrus blubbered and dropped his polishing cloth, bent to pick it up, and bumped his head against a telescopic panel.

Redd tried to pinpoint Alyss' location in her imagination's eye, saw a confusion of foliage and trees. A forest of some kind. But there were many forests in the queendom.

"Where is Bibwit Harte? I want the royal secretary here, now."

"I'm sorry, Your Imperial Viciousness," said the walrus, rubbing his head, "truly very sorry, but Bibwit Harte is not here. No one's seen him since—"

"He's with the Alyssians now." The Cat had regained consciousness and lay on the floor watching his wound heal.

"No more unwelcome news out of you, my feline friend," Redd threatened. She motioned with her fingers and The Cat found himself standing upright. "Come with me."

She swooped out of the room, her heels click-clacking on the polished floor. Casting a last, squinty-eyed glance at the walrus, The Cat followed Redd down the spiraling hall, through dim rooms of questionable purpose to the vacuum shaft that shot them into the bowels of the fortress. They entered an enormous room in which an army of Glass Eyes stood in columns, waiting for orders. As Redd opened her mouth to speak, she projected her holographic, anger-gnarled face onto Wondertropolis' billboards and government-sponsored poster-crystals, Wonderlanders pausing amid their various jobs and activities to listen to her spew the words she spoke to the Glass Eyes at Mount Isolation.

"Loyal subjects, there is a pretender to the throne in our midst. She calls herself Alyss Heart. Your assistance in her capture—in her death—is hereby commanded. She is in one of our forests. Find her by the time my moon sets or I will burn every forest in Wonderland. Whoever accomplishes this will be rewarded with the knowledge that she or he has earned my eternal favor."

Redd's face vanished from the city's billboards and posters, replaced by the usual advertisements for Redd's Hotel & Casino, Redd Apartments, jabberwocky matches, and reward offers for reporting followers of White Imagination. Wonderlanders went back about their business—though, to be sure, there were some who considered Redd's eternal favor worth having and would do what they could to find Alyss Heart.

Back at Mount Isolation, the last of the Glass Eyes streamed out of the fortress into the desert.

Redd turned to The Cat, her voice echoing through the empty room. "Tell Jack of Diamonds it's time he proved his loyalty once and for all."

CHAPTER 35

SHE HADN'T really intended to sleep, had just wanted to be alone to think things over. *How long since I was standing beside Leopold in Westminster Abbey?* It seemed so long ago, such a terribly long time ago. *What's become of him? And the Liddells? What do they think has happened to me? What are they doing this very moment?* She had grown to love them, perhaps as a kidnapped person grows to love those who hold her captive, but it *was* love. Alyss knew that now.

All of this thinking solved nothing and it was a relief when Bibwit entered the tent carrying a small, neatly folded stack of clothes.

"Please put these on, Alyss," he said. "I'll wait for you outside."

It was an Alyssian uniform, makeshift as all things

Alyssian had to be in the Redd-controlled queendom. The shirt and trousers didn't match in color. Their particular weave of nanofibers was coarse by Wonderland standards, and yet, rubbing the hem of the shirt between her index finger and thumb, Alyss knew it to be smoother and softer than the finest silk in England. Yes, they were plain garments, as plain as anything worn by the poor in Genevieve's time, but with one difference: the faded badge of a white heart on the end of the right shirtsleeve.

Alyss stripped out of her wedding gown and, torn as it was, carefully laid it on the general's cot. She dressed herself in the Alyssian outfit and wanted to know what sort of figure she made in the unfamiliar clothes, but there were no looking glasses in the tent.

Nothing left to do. Must face the future, whatever it holds.

With a decided breath and a firming up of the shoulders, she stepped out of the tent. Bibwit came forward with beaming countenance and took both her hands in his. He looked her up and down, approving of what he saw.

"Were you to wear one, Alyss, you could make the saddle blanket of a spirit-dane look regal."

"Thank you, Bibwit, but—"

"Ah, ah, no buts. You've just returned to us and it is too soon to express whatever doubts you undoubtedly have with that most cowardly of words, that qualifier of qualifiers, *but*."

Alyss smiled—more a matter of facial muscles than of feeling. "It's good to see you're still the same old Bibwit

Harte," she said. "After our recent clash with The Cat, I thought you might have become a man of heroic action and no longer cared for the subtleties of the intellect."

"I, a man of heroic action? Tut tut. I leave such things to others. But of course I am the same old Bibwit Harte, Alyss; I am the same precisely *because* I am old. I tutored your great-grandmother's grandmother, and—"

"Yes, I remember."

"—I've seen enough political upheavals to fill countless heads. Nothing has changed me yet. I admit that this Redd business is the worst I've experienced, but I'm much too old to change. Now enough about me, though I am a fascinating subject. Come."

He led her to an arrangement of weathered, empty ammunition containers that served as a seating area. Lowering himself onto a container that had once held orb generators fresh from Redd's factory, Bibwit's expansive, brown robe puddled around him. He looked like a small brown volcano with a white head. Tea was brought by a young girl wearing a homburg hat and cracked leather overcoat, so timid in Alyss' presence that she didn't dare raise her eyes to look at the princess.

"She's a shy one," Alyss said after the girl had hurried off.

"Not usually. It's you that makes her so. She was born here, in this very camp. Do you know what they call themselves, all of these people?"

Alyss shook her head. How could she know?

"Alyssians." Bibwit spelled it out.

Her heart gave a little jump. *Alyssians? They ask too much of me.* "I don't think I'm ready for all of this," she said.

Bibwit studied her a moment. His ears twitching and swiveling in response to every passing sound, he described the changes that Wonderland had suffered in the past thirteen years, and though his wisdom covered many subjects, there were things even he didn't understand, most of which concerned her. So then it was her turn to talk, to try to explain what felt inexplicable.

"I had to turn my back on all my Wonderland memories," she said. "I had to shut my mind to them in order to survive in a world that didn't believe. I resisted for a long time, but it became . . ."

"So that's why you were to be married?"

Alyss nodded. "I will always belong partly to that other world now."

"Wisely put. You can't spend so much time in a place and not carry a bit of it inside you. But this is your rightful home, Alyss. This is where you belong."

"Is it?" She looked around. *How can they call themselves Alyssians when I hardly feel Alyssian myself? It's too much. They ask too much.* "It seems to me that I no longer quite belong anywhere. And what about the family I left behind? What about Leopold, the man I was to marry?"

"We will provide for the people who nurtured you as

234

their own, if we have the luxury to do so in the future. As to this Leopold character, we have more important things to consider than one man's love, be he of this world or any other."

Alyss caught sight of Dodge staring at them from behind a tent. She raised a hand to wave, but he ducked out of sight and didn't show his face again.

"You have a powerful imagination, Alyss," said Bibwit Harte. "The Alyssians will need it, and the fate of the queendom depends on it. In what little time we have, my job is to educate you in its uses and limitations, according to the precepts of White Imagination."

"It's gone."

Bibwit's large ears crimped in perplexity. "Your imagination has not gone, Alyss, because there is nowhere it can go *to*. It is within you whether you like it or not. You will see. You were born to be a warrior queen, like your mother." But here the wise tutor paused, remembering Alyss sitting backward on the spirit-dane after she'd emerged from the Pool of Tears. She had been disorientated, of course. Yes, better to think positive thoughts. "You will fight alongside your army," he continued, "and you will face Redd because only you have the strength and power to defeat her."

"A warrior queen?" Alyss guffawed. "What do I know of warfare or weaponry? The only time I've lifted a sword was when Dodge and I used to play our juvenile games."

"By successfully navigating the Looking Glass Maze, you

will evolve to warrior queen. The maze will release what's inside you."

Alyss shook her head, doubtful.

"How the Looking Glass Maze will accomplish this, even I can't say," Bibwit continued. *"In Queendom Speramus* once stated, 'Only she for whom the Looking Glass Maze is intended can enter.' I look forward to the day when you can tell me what's inside."

"I don't know, Bibwit. I just don't know."

Wasn't it possible that she might no longer be the rightful heir to the crown? Her years and experiences in that other world had severed the girl she was from the woman she was supposed to have become. *Redd did away with two generations of Heart rulers that horrific afternoon.*

"Tell me about Dodge," she said.

Bibwit was quiet for a long time. "None of us is the same since Redd's return. Some of us are more changed than others. As to the man Dodge Anders has become, I think it best to let you discover that for yourself." The tutor hopped to his feet. "Well, we'll soon be making a trip to the Valley of Mushrooms, where the caterpillars will instruct you. Finish your tea, collect your thoughts, and then we will begin the lesson we should have begun thirteen years ago."

Alyss watched Bibwit scurry off. Not having touched her tea, with no thought to what she was doing or where she was going, she stood and walked through the camp. Alyssians gathered outside their tents or cooking food over

gemstone fire pits bowed to her as she passed. Some shouted, "In Alyss we trust!" Others declared, "May the light of White Imagination again shine on Wonderland, my princess!" Alyss tried to look as hopeful as she could under the circumstances.

Alyssians. They call themselves Alyssians. Now see where I've ended up.

She stood outside a tent, not just any tent—*his*—her feet carrying her there almost without her knowing.

Should I announce myself or . . . ?

But no need. Here he was, stepping out of the tent.

"Hello," she said.

Dodge tensed, pushed out his chest, and stood with his back straight. "Princess."

He was surprised, caught off guard—she could see that.

"Was there something you wanted," she said, "before, when I—"

"Bibwit's told you that we'll have to risk a journey to the Valley of Mushrooms?"

"Yes." *Had thought, hoped, it was something else. But what, exactly?* "Dodge, do you really think I can lead a battle against Redd's forces?"

"I do."

"That makes one of us. I'm sure it's too late for whatever Wonderland expected of me. I'd ask you to take me home, but I no longer have any idea where that is."

She felt unbearably sad all of a sudden and wished that

someone, *anyone*, would put a comforting arm around her. But her pout only seemed to harden Dodge, to make him even more callous toward her. "There's something you need to see," he said.

If the future of the queendom weren't at risk, and if Dodge weren't being so cold and distant toward her as he led her out of the Alyssian headquarters, Alyss might have been able to convince herself that they were heading off on a harmless adventure, as they used to do in simpler times.

CHAPTER 36

JACK OF Diamonds tramped through the Everlasting Forest carrying a case the size and shape of a bread box.

"Prove my loyalty? Haven't I proved it time and time again? Haven't I turned in traitors who dared to steal her weapons? Haven't I kept her informed of Alyssian activities? If just once she didn't let herself be governed by her temper . . . A summit—that's how *I* would've dealt with it. Pretend to grant the Alyssians statehood, lull them into complacency. I would marry the princess while remaining loyal to Queen Redd and she'd control the Alyssians through me. *That's* the way to handle things. But all anybody around here wants to do is fight."

A kitten the color of burnished gold poked its head out of the top of the case.

"No, you don't," Jack said to the animal. "You'd better stay out of sight altogether."

He put a fat palm on the kitten's head and tried to push it back into the case, but the kitten hissed, openmouthed, and scratched him with a nimble paw.

"Ow!"

Jack tossed the case to the ground, sucked at his wounded hand. The surrounding trees twittered. Jack could see the kitten's tail whisking back and forth out the top of the case, but the animal made no sound. Wasn't he in a favorable position here? He had his archrival stuffed in a bag! He could easily do away with a little kitten. Yes, yes. Then Redd would have to rely on him and him alone for counsel, and he'd convince her to enact plans of which he could take better advantage. But what of the task at hand—the ambush? And what if Redd were watching him right now in her imagination's eye? No, he'd better wait. To get rid of the kitten was too risky at present. But at the first opportunity . . .

He picked up the case and continued on through the forest. The kitten's tail, still snaking up out the top of the case, brushed against his hand. He paused and looked around. Now, where was the Alyssian headquarters? He always had trouble finding it. To the left maybe? Yes, definitely to the left. But after going a couple hundred paces, he decided it must have been the other way. But four hundred or so paces in the opposite direction seemed to bring him no closer. He was lost. The kitten growled. But then a wink of sunlight on a crystal shooter caught Jack of Diamonds' eye: two Alyssian guards patrolling the perimeter of the headquarters. Aha! He knew it had been close. But perhaps, now that violence was near, it would have been better to stay lost?

He approached the guards with a cautious tread, the color draining from his face, making it almost as pale as his beloved wig. "We must increase security now that Alyss is here," he said, coming upon them. "I have requisitioned more perimeter guards."

"If you believe it necessary, Lord Diamond."

"Obviously I do."

"Yes, sir."

"Is . . . the mirror keeper about?"

"Not at present, sir."

"Ah, well."

Jack shifted his weight from one leg to the other. He had started to sweat; his scalp itched horribly. "Any idea when he'll be back?"

"No, sir."

"Oh." He felt the kitten moving inside the case, impatient. "I, ah . . . I have something for him."

The guards said nothing.

"Maybe one of you should take a look at it?"

If the guard who volunteered had had the time, he might have noticed that Jack of Diamonds was trembling. But as soon as the unfortunate fellow held his face over the opening of the case to see what was inside, out came the two

manly arms of The Cat. Jack stumbled backwards, dropping the case. But before it hit the ground, while the guard was screaming, The Cat morphed into full assassin and did away with both guards. A wave of alarm passed through the trees and shrubs of the forest.

The Cat turned to Jack, his claws dripping blood. "Summon The Cut."

Jack reached into a pocket with bumbling fingers. He raised a marbled crystal bubble to his lips and blew into it. Nothing. It was a sound for The Cut alone. He heard them coming, the scissor-sound of their stalking limbs: three decks in all, 156 soldiers.

"I, ah . . . think I should wait out here," Jack of Diamonds managed. "I don't want my position with Redd to be compromised, which it will be if I'm seen by General Doppelgänger or any of the others."

The Cat knew better. But it was all right; the cowardly Jack of Diamonds would only get in his way. "Do what you want," he spat, and accompanied by the high cards of The Cut, he pounced into the Alyssian headquarters while the lower numbers began smashing its perimeter mirrors.

CHAPTER 37

DODGE HADN'T told her that they'd be leaving the forest. They should have informed somebody. *Bibwit, the general, Hatter. We should have told them we were going. That's what the old Dodge would've done . . .* The ten-year-old Dodge Anders who had prided himself on strict adherence to military procedures and the importance of communication among members of a fighting force. But a lot about the adult Dodge was unlike the child Alyss used to know.

He kept in front of her, moving at a rapid pace, and she often had to trot just to stay in sight of him. He turned around every now and again to make sure she was still following him, but really, he could have been more considerate. *Wouldn't hurt him to slow down a little.*

They came to the edge of a shabby city, the one she had

already passed through this day. The pawnshops and military checkpoints, the ear-clutter of recorded voices declaring "Better Redd than dead" and "The Redd way is the right way." The barrage of gaudy, flickering advertisements for products and places Alyss had never heard of. *I can hardly . . . is it really my once-gleaming city?* The only landmark she recognised was The Aplu Theater, where she'd seen performances by the Merry Pretenders, an acting troupe favored by her parents. It was boarded up and had been left to rot. The few Wonderlanders she saw passed through the city like shadows, flitting and ashamed.

Dodge was waiting for her up ahead. *About time he showed some consideration.* But when she stepped up beside him, she found that it wasn't manners that had made him stop and wait for her.

"That is your home," said Dodge. "Redd left it standing to show how far the Hearts and White Imagination have fallen."

She grew dizzy, looking at the ruins of Heart Palace, her mind suddenly aswirl with memories. *Where Father and I used to play tag in the halls and he could always catch me by making me laugh. "The letters of my name spell 'alnon' or 'onnal' or 'lonan'when shuffled around," he'd say. And laughing, I'd say, "But those aren't words," and he'd know where I was from hearing my voice, and he'd tag me, saying, "Why, Alyss, I never claimed they'd spell actual words!"*

And where there were all sorts of nooks perfect for spying on

244

him and Mother, and I saw him massage the nape of her neck as she sat on her throne, she lifting her face to his for a kiss.

"Can we go inside?"

"If we're careful."

The grounds appeared deserted—no Wonderlanders looting the place, hurrying past with goblets and cutlery in their fists, because there was nothing left to take. But Dodge unsheathed his sword all the same, and he guided Alyss carefully to the palace entrance, keeping his voice to a whisper.

"The poor and desperate sometimes live here for a while, until they die from imagination-stimulant addiction or Redd sends them to the Crystal Mines."

Entering through the broken front gate, Dodge's heart pumped as quickly as if he were in battle. He hadn't personally set foot in the palace since the day he and the rook buried his father—hadn't wanted to return, afraid of what he might feel. He held his face turned away from Alyss, wrestling with emotions he was no longer used to experiencing.

Inside, the once-great halls were scarred with obscenities, and what little that had remained of furniture and decorations lay in charred piles throughout, evidently used as fuel for fires.

"It's empty because people stole things," Dodge said. "Right after, you know . . . that day."

Alyss reached out, ran a hand along the cold stone walls. "It's not empty," she said. The place was full of the past. At a bend in one of the halls: *Here is where I imagined the floor covered in squig berries and the walrus slipped on them and dropped the tea platter and squashed the berries, rolling in them and turning himself squig color.* In the anteroom of her mother's throne room: *Here is where I used to charge toll to the servants, not letting them pass unless they gave me a treat of jollyjellies or tarty tarts.*

Skeletons of card soldiers and chessmen littered the dusty hall approaching the South Dining Room. Many more skeletons were in the dining room itself. The air tasted as if it hadn't been breathed by the living in more than a decade. The walls were pockmarked from Redd's attack, but no weapons were anywhere to be seen. Silent tears coursed down Alyss' cheeks. She turned to see if Dodge was crying, feeling the sorrowful weight of the scene, but it was difficult to tell in the dimness of the room.

"Your father," she whispered.

"He's . . . buried in the garden."

Dodge's voice sounded choked. He was taking deep, even breaths in an effort to remain calm. Anger birthed from grief. He wanted to punch something. He wanted to make someone feel the pain and loss he felt standing in this place.

Alyss bent down and picked up off the floor a triangular-shaped, weathered, chipped piece of bone. It hung on a bit of chain. "Do you remember this?"

He wasn't sure. It couldn't be—

"You gave it to me. I said I would keep it forever."

The jabberwock tooth—the one he had given to her as a

246

birthday present. She unclasped the necklace and secured it around her neck. The tooth hung at her throat.

"I never thanked you for saving my life, so . . . thank you."

He winced, as if the thanks physically hurt him.

"Dodge, I know it's hard seeing each other after all this time. So much has happened. We've both grown into adults we never imagined becoming. But I would have expected a friendlier reception from you, of all people."

"I'm sorry to disappoint you."

"That's not what I'm saying. It's just . . . we were friends, Dodge. We were more than friends. Wasn't that why you came for me in that other world?"

"To defeat Redd, to face The Cat, I would do anything."

Annoyed, Alyss clicked her tongue. "Is that why you danced with me at the masquerade? Was that to defeat Redd too? Did you do that for The Cat?"

Dodge didn't answer.

Alyss turned from him and examined her reflection in a sliver of looking glass, the only fragment left in the frame of the large decorative mirror that had once hung on the east wall. "If you no longer care for me, why did you bring me here?"

"I never said I don't care for you." But Dodge didn't trust himself to say more. He held his tongue, began again. "I brought you here to remind your heart of what Redd's done. To spark your vengeance. You're the agent by which I'll have my revenge. That's what you mean to me now. That's all you *must* mean."

"Touching." Her fingers toyed with the jabberwock tooth at her throat. *Take it off. Take it off and show that if it means nothing to him, it means nothing to—*

Her reflection in the looking glass suddenly rippled and morphed into an image of Redd. "So glad you could visit us. Now off! With! Your! Head!"

Dodge snatched Alyss' hand and pulled her away as the glass broke into sharp piercing pieces—tiny daggers meant for the princess. The floor shook beneath them, the walls shivered, the thick ceiling beams creaked and cracked, and mortar dust and skull-sized stones began to fall. They ran, each with an arm over their head to protect themselves from falling debris. They hurdled smashed wall stones and ducked fallen beams as the old palace collapsed around them, sending stinging pellets of rock into the backs of their legs. They barely managed to make it outside to safety.

Alyss stood bent over, coughing from dust and wiping her mouth. Where Heart Palace had stood only moments before: a pile of rubble.

"She's destroyed everything," Dodge said.

Resignation to the past, defiance of the present, hope for the future—Alyss felt them all at once. "Not everything," she said.

Not if she had hope.

CHAPTER 38

SOMETHING WAS wrong in the Everlasting Forest. Tuttle-birds were shrieking, jabbering, making a din. In a moment the problem became clear: trees and shrubs had been hacked, clubbed, chopped, cracked in half, or ripped from the soil. Flowers lay stamped into the ground, silent. What foliage happened to still be alive warned, "Don't enter! Don't enter!" An unfamiliar sound filled the forest, a steady, mechanical beat: endless columns of Glass Eyes marching toward the Alyssian headquarters. The bodies of Alyssian guards were scattered pell-mell on the ground, the looking glasses that had once camouflaged the headquarters smashed, some cracked and left half standing, others completely destroyed.

"Bibwit and the others," Alyss breathed.

She took a step forward, but Dodge grabbed her arm, stopping her.

"We can't go any closer. It's too dangerous."

They were already too close. A Glass Eye shot clear of a nearby thicket, deadly blades sticking forward from the back of its hands, and flew at Alyss. Dodge tackled her. Missing its target, the Glass Eye smashed headfirst into a dead tree. But more of its kind were already upon them. Dodge fought with a sword in each hand. Alyss focused her energy on imagining the Glass Eyes . . . *What? Dead? Forever inactivated? Can they be killed like ordinary Wonderlanders? Concentrate, concentrate.* She focused on Dodge, imagined him with increased strength and skill, but the Glass Eyes had been engineered for this sort of combat. Dodge was overpowered; a few moments more and he wouldn't be able to protect himself, let alone her.

A weapon. I need a weapon. Alyss crawled to the Glass Eye lying motionless in a shatter of tree bark. *Must be a weapon on it somewhere.* She reached for the avocado-like object hanging from its belt—a whipsnake grenade, one of Redd's newest inventions. She pulled the ring at the top of the grenade, threw it at the Glass Eyes, and it blew open, releasing a nest of snakelike coils, alive with electricity and whipping through the air. Dodge dropped to the ground and rolled.

Swaap!

A coil whipped a Glass Eye's cheek, short-circuiting it.

Swaap! Swaap-swaap! Swaap!

The Glass Eyes fell. Dodge and Alyss were up and running before the coils of the grenade lost their power and sizzled on the forest floor. A fresh pack of Glass Eyes stepped free of their marching column and darted around smoldering tree trunks and broken, low-hanging branches after them.

The rapid thunder of their approach . . .

Dodge raised a sword to strike, was bringing it forward with all the strength left in him when, out of the surrounding foliage, burst—

Not the Glass Eyes, but Generals Doppel and Gänger on galloping spirit-danes. Dodge tried to check his swing. Too late. General Doppel instinctively raised his sword in defense and it clanged with Dodge's.

"Dodge!" cried General Doppel.

"Alyss!" exclaimed General Gänger.

The white knight, the rook, and a platoon of pawns hustled up behind them.

"We've been casing the perimeter in hopes of finding the princess," the rook explained to Dodge. "Though we feared the worst."

The Glass Eyes converged and Dodge and the chessmen lost themselves in the urgency of battle. The generals took up positions at Alyss' flanks, their spirit-danes affording her momentary protection.

Concentrate, Alyss. Imagine.

With a war cry that sounded like ripping metal, a Glass Eye knocked aside the pawns and sprinted toward her, but

General Doppel, leaping from his spirit-dane onto General Gänger's, shot a cannonball spider at it. On impact, the over-sized spider bit an unhealthy gob of synthetic flesh off the assassin and chomped at its vital circuitry. Spooked, the rider-less spirit-dane reared and took off. Dodge, entangled with a Glass Eye, kicked it in the groin. The Glass Eye looked down, confused, because it didn't have anything sensitive in that area. The assassin's confusion lasted only half a moment, but it was enough time for Dodge to reach out and grab the reins of the frightened spirit-dane as it hurtled past. The animal ran, dragging him alongside until he managed to climb onto its back.

"Princess! Catch!"

Alyss turned, caught the weapon tossed to her by the white knight—the Hand of Tyman, five short sword blades rising from the handle grip. She raised it as a Glass Eye leaped toward her. One of the blades lodged into the assassin's left ocular opening and stuck there. The Glass Eye fell to the ground and, as the rook finished it off, Dodge galloped over on the spirit-dane and lifted Alyss up behind him, into the saddle.

"Go!" the rook shouted. "We'll hold them off *again*!"

Even with the fighting raging all around, Dodge had to smile. "Again": a little joke among battle-scarred warriors.

Generals Doppel and Gänger merged into one as they spurred their animal away from the fight. The spirit-dane car-rying Dodge and Alyss galloped alongside.

"Hatter and Bibwit have gone ahead to clear the emergency portal," General Doppelgänger panted.

But no matter how fast they traveled, their escape would be as fleeting as a wisp of smoke in a fog. More Glass Eyes were already after them.

CHAPTER 39

THEORETICALLY, IT was possible for inexperienced Continuum travelers to discover the rebels' emergency portal; they could have been inadvertently reflected out of it. But the portal was connected to the Continuum by such an unlikely arrangement of crystal byways (courtesy of strategically placed looking glasses) that no traveler who wasn't Alyssian had ever determined its location or even learned of its existence.

Hatter Madigan and Bibwit Harte hurried to clear the dried brush from the portal entrance—a thick, ancient-looking glass with bevelled edges located in a part of the forest rarely frequented by Wonderlanders. Hatter pressed his face through the glass, peering into the Continuum, and pulled it out as General Doppelgänger, Dodge, and Alyss raced up on their spirit-danes.

"It's clear," Hatter said.

"I'll go first," Dodge said and, without another word, he jumped into the glass.

"Be quick," Bibwit said, his ears trembling. "I hear our enemies approaching."

The tutor guided Alyss through the portal's liquid-crystal surface and into the Continuum. General Doppelgänger followed, and Hatter brought up the rear. It was only the second time in her life that Alyss had been inside the Continuum. For a moment, wide-eyed and entranced by the beauty of the luminous surfaces surrounding her, she navigated it as well as anyone, zooming through this kaleidoscopic lifeline at pace with Dodge and the others. But as soon as she realized that she'd only been in the Continuum once before . . . *Whoa!* . . . She lost control, floated up and back, bumping into General Doppelgänger.

"Focus your will and think heavy thoughts," shouted the general, "or you will be reflected out!"

Heavy thoughts? What are . . . ?

The general let go of her.

Uh-oh.

Again Alyss lost speed, would have been sucked up out of the Continuum if Hatter hadn't caught hold of her. With the princess in tow, he steered his body toward Bibwit.

"Hold on to him," the Milliner instructed.

So she did, traveling through the Continuum piggyback.

"Glass Eyes incoming!"

Without slowing, Hatter flicked his top hat; it morphed into deadly spinning blades and he flung them at the Glass Eyes racing up fast at his back. The blades cut into one after another, ricocheting among them, then returned to him.

Still the Glass Eyes closed in, firing orb generators. Hatter deflected them into crystal byways by spinning his top-hat blades so quickly that the force of their wind sent the orbs reeling. If he'd been alone, he would have reversed directions and attacked the Glass Eyes, but his duty required him to stay close to Alyss. He would have to fight them nearer to her than he liked. He slowed his pace. The saber blades of his belt snapped open and he twirled, letting the Glass Eyes come at him. Sliced and batted by his sabers, they became disorientated. Unable to maintain their equilibrium inside the Continuum, they were sucked from its main artery and reflected out of looking glasses.

"More coming!" Dodge shouted.

From in front of them this time.

"Out of the way!" warned General Doppelgänger.

Dodge steered his body to the Continuum's edge and the general shot a cannonball spider at the attacking Glass Eyes. Mid-shot, the cannonball cracked open and the emerging spider latched on to the entire pack, holding each of them fast with a sticky leg while its pincer-mouth pecked at them in rapid fire, reducing them to lifeless husks. *Shoosh!* They were reflected out of the Continuum.

The cannonball spider now came careening up fast toward

the Alyssians. Dodge threw himself at it to prevent it from targeting Alyss. The spider held Dodge's arms and legs, and though it wasn't designed to live long—would soon fold into itself and die—it had time enough to end Dodge's life. Its pincers opened and moved in toward Dodge's stomach.

Concentrate, think, imagine.

A muzzle formed out of nowhere—a rust-colored contraption that covered the spider's pincers, rounding their pointed ends.

"Ha!" Alyss shouted, ecstatic.

Frenzied, the spider tried to shake the foreign object from its mouth. Dodge managed to free an arm and, with a single wide, circular swipe of his sword, chopped off the spider's legs, then plunged the weapon into its vitals.

"Did you see that?" Alyss cried, holding on to her tutor's back. "I imagined that!"

"I saw it," said Bibwit Harte. "Very impressive."

But it would have been a whole lot more impressive, thought the tutor, if Alyss had conjured a happy end to this nightmare. Glass Eyes were again coming at them, simultaneously closing in on them from in front and behind, and General Doppelgänger was out of cannonball spiders.

CHAPTER 40

"HOW COULD she not have been there?! Where else would she be?!"

Banging the end of her scepter on the floor with every other word, Redd sent long-stemmed, flesh-eating roses slithering around the feet of Jack of Diamonds and the thick-padded paws of The Cat, both of whom had to keep moving to prevent the flowers from climbing up their legs.

"Maybe the Jack of Diamonds isn't as loyal as you supposed?" said The Cat.

Redd turned on Jack. "Yes, perhaps."

"My queen—I mean, Your Imperial Viciousness—the most important Alyssians were there and could have been done away with if The Cat hadn't been concerned solely with Alyss."

"I demanded that he be solely concerned with her!"

"But I don't think she's as dangerous as—"

"Who asked you!" Redd bellowed. Her scepter lifted into the air, its pointed end poised at the pulsing hollow of Jack of Diamonds' throat. "You don't, by chance, have nine lives?"

Jack swallowed, hard. "I have only one, which I devote to you, Your Imperial Viciousness."

"Hmmph." Redd twirled her scepter like a baton and stood it at her side. "Cat, why is there an empty box of orb generators in the hall?"

An ammunition container slid into the room, moved by Redd's imagination.

"Oh, that?" The Cat had been waiting for her to ask. Jack of Diamonds was in for it now. "We found it and many more at the Alyssian camp. I checked their manufacture codes. They were stolen from your factory three and a half lunar cycles ago. The thieves were interrogated and punished, but the twelve containers of stolen weapons were not where they informed us they'd be."

"Get to the point, Cat, or you will feel one in your guts."

The feline assassin bowed in acknowledgment. "Your Imperial Viciousness, you captured the thieves because of intelligence received by Jack of Diamonds. You allow the pudgy lord to have dealings with the Alyssians. How could the Alyssians have come into possession of these weapons if not from him? He knew where to find the thieves, he must have known where to find the weapons."

"Interesting," said a thoughtful Redd. "So, my well-fed informant has been taking advantage of the freedoms I grant him by supplying weapons to my enemies?"

"No! Absolutely not!" declared Jack. "Your Imperial Viciousness, this is ludicrous."

"We'll see how ludicrous it is."

Again, the sharpened point of Redd's scepter was at Jack of Diamonds' throat. But thoughts of Alyss had never completely left her head and, in a blink of imagination's eye, she saw the princess surrounded by sparkling, effervescent surfaces.

"She's in the Crystal Continuum!" Redd shrieked. "Smash the looking glasses! Every last one!"

Redd's face, wild with rage, flashed onto the billboards and government posters of Wondertropolis.

"Every looking glass in the queendom is to be smashed! *Now!*"

But the force of her anger beat most Wonderlanders to it. In pubs and stimulant dens throughout Wondertropolis, in the homes of ordinary Wonderlanders, in the gated and patrolled mansions of ranking families, looking glasses exploded. Wonderlanders eager for havoc ran through the streets, breaking windows and anything that could even remotely serve as a reflective surface.

CHAPTER 41

THEY WERE trapped, marooned. They would be killed for sure: Glass Eyes ahead of them, Glass Eyes behind.

The Continuum, it's . . . it's . . . disappearing!

With every looking glass in the queendom smashed, the crystalline pathways that made up the Continuum were vanishing. The Glass Eyes advancing upon Alyss and the others were themselves being chased by a void. And the void was gaining.

To be swallowed by nothingness is to become nothing.

At least they wouldn't suffer; one felt nothing upon becoming nothing.

The void rushed at the Glass Eyes, consumed the rear guards first and moved quickly up their ranks. No more Glass Eyes.

And still the void came fast.

"Anyone have a pocket looking glass?" Dodge asked.

Alyss and the others glanced at him, not understanding. "Quick!"

Bibwit reached into the folds of his robe and pulled out a looking glass no bigger than a tuttle-bird's wing. Dodge took hold of it. No Wonderlander had ever attempted what he was about to do. There had never been a need.

He held the looking glass at an angle, aiming it so that it reflected a small portion of the Continuum, regenerating it. As fast as the void swallowed up what was behind them, the modest little mirror added the corresponding length of Continuum ahead of them. But now what? Were they doomed to race through the void, safe in this small portion of Continuum—which, had he been at leisure, Bibwit would have pointed out was no longer strictly a Continuum since it connected to nothing, and without the pocket glass it would not, in fact, *continue*. Were they destined to be imprisoned in this mobile prism, zipping this way and that through pure emptiness until they perished from starvation, or fatigue caused Dodge to drop the glass?

What's that? Is it . . . It is. A way out.

At least one looking glass in the queendom must have still been intact. Ahead of them in the void, a short distance off, was a crystal byway, a dead end. Where it had once connected with the Continuum's main thoroughfare, it now simply stopped, connected to nothing.

"Dodge!"

"I see it!"

With subtle shifts of angle in the way he held the looking glass, Dodge steered them over and they linked up with it. The additional light and increased play of translucent colors were like the dance of life itself. Dodge, Bibwit, and Alyss, General Doppelgänger, Hatter—they emerged from the Continuum in the same order in which they'd entered, discovered themselves in a landscape resembling the open belly of a volcano, with clouds of sulphurous smoke drifting lazily into the upper reaches of the sky, and jets of flame spouting from the rocky ground between streams of bubbling lava: the Volcanic Plains.

CHAPTER 42

THEY TREKKED single-file along a volcano's narrow ridge, their noses and mouths covered with cloth torn from Bibwit's robe to protect them from airborne ash. It was too hot to speak, almost too hot to breathe. No one had said a word since they first emerged onto the Volcanic Plains and Dodge had suggested they smash the exit portal *just in case*. Redd's diabolically inventive mind was not to be underestimated; any remnant of the Crystal Continuum might cause her to reconstruct it in its entirety, providing her with the means to reach the plains that much sooner. Now Redd and her armies would have to travel on foot or by beast.

"The looking glass must have been used by jabberwocky poachers," Bibwit Harte had said. "Lucky for us, it was overlooked or we'd still be . . ." He'd shivered with the thought of the void.

"If Redd saw us in the Continuum, she might still be watching us," General Doppelgänger had observed.

"Can't be helped," Hatter had said.

Dodge had been impatient. "Then let's stop standing around and get to where we have to go."

So Bibwit, who carried detailed maps of the queendom within his bald head, led them toward the Valley of Mushrooms. Picking their way along the rocky, irregular ridge, they constantly had to look down to be sure of their footing, all the time reminding themselves of how high they were and how dangerous their passage.

"Ah!"

A hardened chunk of lava hit General Doppelgänger on the shoulder. The Alyssians paused, looked up. Another chunk of lava rock fell. Another and another.

The volcano's moving.

Not the entire volcano, just the topmost layer of rock and earth on the steep slope above them. The ridge gave way, crumbling beneath the Alyssians' feet, and they tumbled and rolled down into a gorge at the base of the volcano. General Doppelgänger was half buried in earth and rubble. Bibwit came to rest completely upside down, his feet in the air, but he quickly righted himself, coughing and spitting, before he was suffocated. Alyss, being the lightest among them, had bounced down the volcano's craggy lower slope and slid to a stop on a bed of gravel. Hatter and Dodge stood wiping lava crud from their coat sleeves as if surviving a landslide was something they did every day.

"Everyone all right?" asked General Doppelgänger.

"Alyss?" Dodge's voice, concerned.

"I'm okay." She didn't want the others to think she considered a few scrapes and bruises serious injuries. She was supposed to be strong enough to defeat Redd. "Someone's watching us," she said.

A pair of yellow-green eyes were peering at them from the black mouth of a nearby cave. Before anyone could speak, the giant reptilian head of a jabberwock thrust forward from between two boulders. Its long tongue lashed at Bibwit, scorching a swath through the sleeve of his robe to his delicate skin.

"Yaow!"

Even in the heat of the plains, Alyss and the others could feel the hotness of the jabberwock's breath, fouled by the stink of carcass meat. The creature opened its slobbery mouth impossibly wide, as a cobra does to swallow a rabbit—a display of menace quite uncalled for, since the jabberwock could have easily fit two full-grown Wonderlanders in its jaws with any old everyday chomp. The Alyssians backed toward the cave. The jabberwock lurched toward them, shot a spitball of fire at Alyss. She dived to the ground and the fireball flared against the gorge wall, but in its brief explosion of light the Alyssians saw that the yellow-green eyes in

the cave belonged to a miniature jabberwock surrounded by gnawed bones: a newborn.

"She's protecting her baby," Bibwit said.

The mother jabberwock rose up on her hind legs, preparing to charge, and in a single swift motion, Hatter took off his top hat, flicked it into blades, and hurled it at the rock overhanging the cave entrance.

Thwink-thwink-thwink-thwink!

Rocks loosened and fell into a pile, blocking the mouth of the cave. Hatter's blades were still boomeranging back to him when the mother jabberwock let out a pained wail and, ignoring the Alyssians, scratched and scrabbled at the fallen debris, clearing it away to save her baby, as Alyss and the others escaped unharmed along the gorge floor.

Each of them knew without saying it aloud: As long as they were on the plains, the threat of jabberwocky still loomed.

CHAPTER 43

SURPRISINGLY, BIBWIT Harte did not have a pair of gemstone fire crystals tucked anywhere in his scholar's robe, so they had to build a fire the old-fashioned way, with the suns and a pile of dead branches. The Volcanic Plains were behind them and they had made camp next to a wide river en route to the Valley of Mushrooms.

Dodge wrapped a dampened leaf around Bibwit's burn and tied it with strong vine. Bibwit tested the movement of his arm, grimacing and perhaps making more of his injury than was necessary, because Dodge, with a quick glance at General Doppelgänger, said, "We might have to cut it off."

Bibwit fell still, too horrified to speak.

"You can tutor just as well with one arm as with two, can't you?"

Bibwit's mouth opened and closed, but nothing came out.

Dodge and General Doppelgänger sputtered with laughter.

"I'm just teasing, Bibwit," Dodge said. "You'll be fine."

"Oh. Ha ha," Bibwit said uneasily. "A bit of levity to ease the burden we're under. Yes. Ha ha." But he hugged his injured arm close until Dodge and the general settled into sleep. Regaining his usual composure, he took a seat next to the princess. "Now, Alyss, we shall have that lesson of ours that keeps getting put off. Lucky for us, I have memorized most of the necessary books."

Alyss nodded, but she was in no mood for a lesson. The day itself had been a lesson—in survival.

"I will close my eyes for a moment," continued Bibwit, "to file through all that's in my head for the appropriate material. It'll just take a moment."

But as soon as the tutor shut his eyes, he began to snore, his ears opening and closing with each breath. Alyss smiled a tired smile and pulled the ends of his robe about him as a blanket. She moved to the other side of the fire to let him sleep undisturbed. As it had long ago, on that first night with Quigly and the orphans in the London alley, her mind was plagued by too much to allow her any rest. *How did it work when I was young?* Her ability to conjure objects from the strength and depth of her imagination. *How had it worked?* She'd been lucky with the muzzle. She hadn't intended to

conjure such a thing, had only tried to imagine Dodge safely out of the spider's sticky clutches.

Hatter sat beyond the fire's glow cleaning his weapons, his top hat beside him. He removed first his left wrist-bracelet and then his right, and set about wiping their blades with a leaf. Alyss had never seen a Milliner without his bracelets. *He looks so much like an ordinary Wonderlander.* Indeed, especially now, as Hatter paused in his work to strip off his long outer coat and lay it on the ground beside him. Without his coat and the tell-tale weapons, there was nothing in his appearance to distinguish him from any normal, adult male Wonderlander. *He must have hopes, dreams, loves, and sorrows outside his duty, as anyone does. Strange that I should know so little about him when he's devoted his life to protecting my family.* He caught her looking at him. She smiled in apology, as if she had been intruding. Hatter went back to his cleaning.

The thing about when she was young . . . she didn't remember her imagination having to *work.* It just was.

"Hatter?"

"Yes, Princess?"

"When you're fighting in a battle, what do you think about?"

Hatter considered. "Nothing, Princess. Nothing at all."

"So you don't tell yourself, 'I'm going to throw my top hat and then I'm going to attack with the blades on my wrists' or anything of that sort?"

"No."

"No," Alyss echoed, "of course not. It just happens. Your body knows what to do."

Hatter nodded.

It's unconscious. To will something into being, the willing of it must be so deep down that no self-doubt is possible. The imaginative power itself must be a given, a thing already proven that cannot be disbelieved.

Lunar hours passed and, at first, Alyss was all too aware of her efforts to conjure, all too aware of the items she attempted to imagine into being. *A platter, a sword, a crown. A platter, a sword, a crown.* She repeated these words over and over again to herself. No crown materialized. Part of a platter did form, but quickly vanished. A sword appeared, but in outline only, plain and without detail, as if the weapon had not been precisely envisioned. With time, the fire died down to a heap of glowing embers. Alyss' mind cleared. While she was in this trance-like state, a large glass cover akin to one you might see over a cake in a bakery formed in the air. Alyss looked at it without surprise. She tilted her head to the left and the glass cover tilted left. She tilted her head to the right and the cover tilted right. Then, without moving at all, she brought it down over the fire. Robbed of oxygen, the embers fizzled out. The glass cover dissolved in the air.

Alyss beamed—for not only had she conjured, but she had controlled her imagination in a way she never had before. *I'll need to practice. I'll need to . . . oh.* Hatter was watching her, had witnessed this first controlled exercise of her power-ful imagination. He bowed his head in respect. Then came a final, honking snore and Bibwit awoke, shivering and hugging himself.

"It *is* chilly without the fire, isn't it?"

CHAPTER 44

WITH THE queendom's looking glasses obliterated, Redd again turned her anger on Jack of Diamonds.

"I grant you a leniency that others don't enjoy. Why? Because it's supposed to benefit *me*. I let you believe you're your own boss. In exchange, you're to provide me with Alyssian intelligence. As queen, I command the better end of all deals and it doesn't fill me with glee, *Lord* Diamond, that you've been profiting from treachery."

"Your Imperial—"

Redd made a shooing motion with her hand and Jack slammed against a wall of the Observation Dome. The Cat's tail whisked back and forth, happy and playful.

"What am I to do with you?" Redd asked.

"M-maybe you could—" Jack began.

The Cat raised a paw. "I know."

"It was a rhetorical question, fools! You don't answer it! Since when do I need help making anyone suffer?"

This time The Cat and Jack of Diamonds knew better than to answer.

Redd stepped up to Jack and stroked his wig. She held one of its long curls against her palm, studying it a moment. With sudden ferocity, she yanked the curl from the wig and tossed it away from her. The lock of hair lay on the floor, growing in size and hairiness. It grew and grew, developing arms and legs, until it stood at twice Jack's height.

"Lord Diamond, say hello to my beast of a wig." Redd yawned.

Before Jack could offer a greeting, the beast dealt him a stinging blow to the stomach. He doubled over, straining for air. The Wig-Beast picked him up and tossed him across the room. He landed with a thud worthy of his girth, and with a single bound the Wig-Beast was beside him, lifting him to his feet, holding him upright with one wiggy limb and slapping him with the other.

The Cat purred, a wide grin on his face as he watched Jack of Diamonds suffer, but his enjoyment was interrupted by the sharp-as-a-claw piercing of Redd's voice raised in anger and disbelief. Redd had turned her imagination's eye on Alyss. She should have seen nothing—Alyss should have been part of the void—but instead she saw the princess, Hatter Madigan, and

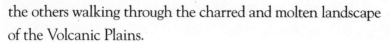

the others walking through the charred and molten landscape of the Volcanic Plains.

"Not dead!" she screeched. "Alyss not dead!"

Jack heard the words too, but it took a moment for his addled brain to understand their meaning. Between slugs from the Wig-Beast, he managed to say, "They're—going to—Looking—Glass—Maze!"

Redd held up a hand and the Wig-Beast halted.

"I must be getting soft, Lord Diamond, if I think you could have said *anything* worth listening to."

It was lucky for Jack that Redd had shrugged off the lessons Bibwit tried to teach her in adolescence. Jack was quick to understand that his knowledge of the Looking Glass Maze could save his life. But he would tell her as little as necessary. His future health and safety might depend on his leaking such valuable intelligence to Redd.

"The Looking Glass Maze, Your Imperial Viciousness. By passing through the maze, Alyss will reach her full potential of strength and imaginative power and be able to defeat you."

"But *I* have the Heart Crystal! She can't reach her *full* potential without that!"

"I'm only repeating what I heard from Bibwit Harte, Your Imperial Viciousness."

He shouldn't have mentioned Bibwit; Redd bristled. Jack cast a quick glance at the Wig-Beast. It was perfectly still, as if it had never been alive. So far, so good.

"What if I pass through the maze instead of her?" Redd asked.

"Ah, very clever, Your Imperial Viciousness. If you pass through the maze, then you'll be that much more powerful. I'm sure Alyss won't be able to defeat you then."

What Jack of Diamonds knew of the Looking Glass Maze could fit in a gwynook's third nostril—which was very little. As a boy, he'd often heard his mother recall in bitter tones how Princess Genevieve had passed through the maze to become queen. But she didn't know that becoming queen was not just a matter of navigating the maze. None of the Diamond clan had been tutored by Bibwit Harte, so none of them knew that only the person for whom the Looking Glass Maze was intended could enter it. But like many young men who grow up as privileged as Jack of Diamonds, he didn't suspect his own ignorance.

"We'll see if what you say is true," Redd said. "Bring me *In Queendom Speramus!*"

The walrus toddled into the dome. "Here it is, Your Imperial Viciousness. *In Queendom—*"

The book flew from his flippers, hovered in the air before Redd as she thumbed through its pages, searching for mention of the Looking Glass Maze. She found none. She saw pages torn from the book and her own words in Bibwit's handwriting.

"Bah!"

She swatted the book and it flew at the walrus, but the

waddly fellow ducked and the book hit the floor and skidded out the dome and down the hall.

"I'll get it, Your Imperial Viciousness," said the walrus-butler, and hurried after the book, never able to leave Redd's company fast enough.

Redd strolled up to Jack, all the more frightening for her nonchalance. "And now, my unworthy servant, you are going to tell me where the Looking Glass Maze is."

"But I don't know where it is."

Redd's fingers twitched and Jack thought he saw the Wig-Beast move.

"The Alyssians don't know either!" he said quickly. "The caterpillars have to tell them!"

The caterpillars: those annoying, oversized larvae. Redd had tried to do away with them and their outdated prophesying when she first took control of the queendom. She didn't need those *things* breeding dissent with their predictions. But every time she tried to attack them, they saw her coming and vanished like smoke. So she had exercised her rage on their beloved Valley of Mushrooms. But what to do now? A raid on the valley would not serve her purpose.

"I have decided to let Alyss meet with the caterpillars," she announced. "We'll maintain close surveillance on that goody-goody little Heart, and when she leads us to the Looking Glass Maze's location, we'll attack and I will enter it myself. Cat, bait the seekers."

"But what about Lord Diamond?" the feline whined.

"He may prove useful yet."

Jack gave Redd's furry assassin a taunting little smile. The Cat was to blame for his trouble, the bruises he felt forming all over his body. He would have to return the favor somehow.

"I see you don't treasure your lives as much as I'd supposed, Cat, or you would have obeyed my order by now," Redd said.

As The Cat sulked off to bait the seekers, Redd again focused her imagination's eye on Alyss. How wonderfully cruel it was going to be! Miss Prissy Heart would serve as personal guide to the Looking Glass Maze and thereby become the agent of her own downfall. How deliciously nasty.

~

The Cat could hear the seekers' frenzied screeching even before he reached the end of the corridor, shouldered open the heavy door, and stepped inside the chamber carved out of Mount Isolation itself. It was impossible to hear his own footfalls or breathing because the seekers' cries—like the sound of pain itself—were so loud. The chamber was dimly lit by faint, glowing crystals embedded in the walls. Hundreds of cages hung from the ceiling, with several seekers in each of them: Redd's bloodhounds, bred out of her distrust and paranoia; creatures with bird-of-prey bodies and the heads of blood-sucking insects.

Walking up and down the chamber, The Cat stopped beneath each cage to wave Alyss' London wedding dress—

278

a souvenir from his raid on the Alyssian headquarters. He teased the seekers with its scent and they pressed eager faces against the bars of their cages.

The baiting complete, The Cat flipped a lever in the floor and a wall retracted—a wall that, from the outside, looked like part of the mountain. The cages fell open and with wild shrieks the seekers flew out into the night, on the hunt.

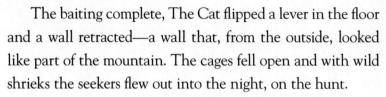

CHAPTER 45

THE ALYSSIANS emerged from a small wood to find themselves on a mountaintop, the Valley of Mushrooms spread out before them. The suns were setting on the distant horizon, their slanting rays shining down on the mushrooms nestled within a ring of twilight-blue mountains. No two mushrooms were alike, their colors ranging from earthy pink to unearthly brown to nearly translucent and, with the play of the suns on their caps and the multihued shadows they cast on the valley floor, the Alyssians were greeted with a sight of impressive kaleidoscopic brilliance.

The colors of the valley were like the sprouting of renewed hope in the breasts of Alyss and her friends and, for a moment, it seemed unlikely that Redd could survive their rebellion. They may have been few in number, but they were strong and

determined. They *believed*. But this optimism lasted only a moment, because as they descended into the valley, they saw that it wasn't as beautiful as it might have been—indeed, as it once was. Mushroom stalks showed the marks of The Cut; mushroom caps lay butchered on the ground. Prayer temples were blasted apart.

In silence, Bibwit led the Alyssians through the unexpected desecration to a clearing, where they came upon five giant caterpillars whose bodies were coiled beneath them as they smoked from the same ancient hookah. Each of them sat on a mushroom as distinct in color as himself: red, orange, yellow, purple, and green. The caterpillars showed no sign of surprise upon seeing the Alyssians, had in fact been aware of their presence for some time.

"The caterpillar counsel," Bibwit informed the others, and then stepped forward to address the oracles. "Wise ones, we are in need of your assistance. We—"

The orange caterpillar raised his frontmost right leg, as if to say *shush*, and all the little legs behind it echoed the gesture. "We know why you've come."

"What sort of oracles would we be if we didn't know *that*?" said the yellow caterpillar.

The hookah burbled, the purple caterpillar inhaling deeply. His eyes rolled up into the back of his head and smoke streamed out his nostrils.

"Whooah."

Dodge and General Doppelgänger exchanged an

uncertain glance. Hatter stood at the ready, a hand at the brim of his top hat, his eyes scanning the surroundings for trouble.

"O wise, all-seeing caterpillars," said Bibwit Harte, "we offer you our humility and respect, and hope that—"

"I'm having the weirdest sense of déjà vu right now," said the green caterpillar.

"Duh!" said the yellow caterpillar. "Do you think, just maybe, that's because you predicted this?"

"Oh, yeah."

The caterpillar counsel tittered.

"We are saddened to see that even your home has suffered from Redd's reign," Bibwit pressed on. "Knowing who we are and why we've come, then you already know . . ."

But here, the caterpillars added their voices to his: ". . . that we come for the health of the queendom, to install the rightful queen on her throne and end these years of brutal tyranny."

Being able to see the future (and/or possible futures) didn't always make the caterpillars agreeable conversation-alists.

"Have you brought us anything to munch?" asked the orange caterpillar.

"Some tarty tarts perhaps?" the yellow caterpillar hoped.

"Well," Bibwit said, checking his robe but finding no tarty tarts.

I'll conjure a dozen tarty tarts. It'll be good practice. Alyss

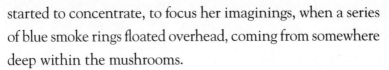

started to concentrate, to focus her imaginings, when a series of blue smoke rings floated overhead, coming from somewhere deep within the mushrooms.

"Blue has summoned Alyss," the orange caterpillar said. "He will tell her everything she needs to know."

The counsel fell silent, puffing intently on their hookah as if able to communicate with one another through it.

"Go on, Alyss," said Bibwit Harte. "It's all right."

The princess followed the trail of smoke rings back through the mushrooms to a ruined temple. Over its front door were the words "Did Lao Tsu Dream the Butterfly or Did the Butterfly Dream Lao Tsu?" Sitting on a blue mushroom out front was the blue caterpillar, smoking from a hookah of his own.

"Thank you for seeing me," Alyss said with a bow.

"Ahem hum hem," the caterpillar grumbled, exhaling a cloud of smoke, in the middle of which Prince Leopold appeared. The prince was in a London drawing room, pacing anxiously back and forth while his mother, Queen Victoria, sat fanning herself in a quilted chair. Dean and Mrs. Liddell were there too, sitting close together on a settee. Prim and erect, the commoners looked uneasy, cowed by the queen. *Is this the past I'm seeing? The present?*

"Even in that world," the caterpillar said, "where no one knew you were a princess, you were to marry royalty. It seems that destiny will not let you deny who you are."

"I don't mean to deny it, Mr. Caterpillar."

The caterpillar frowned, puffing at his hookah. "Call me Blue."

"All right. I don't want to deny it, Blue, it's just that my time away from Wonderland has confused me. I've been through so much and all I do is run from those more powerful than myself, which doesn't strike me as being . . . well, as very *queenly*."

"Ahem hum mmm," Blue said, and in the cloud of smoke he exhaled from his caterpillar lungs appeared the words: *It is sometimes braver to run.* "By running, you live to face further uncertainty and trouble," he explained. "It would be much easier for you to give up. You should not doubt your courage, Alyss Heart. She who runs from her enemies until she has the strength to do otherwise is both brave and wise."

Funny that it should feel like cowardice. "You know why I'm here?"

"You seek the Looking Glass Maze, as your mother did before you."

Alyss said nothing, remembering the surprise of seeing her mother engage so readily in combat. *She must have stood before Blue just as . . . just as I am now.* Indeed, and like then, the future of the queendom had been threatened by Redd.

Blue seemed to know what she was thinking. "Alyss Heart, your mother was a warrior queen, as you discovered the hard way. She passed through the maze to assume the throne and to make the most of what she innately possessed, but her strength could only carry her so far. Redd was always the stronger of the two. But you, Alyss Heart, have the strength of generations in your blood. Successfully navigate the maze and you will discover this for yourself."

"And if I'm unsuccessful?"

Blue ignored the question. "Everything you have experienced up until now has *had to be* if you are to become the strongest queen Wonderland has ever known. It has been necessary to forge in you the wise and judicious temperament that will guide you as protector of the Heart Crystal. Hatter Madigan will lead you to one who knows where to find the maze. Look for a puzzle shop. You will know the key to the maze when you see it, but you will have to return to Wondertropolis." Blue formed an O with his lips and exhaled a thick stream of smoke directly at the princess.

~

When Alyss awoke, she was alone. She walked back through the mushrooms to Dodge and the others. The caterpillar counsel sat coiled on their mushrooms, smoking contentedly. Their expressions did not change at the sight of Alyss, but the Alyssians looked at her, expectant.

"It's back in Wondertropolis," she said.

There were groans all around.

"That's like entering the jabberwocky's lair!" fretted Bibwit. "Or stirring up the seekers' nest, or—"

The green caterpillar puffed a cloud of smoke at the royal tutor. The smoke enveloped him and his expression slackened, relaxed.

"Oh, well." He grinned, dreamy. "I suppose we must do what we must do."

"Where in Wondertropolis?" Dodge asked.

"I was told only that Hatter can take us to someone who will know."

The others turned to the Milliner, but even he, who was able to maintain his composure in battles that would have sent most Wonderlanders running for their mothers' skirts, was a little exasperated by this.

"Me? How can I know anyone? I've hardly been in Wondertroplis in thirteen years. The people I knew are all dead."

Bibwit, still feeling the effects of the caterpillar's smoke, put a hand on Hatter's shoulder. "Relax, my good fellow. The oracle wouldn't say it just to hear himself talk. There's got to be a reason. Relax and *think*."

So Hatter thought. What would he have done thirteen years ago? To whom would he have turned for help? *Where* would he have gone?

"There is one place," he said finally. "I don't know if it still exists, but I used to go there whenever official sources didn't yield the information I needed."

"Well then, that's where we'll go," General Doppelgänger said.

"Let's *go* already," fumed Dodge. He didn't much care if they stirred up the seekers' nest; on the contrary, he rather welcomed it.

CHAPTER 46

IT WAS a long, exhausting journey without the ease of travel once afforded by The Crystal Continuum. Not wanting to risk further encounters with jabberwocky, the Alyssians skirted the Volcanic Plains, and luckily—though strangely, considering Redd's usual aggression—their trek was uneventful. They hadn't seen a single Glass Eye or card soldier, just the occasional flock of seekers circling high overhead.

They stood gathered at the base of an abandoned building, gazing out at a dingy Wondertropolis alley.

"Where is it?" General Doppelgänger asked.

"There."

Hatter pointed as two Wonderlanders tripped up the front steps of a basement tavern and stumbled into the alley, drunk.

"That's the place?" General Doppelgänger asked. "It looks more than a bit . . . unsavory."

"It's the only place I know," Hatter said. He cast a studious eye over his confederates: Bibwit in his scholar's robe; the general, Dodge, and Alyss in their Alyssian uniforms. No amount of camouflage could hide the fact that they were not average Wonderlanders. Still, they didn't have to bring unnecessary attention to themselves by *flaunting* their rebel colors, so Hatter folded his top hat into a stack of deadly blades and placed it in his inside coat pocket. He removed his coat and draped it over his arm. "Ready?" he asked.

Alyss nodded, conjured hooded cloaks for herself and the others, and the Alyssians crossed the alley and entered the tavern. They paused in the doorway to let their eyes adjust to the gloom, giving the bartender and a toothless old smuggler at the counter an opportunity to size them up. The rest of the patrons were too absorbed in their drink to notice the newcomers, slumped half-conscious on their tattered bar stools or passed out altogether.

"We don't have to put ourselves on display, do we?" Dodge said. "Let's sit down."

They had hardly settled around the nearest table when the bartender jerked his head toward a corner of the tavern, and out of the vacuous dark stepped a girl wearing a homburg hat and a long overcoat not unlike Hatter's. She approached the Alyssians to take their order.

The shy girl I saw at camp, who brought tea when I had my first talk with Bibwit.

"You?" Bibwit said, surprised.

"Me," the girl confirmed.

"But . . . how did . . . I don't . . ."

It was the first time any of them had seen Bibwit Harte at a loss for words.

"My child," he said, recovering himself, "I don't know how you survived the raid on our camp, and of course it's pleasing to discover you, as it would be pleasing to find any of us alive, but . . . what are you doing here? You're too young to be working in a place like this."

"I'm thirteen. Old enough, I think. And lucky to be working at all."

Alyss glanced at Dodge, and the questioning, slightly perturbed expression on his face told her that they were thinking the same thing. *Is this who we're supposed to meet? It must be. It's too much of a coincidence.* But the girl was so young—not at all what Alyss had been expecting.

"How well do you know the city?" General Doppelgänger asked.

The girl shrugged. "Better than most."

Hatter caught sight of a vein in the shape of an *h* below her left ear. His face hardened. "She's a halfer. Civilian and Millinery spawn. Not to be trusted."

"Hatter—" Bibwit began.

"I don't need *your* trust," the girl said. "I serve the

princess . . . if she'll let me." With a bow too subtle for those around them to notice, she directly addressed Alyss for the first time: "Homburg Molly, at your service, Princess."

Alyss dipped her head in response. "We are looking for a certain puzzle shop. Do you know of it?"

"I think I do."

"How can we be sure you won't lead us into a trap?" The question came from Hatter.

"You can't."

"Hatter, I don't think we need fear the girl," said Bibwit Harte. "And judging by the looks we're getting from the other patrons, we could use a friend in this place."

The longer the Alyssians remained in the tavern, the more the regulars woke from their alcohol dreams and squinted menacingly at them. Alyssians were not welcome. The toothless smuggler heaved himself away from the bar and hurried out, glaring at them.

"I wonder where *he* could be going," Dodge said, sarcastic.

"If you're afraid," Molly said to Hatter, "you can stay here."

"Afraid?"

"It happens to everyone."

"Keep it lively, you!" the bartender shouted.

"You better order something," Molly said.

"Bring us whatever will keep you out of trouble," Bibwit said.

Molly went to fetch the order and received an earful of

abuse from the bartender for her so-called laziness—he filling five cracked mugs with frothy, steaming brew all the while.

Bibwit shook his head. "What sort of world is it when a youngster must become a barmaid in a place like this to survive?"

"She's a halfer," Hatter repeated, as if the fact in itself was enough to ward them off the girl.

"We had halfers at the Alyssian headquarters, Hatter," said General Doppelgänger. "After the Millinery went down, several members lived with us for a time. Many halfers were born under our care. They're not as disloyal as you suppose."

"Their only duty is to their own self-interest."

"She says she knows the puzzle shop," Alyss said, and the table fell silent. "She's the only one the caterpillar could have meant. Look around. There is no one else."

"Assuming this is the place the caterpillar meant for us to be," Dodge said.

But Alyss had made up her mind. This was the place. Homburg Molly was the one. "It is," she said.

Molly returned with their drinks and began setting them on the table.

"You see that poster over there, Princess? The one for Redd's Hotel and Casino?"

"Yes."

"It's a false wall. Behind it is a way out. We use it whenever we're raided. The Cut is already on its way."

"Thanks to our friend with no teeth," Dodge said.

292

Indeed, a division of The Cut was at that moment rounding the corner into the alley, led by the toothless smuggler. The unmistakable rasping of the card soldiers' marching, steel-like legs echoed off the buildings. By the time it was heard inside the tavern, it was almost too late. The Cut burst in and the suddenly sober patrons overturned tables and trampled one another in their efforts to flee. Fighting broke out. Dodge, Bibwit, General Doppelgänger and Hatter formed a circle around Alyss—the first three with their swords drawn, Hatter with his wrist-blades spinning. Homburg Molly steered them through the brawling soldiers and patrons, ducking to avoid the reach of pummeling fists, her homburg flattened into a razor-edged disk to shield her from the soldiers' swords. *Dink! Clank! Pong!* In close formation, the thirteen-year-old guided the Alyssians to the false wall, down a dank tunnel, and safely outside.

The street was quiet, no hint of the violence from which they had just escaped. It could have been an ordinary night in Wondertropolis. Molly kept walking, calmly continued down the street, knowing exactly where she was going. The Alyssians stood watching her until the girl stopped and turned to them.

"Well? Come on if you're coming."

CHAPTER 47

EMERALD DRIVE was one of the oldest streets in the capital. In Genevieve's time and before, it had been a grand thoroughfare of upscale shops and restaurants, but the wealthy and privileged gradually moved elsewhere as the surrounding streets became havens for looter gangs, imagination-stimulant manufacturers, and Wonderlanders engaged in other illicit but profitable employment. The squalor had at last reached its fingers into Emerald Drive itself, and the once-celebrated promenade was now indistinguishable from the scum-heavy streets around it.

At scattered points along the drive's ruined glory, the homeless warmed themselves around pits glowing with fire crystals, their mumbled conversations brought to a pause by the sight of a strange array of Wonderlanders approaching a shop that hadn't been open for business in many lunar cycles.

"ZZLES &" was all that remained of the sign that had once declared the shop's wares. Its massive front door, through which two spirit-danes could have easily passed side by side, was locked. The single front window was covered with dust and revealed nothing. Dodge pounded on the door.

"I doubt anyone's in," General Doppelgänger said.

Bibwit's ears twitched. "I hear trouble." Paler than usual, the tutor removed a sword from beneath his robe and gripped it with two hands.

It wasn't long before they all heard it. The dark sky turned darker as Redd's moon was eclipsed by a screaming swarm of seekers.

The homeless Wonderlanders scattered as *kreeeeech!*— the seekers attacked. Dodge, Alyss, Bibwit, and the general slashed at the creatures with their swords while Hatter sent his top-hat blades into the thick of them. *Thimp thimp thimp! Thimp thimp thimp!* The blades sliced through the flock, wounding and killing several, and returned to him. Molly flicked her own hat flat and used it as both shield and offensive weapon, digging its sharpened edges into the alien creatures when they shot toward her out of the sky with their hungry insect mouths.

"Aah!"

One of them swiped Dodge on the shoulder, knocking him to the ground and sending his sword clanking out of reach. The seeker circled, was coming in for the kill with its talons drawn when someone kicked Dodge's sword back to him.

"Seek this!" Dodge hissed through clenched jaw, stabbing the beast. He rolled away from the creature as it writhed in its death throes, saw the rook and white knight battling alongside him, together with a small platoon of surviving chessmen.

"Hope you don't mind us always showing up unannounced like this," the rook said.

"We followed the seekers," explained the white knight.

Next to each other now, standing, Dodge and the rook whirled, aiming their swords skyward just in time for an attacking seeker to impale itself on them and perish with a hideous howl. A division of Redd's Cut appeared at the end of Emerald Drive. A few of the card soldiers were armed with AD52s—automatic dealers capable of shooting razor-sharp projectiles the size and shape of ordinary playing cards at the rate of fifty-two per second. Hardly had the soldiers rounded the corner and spotted the Alyssians when a Four Card let loose with a spray of razor-cards.

"Incoming!" General Doppelgänger shouted.

The Alyssians dropped facedown in the street, all except Alyss and Homburg Molly, who flattened themselves against the front of the puzzle shop as the first of the razor-cards sliced past. Hatter jumped in front of them and, with his wrist-blades activated and his arms moving in a blur, knocked the rest of the razor-cards to the ground.

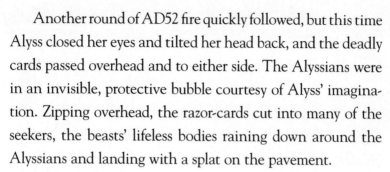

Another round of AD52 fire quickly followed, but this time Alyss closed her eyes and tilted her head back, and the deadly cards passed overhead and to either side. The Alyssians were in an invisible, protective bubble courtesy of Alyss' imagination. Zipping overhead, the razor-cards cut into many of the seekers, the beasts' lifeless bodies raining down around the Alyssians and landing with a splat on the pavement.

With Redd's Cut closing in, Hatter hurled his top-hat blades at the puzzle shop window. Hitting the glass, the blades rotated and cut a hole large enough for Alyss to fit through.

"Go!" he shouted.

General Doppelgänger split into Generals Doppel and Gänger, swords held at the ready.

Dodge glared at the advancing card soldiers, his words directed at Alyss: "We'll keep them busy. You just find the maze."

But there are too many. Even with the chessmen, we're outnumbered.

Homburg Molly tugged at her sleeve.

No choice. No choice but to go.

Before Alyss followed Molly into the shop, she imagined the AD52s plugged up, useless, and could only hope her imagining had been successful, because she didn't wait around to find out. She dived through the window into the shop.

As was perhaps appropriate for any shop specializing in the sale of puzzles and games, this one was itself built in the shape of a puzzle. Hand-crafted bookshelves were arranged to form a simple maze. Alyss and Homburg Molly ran up and down the narrow passages but found nothing. Every shelf was bare. They began toppling bookcases, opening every cabinet, trapdoor, and dummy window they came across.

"What are we looking for?" Molly yelled.

Alyss could barely hear her over the battle noise from outside. "I don't know!" But then a bluish twinkle, a wink of colored light, caught her eye. She looked up and saw it: on the edge of the tallest bookcase in the shop, a glowing crystal cube.

"Up there!"

"I'll get it!"

Molly didn't climb more than halfway up the bookcase before it tilted, started to fall. She jumped to the ground, scurrying out of harm's way, but the crystal cube was in the air, falling hard and fast.

"Nooooo!" Alyss screamed.

The princess leaped, arms outstretched, as the bookcase crashed to the ground and splintered apart. But she'd caught it; the crystal cube was safe. Alyss turned it over in her hands, looking for a clue as to how it worked. *What am I supposed to—?*

Kabooooooorrrchk!

The shop door imploded and, still holding on to the radiant cube, Alyss fell back through a looking glass painted to appear like part of a wall. The fighting had spilled into the shop. But floating weightless inside the looking glass,

Wonderland's rightful princess saw the battle scene freeze, stopped in time. There was Dodge with his sword raised, attacking a Two Card. There was Hatter in midair, the saber blades of his belt open to fight three card soldiers at once (a pair of Fours and a Two). There were the generals, come to help Bibwit, who had somehow lost hold of his sword. And there was Homburg Molly, staring wide-eyed at the spot where the princess had fallen through the looking glass. Alyss saw it all as if through a watery film, and despite the mortal threat she and the Alyssians were facing, despite the uncertainty of everything, she felt almost serene as she drifted down into the Looking Glass Maze.

CHAPTER 48

SHE LANDED gently on her feet in the middle of what appeared to be a prison—a looking glass prison. On every side of her were looking glasses as tall as forever, and no matter what direction she turned, she saw her reflection infinitely repeating into the mirrored distance.

"This is a maze?" she said aloud, but instead of hearing just her voice, she heard a chorus of voices, all of them hers.

Something was wrong—besides that she wasn't in a maze. *I must have found the wrong key but . . . Odd, that looks like me and yet it doesn't.* The reflection directly in front of Alyss was off somehow, inexact. She reached out toward the looking glass and—*Ah!*—the reflection grabbed her and pulled her into it.

"We have to hurry," the reflection said. "Lots to do and many people to see. So little time."

"But . . ." Alyss couldn't think what to say.

The reflection wouldn't let go of her wrist and pulled her at a fast clip past looking glass halls that branched and snaked into the distance, past mirrored alcoves and dead ends. Even the floor was made of looking glass. Being led first one way and then another, Alyss felt sure her reflection was taking this complex route only to confuse her. *Better not have to find my way back.* Because there was no chance of that; Alyss had lost all sense of direction.

The reflection brought her to a stop in what appeared to be a rest area, a mirrored room wider than the corridors along which they'd passed. "Wait here," the reflection said. "Someone will be with you shortly."

"Don't leave me!" But Alyss was already alone. Or was she? Her likeness looked back at her from every surface.

"Hello?" she said, and again a chorus of voices said it with her—the voices of her reflections. She lifted her hand toward the one closest to her, to take hold of it, but her fingers couldn't penetrate the looking glass and stubbed themselves against its cold quicksilver surface.

Maybe I was supposed to follow her? But Alyss could no longer be sure in which direction the reflection had gone. *Imagine a way out. That must be what I'm supposed to do. It's a test.* Alyss gathered herself tight for the effort her imaginings required, but between the flicker of her eyelids she saw someone approaching from the distance of a looking glass. Closer and closer the person came, and even before

Alyss could make out the woman's face, she recognized the clothes.

"Mother!" she and her reflections gasped.

Genevieve was dressed as her daughter had last seen her but without the crown. She came right up to the other side of the looking glass.

"Alyss," Genevieve said, and the wistful, proud smile that formed on the dead queen's face caused tears to well up in her daughter's eyes.

"She's become as beautiful as I imagined," said a man's voice.

Alyss turned to see her father, Nolan, beaming at her from one of the looking glasses in place of her reflection.

"Dad!" she said, running to embrace him, wanting to feel the touch of her long-gone father. *I don't care about any maze or about Redd or the Heart Crystal! I want us all to be together again! I want my family back! I WANT MY FAMILY BACK!* But Alyss couldn't pass through the looking glass. "What *is* this?" she cried. "Where *are* you?"

"We're in you, dear," Nolan said.

Genevieve gave a little sigh. "If we are successful against Redd, no one can say that our success has been without sacrifice. But I sometimes wonder if it has required too much of us."

"Of all involved who fight for White Imagination," said Nolan.

"Yes, of course," said Genevieve. "The path to a victory

of this magnitude is doomed to be littered with defeats and failures."

With a soft look of sympathy, Nolan walked from one looking glass to another to stand next to his wife. He put his arm around her and kissed her on the forehead, which seemed to raise her spirits.

"Alyss," Genevieve said, "it is good that you have taken it upon yourself to exercise your imagination. You are well on your way to reaching your potential of imaginative power and control. But all you have experienced and discovered about yourself is not enough. Not yet."

"Look at her." Nolan chuckled. "She's an adult. She doesn't need her parents nagging her. Alyss, my sweet, have half as much faith in yourself as others have in you and you'll be fine."

The royal couple turned and began walking off into the distance of the looking glass.

"Wait!" Alyss shouted. "Don't go!"

But Genevieve and Nolan kept walking.

"Wa-ait! Will I ever see you again?"

They stopped, apparently surprised by the question.

"Again and again and again," said Nolan.

"If you know where to look for us," said Genevieve.

Then they were gone and Alyss' reflection once again occupied the glass.

All strength left the princess. She fell to her knees and buried her face in her hands. She would never get over the

sudden, violent loss of her parents, never be able to accept the absence their deaths had left behind. *How can I? How could anyone?* Her sobs were magnified tenfold as her reflections cried with her.

The worst of it had passed, and all that was left of Alyss' swell of unhappiness was the occasional hiccup. Someone touched her shoulder.

"Tag, you're it."

Alyss lifted her head and saw a little girl. *Is that . . . ?* She brushed the hair out of her face and wiped her eyes to be sure. *She looks exactly like me.*

It was: Alyss Heart, age seven, wearing her birthday dress.

"You want me to chase you?" Alyss asked.

The girl clicked her tongue, annoyed. "Haven't you ever played tag before?"

"Yes, but . . . not in some time." The princess got to her feet. It wasn't every day that you met up with your younger self. Who knew where it might lead? "Okay," she said. "You'd better run then."

With a cry of pleasure, the girl sprinted down the corridor. Alyss chased after her, and corridor after corridor of the Looking Glass Maze was briefly visited by the running pair. As much as Alyss had wallowed in the depths of her sorrow moments before, she now entered into the buoyant pleasure of the chase, laughing with each near-tagging of her younger self. She approached a corner in the maze and the younger

Alyss jumped out from behind it, teasing the princess with her capture.

"Hah!"

They both laughed so hard that it became difficult to run, and when the girl stopped to catch her breath, Alyss hurried up and took hold of her.

"I've got you now!" she said, tickling the girl.

"No, don't! Stop! Stop!"

The younger Alyss squealed in delight because of course the princess knew where she was most ticklish. But the girl suddenly became serious, pushed Alyss' hands away, and looked off at something. Alyss turned to see what it was. A diamond-encrusted scepter topped with a white crystal heart at the far end of a wide corridor.

"Do you think you can get the scepter?" the girl asked.

It looked easy. Alyss only had to walk down the corridor and take it.

"Why not?"

The corridor walls consisted of looking glass panels that lined up perfectly, facing each other. Alyss stepped between the first pair and her reflections swirled and swirled to form a sort of vortex, and then she was no longer in the Looking Glass Maze. She stood in a featureless Nothing with a tornado of images whipping around her, the words and gestures of the people in them wounding as much as any made by beings of flesh and blood.

"Off with her head! Off with her head!"

Redd swooped toward the princess. Alyss jumped out of the way, her heart thumping when—

There was Dodge Anders, as a boy, wearing his guardsman uniform and receiving a lesson in the etiquette of palace guardsmen from Sir Justice. But like Redd before them, they too vanished. Quigly Gaffer stood before her now, pointing and laughing in her face as if she were the most ridiculous creature he'd ever seen.

"Stop it," she said.

But Quigly was joined by the rest of the London orphans—Charlie, Andrew, Otis, Francine, Esther, and Margaret—as well as some of the wardens she'd known at the Charing Cross Foundling Hospital.

"Stop! It!" she screamed.

Their laughter continued to echo in her ears even after they'd faded from sight and she was gazing upon a silent but confusing scene: she and Prince Leopold surrounded by what appeared to be their four children, picnicking in the Everlasting Forest with Dean and Mrs. Liddell. Two of the children were infants, but they had the faces of Genevieve and Nolan. Alyss wanted to call out to her family, but she couldn't get her voice to work. The Cat stood over her oblivious, picnicking family, licking blood off his paws until a single drop fell to the ground and became a roiling, bloody sea in which her family was drowning. The Alyssians were in it too—Dodge, Bibwit, Hatter, General Doppelgänger, the chessmen. All were drowning. But then the sea drained out

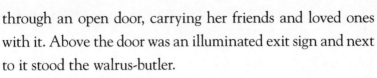

through an open door, carrying her friends and loved ones with it. Above the door was an illuminated exit sign and next to it stood the walrus-butler.

"Oh my, oh dear," said the walrus. "It's only going to get worse, Princess. You don't have to put yourself through this. It's not necessary. Please, I beg you to leave while you still can." With his left flipper, he urged her to use the exit.

But Alyss knew better. The maze had shown her these things to soften her up, to make her more vulnerable for whatever she might face next. She was determined to face it.

She turned her back on the walrus, lifted her foot to step forward into the nothingness before her, and found herself back in the Looking Glass Maze, in the corridor leading to the scepter.

She had made it past the first pair of looking-glass panels.

She moved forward to stand between the next pair of looking glasses, but no sooner had she done so than the maze melted away and she found herself in the South Dining Room of Heart Palace, the scene of Redd's invasion.

"I don't need to see this," she said.

Everyone in the room was staring at the kitten that had begun to morph into The Cat as—

"No!" Alyss cried.

Kraaaaawbooosh!

An explosion blew the doors apart and Redd and her rogue soldiers spilled into the room. Alyss was forced to relive the horror of that ungodly hour, to experience all over again Sir Justice's murder and the destruction of her home, her own near death at Redd's hands. *Once was too much! No one should have to experience such horribleness!* She watched with steadily rising anger as her seven-year-old self and Hatter jumped into the palace's emergency portal (that wrenching, final separation from her mother!) and Genevieve turned to face her sister alone. Then she saw what she had never seen before: her mother bound by Redd's carnivorous roses, Redd cutting off Genevieve's head with a single swing of the scarlet energy bolt.

"Aaaah!"

She ran at Redd, fury in her heart. But the way to Redd became long, and suddenly the twenty-three-year-old Dodge was running alongside her, saying in a voice tight with rage, "Hate makes you strong. Forget restoring White Imagination to power and Wonderland to its past glory. There's no justice except the justice of revenge. The only way to defeat Redd is to embrace your anger."

The Cat jumped in front of them and Dodge plunged his sword into the beast again and again. But he seemed no less angry for it, as if his anger would remain no matter how many times he killed Redd's vicious henchman.

Alyss was almost within striking distance of Redd when her mother's head, lying in a corner where it had rolled, opened its eyes and spoke.

"Black Imagination feeds on anger, Alyss. Give in to your

anger and you merely become a pawn of Black Imagination, which may triumph for a time but never for eternity."

"But look at what happened to you!" Alyss said.

"Yes, look at me. It should tell you a lot that I'm the one saying this."

But the pressure of hate in Alyss' skull was too great. "It tells me that you were weak and that's why you lost!" she screamed, snatching Redd's scepter and cutting off her aunt's head with a single swing, just as *she* had killed Genevieve.

Redd and the roses faded into the floor and Alyss discovered herself standing in a circular room with walls of telescopic glass that allowed her to see the Chessboard Desert and Wondertropolis in their entirety.

Bibwit rushed into the room with an open book in his hands, reading from it with great urgency, wanting her to understand. *"Fleg lubra messingpla gree bono plam,"* the tutor read. *"Tyjk grrspleenuff rosh ingo."*

"Bibwit?"

"Zixwaquit! Zergl grgl! Fffghurgl grgl!"

The tutor continued spouting gibberish, growing more and more agitated with Alyss' lack of understanding, which was when she glimpsed herself in a looking glass. Instead of her usual features, she saw Redd looking back at her. She had become Redd.

"No!"

She smashed the glass, and her entire surroundings—the circular room, the nonsensical Bibwit—showered down around her in fragments, leaving her standing before the entrance glass in the maze; on the other side of the glass, the clash between Alyssians and Redd's soldiers was stopped in time.

"Why am I here? What does this mean?"

"Ahem hum."

A stream of smoke crossed her vision. She turned and saw the blue caterpillar puffing at his hookah.

"It means you failed, Princess."

"I—?" *Can't fail. The maze is intended for me.* "But—"

"You were unable to navigate the maze. It is unfortunate for all of us, but nothing can be done. You must leave through the glass and re-enter the battle."

Failure's not an option. She would rather have been anywhere else, but she couldn't leave yet. Not as a failure. "Unacceptable," she said. "I don't accept it."

And before Blue could blow smoke into her face, she ran deep into the maze. She was quickly lost, but *all* was not lost so long as she remained here. She could still succeed. She *would* succeed, otherwise what would become of—

A figure strode into the corridor up ahead.

"Hatter!"

Oh, she was glad to see him. But the Milliner said nothing, raised a sword and rushed at her.

"Wait! What are you—?"

She had to do something quick. She imagined a sword in her hand and, almost before she realized it, she and Hatter

were fighting—he the aggressor, she surprising herself with a defense that relied on mirroring his moves.

Hatter at last lowered his weapon and stepped away, approving. "Good."

So he was assessing her, Alyss understood, developing her warrior skills—or rather, he was training her imagination in the service of her warrior skills. Still, when a second Hatter Madigan appeared . . .

I have to fight two of them?

In addition to the sword, Alyss armed herself with a Hand of Tyman. She parried with the two Hatters. *Clangk! Shwink-ding-shlank!* Whenever one of them made a move she had never seen before, she quickly appropriated it—imagined it as part of her own repertoire. But merely conjuring herself into a better swordswoman wasn't going to be enough; she had to employ her imagination in other ways, because a third and fourth Hatter appeared, then a fifth and a sixth. Clashing weapons with one Hatter, she imagined that the others felt it. But this proved insufficient as more Hatters stepped forward, so she conjured her numberless reflections to her aid. They jumped from their looking glasses, swords in hand, and for every Hatter Madigan there was now an Alyss Heart to battle him.

"Excellent," one of the Hatters said, and at his signal the Milliners gave up their swords and activated their wrist-blades, employed their boomeranging top hats.

Alyss imagined razor-cards shooting from the sleeves of her uniform, but the Hatters batted them down easily enough.

Never had she wielded her imaginative powers so precisely, so intensely, or for so long a time.

Getting tired, not sure how much longer I can . . .

Sensing her own defeat, she shot wads of a thick, gummy substance from the sleeves of her uniform. The wads hit the Hatters' weapons and stopped up their rotary workings and, in the same instant, Alyss took a deep breath and exhaled, causing such a wind that the Hatters were blown off their feet, lay sprawled on the floor throughout the combat arena.

The fighting was over. Alyss was alone among the defeated Hatters, her reflections back in their looking glasses.

"Control and power aren't everything," one of the Hatters said. "Allow yourself to be the agent by which a cause greater than any single individual triumphs. Then perhaps you'll be worthy of the Heart Crystal."

The Hatters picked themselves up, bowed, and backed away down the maze's various corridors. After a short rest, Alyss felt infused with power and health, better than she had before running into the Hatters.

Better than I have felt in a long, long time—maybe ever.

It was a lot like she used to feel before her seventh birthday, when she thought herself capable of anything and the world was a beautiful place.

What was that?

A creaking sound, like something being hoisted. And voices.

Off to the left? Yes, there they are again.

She followed the sounds and, coming to the end of a shallow passage, found Dodge, Bibwit, Hatter, General Doppelgänger, the white knight, and the rook kneeling with their hands fastened behind them, their heads locked in an enormous guillotine. Queen Redd and The Cat were standing by the lever that would drop the blade, waiting for her.

"But I killed you," Alyss said.

"Did you?" Redd turned to The Cat. "Why wasn't I informed?"

The Cat shrugged.

Is this real or a figment? Can't be real since she's not dead, so there's no danger to anyone if I walk away. Just walk away.

But Alyss couldn't; the sight of the captured Alyssians kept her rooted to the spot. She couldn't chance it, however much reality the scene might contain. Redd's (apparent) multiple lives notwithstanding, who could be sure that if one died in the maze, he or she would still be alive on the outside?

"I'll kill you again if I have to," Alyss said, stepping forward.

"Perhaps," said Redd, "but that won't save your friends."

Alyss again imagined wads of the sticky substance shooting from her sleeves, gumming up the guillotine's works and keeping its blade from falling.

Nothing.

She imagined the blade turned into water and splashing down on the Alyssians' heads.

Nothing.

Redd laughed. "The lovely thing about being here," she said, gesturing at the maze, "is that I'm able to imagine your imagination powerless. Ah, if only that were the case on the outside. But enough chitchat. If you're going to die—which you are—I'm sure you'd like to get it over with. These people are no threat to me without you. There is only one way you can save them: Give yourself up. You might as well. I'll eventually kill you anyway. Then you *and* your friends will be dead. However, to save myself some trouble, I'm giving you a choice."

But how could Alyss be sure that, if she sacrificed herself, Redd would allow her friends to live, let alone live freely? Wasn't it more likely that once Alyss was dead, Redd would kill the Alyssians *because she could*? But what if, because of some unknown leniency in Redd, she *did* allow them to live? They had fought on behalf of White Imagination for thirteen years without Alyss. If, by sacrificing herself, she could secure for them the promise of longer lives, didn't duty demand her sacrifice? They might yet manage to escape; Hatter might find a way. The spirit of White Imagination would live with them. It lived only so long as they did.

Thinking it the final act in her short, troubled life, Princess Alyss Heart knelt down before her aunt.

"Here's to my legacy," Redd said, lifting her scepter. But the moment its cold blade touched the tender back of Alyss' neck—

314

Zzzomp!

—the scene vanished and the princess stood directly in front of the white heart scepter. She reached for it and, as her fingers closed around the scepter's shaft, she was transported by the magic of the maze back into the puzzle shop, amid the chaos of battle once again raging between the Alyssians and Redd's soldiers.

CHAPTER 49

THE KEY to the Looking Glass Maze pulsed with radiance. Alyss was surprised to see it in her palm, but an Intended never left the maze with less than when she entered—although hopefully, as in Alyss' case, she left with much more.

Holding the glowing cube in one hand and the white heart scepter in the other, Alyss stood unflinching amid the fighting. A Four Card tried attacking her but she blew at him and he went crashing back through a wall of the puzzle shop.

"Princess!" Homburg Molly shouted.

"She has the scepter!" Bibwit's joy would have had him speared on the end of a Two Card's blade if Molly hadn't jumped in front of him with her hat-shield.

A couple of Three Cards broke away from Hatter, but

before even he could react, with a quick one-two, Alyss jabbed the pointed end of her scepter into the medallion-sized area above their breastplates. The card soldiers folded up, forever inactivated, as a seeker careened into the shop and snatched the glowing cube out of Alyss' hand. Molly was about to throw her hat at the creature when—

"Let it go," Alyss said. "We don't need it anymore."

She could hear the seekers disperse through the sky, heading back to Mount Isolation. *Now for the rest of the card soldiers.* Alyss banged her scepter on the floor and it splintered into many smaller, identical scepters. With a sweep of her hand, the miniature replicas launched themselves into the vulnerable spot of every single card soldier, each of which folded, no longer a menace. The Alyssians stood in sudden peace with the dead members of The Cut scattered about them.

Dodge, General Doppelgänger, the chessmen—all turned to their princess. The vaguely luminescent quality she'd had as a child was now unclouded by immaturity, uncertainty, or reluctance. She stood like a sun among them, radiant with newfound strength, and any lingering doubt in the Alyssians' minds about her ability to lead them vanished at the sight of her.

"I'd say she's ready, wouldn't you?" the rook said.

The Alyssians cheered, all except for Dodge, whose opportunity for revenge had never been so close. Alyss' luminescence faded to a steady glow as she studied her childhood friend. Her experience in the maze had made her more wary of his behavior. She would have to keep an eye on him, as she would on anyone who stoked their potential for Black Imagination with the tinder of hatred.

"More of The Cut will be coming," General Doppelgänger warned.

"Let them come," Alyss said.

She left the puzzle shop and the Alyssians followed. She walked out into the middle of Emerald Drive and gazed up at the rotted buildings and towers of the surrounding neighborhood, as if able to feel the pain of these inanimate structures, the toll exacted by Redd's rule on her beloved Wondertropolis. Then she turned her imagination to the holographic billboards around the city. Without so much as a wince of effort, she imagined her own face in place of their usual advertisements and reward offers.

"I've finished running from you, Redd. It's time for you to run."

As Alyss spoke the words in Emerald Drive, her holographic images voiced them on every street. Wonderlanders paused amid lawful and unlawful pursuits to stare at the beautiful woman speaking from signs on which, until now, they had only ever seen Redd. More than a few wanted the mistress of Black Imagination to remain in power, knowing how to profit in a world such as hers, but most, though not yet daring to cheer aloud, celebrated Alyss' rise in their hearts.

CHAPTER 50

"I, RUN?" Redd guffawed. She squinted out the Observation Dome as Alyss' transmission ended. "Alyss Heart's misplaced confidence will be the death of her."

"Today, Wonderland will be rid of Alyss Heart for good!" Jack of Diamonds asserted with a puffing out of his already puffed-out belly. He was perhaps too eager to please, because Redd flicked an annoyed glance at the Wig-Beast. "I . . . I beg your pardon for speaking, Your Imperial Viciousness," he said.

"Beg all you want, you powdered and pampered idiot. If I don't get into the Looking Glass Maze soon, it will make no difference to your fate."

The Cat grinned and smoothed his whiskers.

The Lord and Lady of Diamonds, the Lord and Lady of

Clubs, and the Lord and Lady of Spades—who together made up Redd's Cabinet of Military Oversight—shuffled their feet, cleared their throats, and in general enacted every nervous tic available to people unsure of how to ingratiate themselves with their moody, unpredictable leader.

"Your Imperial Viciousness?" the Lady of Clubs ventured. "With all due respect, even if Alyss is not a threat, we think you should move the Heart Crystal to a more secure location."

Redd thought this funny, in a pathetic sort of way, since neither the Lady of Clubs nor any of the other cabinet members knew where the Heart Crystal was.

"'We'?" protested the Lady of Diamonds. "The Lady of Clubs speaks for herself, Your Imperial Viciousness."

"Absolutely speaks for herself," seconded the Lord of Spades.

And Redd, raising an eyebrow, asked the Lady of Clubs, "Did you just tell me what I *should* do?"

"I apologize, Your Imperial Viciousness. I spoke out of—"

"You think my strength is not protection enough for the Heart Crystal? Do you, in fact, suppose that my reign is in danger?"

"No, of course not. What I meant—"

The Lady of Clubs was fortunate that the strangled-baby cries of homecoming seekers interrupted them. The Cat bounded out of the dome and returned in less time than it took Redd to grow impatient. In his paw he carried the

glowing cube, key to the Looking Glass Maze. Redd held out her hand and it flew to her.

"In any case," she said, pressing each of the cube's sides, squeezing it all over, turning it this way and that, "none of you need worry about the Heart Crystal. It's not here at the fortress. Why can't I get this to work?"

Jack of Diamonds stepped forward. "Allow me, Your Imperial Viciousness."

Jack took the cube. He pressed each of its sides, squeezed it all over, turned it this way and that. He began shaking it close to his ear, listening for loose parts inside, while Redd addressed her cabinet.

"I refuse to leave this fortress. It would look cowardly when I have nothing to fear. If Alyss wants to fight me, so much the better. I'll put an end to her. But let no one say that Queen Redd is insensitive. If I have no power, you people have even less than I let you believe. Alyss wouldn't spoil you as I do. If it will make you all feel better, order The Cut to prepare a defense. The Cat will see to the Glass Eyes."

"Your Imperial Viciousness?" The Cat said, and drew Redd's attention with a nod to Jack of Diamonds, who was still tinkering with the glass cube.

"What?" Jack said. "It's not broken. It takes a minute to decipher the code, but I'll have it soon enough. It's not broken, I say."

"It had better not be," Redd warned through thin, bloodless lips.

She swooped out of the dome, down the spiraling hall, and across the open expanse of a ballroom that had never been used. The far wall of the ballroom was decorated with a huge quartz and agate mosaic of the queen's face and, as Redd approached it, the portrait's mouth opened and she entered a secret passage known only to herself and The Cat. The passage led to a balcony overlooking the hollowed-out heart of the fortress. It was here, in the secret heart of the fortress, girded about by supports, that the Heart Crystal burned a dark crimson, as it had since Redd's assumption to power. She leaned over the balcony's edge and placed her hands on the crystal, its power surging through her, strengthening her for the coming battle.

CHAPTER 51

PRINCESS ALYSS Heart was spotted ordering a mug of cider in a brewhouse near the city center. She was seen nibbling a gwynook-kabob in Tyman Street and skulking along the avenue outside the Redd Apartments complex. She was glimpsed entering a tube station at Redd Square, on a safari in Outerwilderbeastia, and at various other locations engaged in a variety of activities. But the Glass Eyes and card soldiers dispatched to destroy these Alysses found nothing because these Alysses were specters, reflections come to life, conjurings from the real princess' imagination that she had dispersed throughout the queendom to confuse Redd's all-seeing eye.

While Redd's forces were occupied with the decoys, Alyss and her companions made it to the outskirts of the Chessboard Desert. The checkered land stretched before them, the promontory of Mount Isolation visible in the middle distance. The white knight and rook were tending to their men, bandaging wounds suffered in the Emerald Drive skirmish, instructing them to double-check all ammunition supplies and be sure weapons were functioning properly. Dodge kept to himself, studying the sword in his lap as if to ensure that it would be able to do what he'd set his mind to: taking The Cat's lives. Alyss should have been entirely focused on developing a sound military strategy, but she couldn't help glancing at Dodge every now and again, her attention divided.

Revenge cannot possibly purge him of hate, but he won't listen to me, won't listen to anyone.

"Alyss?"

"Yes?"

From the expressions of Bibwit Harte, Hatter Madigan, Homburg Molly, and General Doppelgänger, it was clear that she had missed something.

"There is a lot of desert still to cross," Bibwit said, indicating the distance to the fortress.

"And the problem of storming Mount Isolation, so ideally suited for defense," added the general. "We'll need an army greater than Redd's."

"Our objective is to remove Redd from power," Alyss said, loud enough for Dodge to hear. "Our objective is the Heart Crystal, not vengeance."

Dodge didn't look up from his sword.

He heard me. I know he heard me.

"Where Redd is, that's where we'll find the Heart Crystal," said Bibwit. "She'll want to remain close to it to maximize her strength."

"But can you conjure a force of the size we'll need, Princess?" asked General Doppelgänger.

"I don't know." To conjure several doubles of herself was one thing, but an entire army?

"You must try," Bibwit said.

She looked to the others. Hatter made a silent, respectful bow. Molly nodded, eager. The chessmen watched, waited. Even Dodge was watching. To conjure an army she would need to be extremely focused and precise. The millions of details of dress and weaponry—if a single one weren't imagined vividly enough, it would compromise the whole and her imagining would fail. She may have felt stronger than ever, but strong enough for this?

Her scepter, once again whole, showed the intensity of her effort. The white crystal heart at its top glowed brighter and brighter, flashed and zapped as it became a cloud of electrical charges with lightning-like bolts of energy sprouting out of it, encircling Alyss. When these fireworks stopped and Alyss again focused her sight on her surroundings rather than her internal visions, she beheld an enormous army of Alyssian soldiers standing in formation and fanned out behind her. The soldiers were a short distance off and she couldn't even see to the end of them, there were so many.

325

I did it. I—

Someone was laughing. Alyss turned.

"I'm sorry, Princess Alyss," Homburg Molly said, slapping a hand to her mouth but unable to keep from laughing.

What had come over the girl? Bibwit, never one to take appearances for granted, approached Alyss' conjured army for a closer inspection.

"Ah."

The army consisted of toy soldiers, figurines no larger than the tutor's ears.

"The princess is too far from the Heart Crystal," he said. "She cannot defeat Redd from here."

General Doppelgänger split into the twin figures of General Doppel and General Gänger and the two of them paced, in perfect step with each other.

"Well, we have to get to her somehow!" General Doppel said.

"But without an army of soldiers that are of a more normal size," said General Gänger, "our cause is lost."

It was Alyss' turn to approach the soldiers. To her, they had looked suitable enough. She picked up one of the toy soldiers and imagined it marching back and forth in her hand. "I have an idea," she said.

CHAPTER 52

THE FORTRESS was surrounded. Regiments of The Cut had been amassed from across the queendom and stood ready to defend Redd's stronghold. Their ranks formed the front line and, behind them, as the second line of defense, were platoon after platoon of Glass Eyes. Both the card soldiers and Glass Eyes were armed with the full array of weaponry available to them in Redd's Wonderland—orb generators, whipsnake grenades, crystal shooters, cannonball spiders, AD52s, all manner of knives and swords.

As the suns rose on a new day, Redd was breakfasting on spicy, crunchy tuttle-bird legs in the Observation Dome. The Cat and the members of her cabinet, none of whom had eaten since the previous midday, looked on with hungry eyes but said nothing. Jack of Diamonds had wisely excused himself from the dome, but more because he feared Redd watching him toy unsuccessfully with the key to the Looking Glass Maze than because of his stomach's grumbling.

Redd's teeth crunched down on the only remaining tuttle-bird leg, the last scrap of night's shadow faded with the day, and they all saw it at once. Gazing out through the telescopic glass, it would have been impossible to miss: An Alyssian army, seeming to rival the population of the queendom itself, massed a short distance off and waiting to attack. Like Redd's forces, the Alyssians were armed with orb generators, whipsnake grenades, cannonball spiders, AD52s.

"How has Alyss gathered such an immense army?" the Lady of Spades asked.

"They'll just have a larger body count," Redd fumed.

Sitting astride a spirit-dane at the head of the soldiers, Alyss raised her arm and held it above her head a moment before bringing it down in a quick motion. The Alyssians charged toward the fortress.

"Deal the first hand," Redd ordered.

Outside, The Cut launched orb generators and cannonball spiders at the advancing Alyssians—direct hits many of them, which should have taken out entire columns of the enemy. The card soldiers followed up the barrage by charging into the smoke and flame. Confident, Redd eyed the scene from her perch in the dome, but when the smoke cleared she saw her soldiers surrounded by tiny Alyssians. Her weapons had had zero effect and the miniature army continued to push toward the fortress.

Redd's face contorted with a sudden realization. "How could I have been so stupid?"

The Cat was trying to decide if this were a rhetorical question when she roared, "It's a construct!"

With a dismissive swing of Redd's arm, Alyss and her army began to shimmer, the billion points of energy that formed them momentarily visible before exploding apart into nothing. Redd scoped the queendom with her imagination's eye. "Where are you, Alyss? Where is my dear little niece?"

~

Alyss and the others could hear the explosions and the rasping, metallic sounds of The Cut racing toward the conjured army as they came upon the fortress from the opposite side. Until now, their approach had been covert; they'd traveled only over the desert's black squares of tar and volcanic rock to camouflage themselves from Redd's lookouts. But to enter the fortress they would have no choice but to show themselves in open warfare.

Under cover of the black rock, Hatter flicked his top hat into blades and winged them at the card soldiers and Glass Eyes guarding the fortress' entrance. While the weapon was still in the air, he activated his wrist-blades and charged. Molly flattened her homburg into its slicing shield and took up his left flank with Dodge, while Generals Doppel and Gänger took up his right, and the chessmen followed.

"We must be getting close to the Heart Crystal," Alyss said to Bibwit.

The tutor looked at her, his ears bent in a questioning manner.

"I feel . . . I don't know how to explain it."

The princess reached out both arms and extended her ten fingers toward the fighting in front of her. Star-bright branches of energy shot out of her fingers, forking and attaching themselves to card soldiers and Glass Eyes until every single one of them was caught on an end while the other ends were, ultimately, still attached to Alyss' fingers. The princess then raised her arms above her head and the card soldiers and Glass Eyes lifted into the air, helpless. She sent them reeling through the sky. Somewhere in the Chessboard Desert it was raining card soldiers and Glass Eyes.

The sound of orb generators exploding on Alyss' conjured army still assaulted the Alyssians' ears, but it stopped almost as soon as they entered the fortress. Silence could mean only one thing.

"She knows," Alyss said.

"Can you see her?" asked Bibwit.

Alyss felt that she was close to the Heart Crystal. Remote viewing wasn't something she'd been able to do before, but Redd was now clearly visible in her imagination's eye, standing in a large, open room at the foot of a spiral hall, beckoning Alyss with a cold smile on her lips. The steady pulse

of the Heart Crystal was behind the queen, obscured some-how.

"She's waiting for me," Alyss said.

"We should split into factions for safety," General Doppel urged.

"Two targets may be harder to combat," agreed General Gänger, "and we can surround Redd if it comes to that. Bibwit, Rook, Molly, you come with us."

"I'm staying with Princess Alyss," Molly said.

Exchanged glances all around. The girl looked quite ada-mant and this was no time for argument.

"Let her come with me," Alyss said.

The generals dipped their heads; whatever the princess wished.

"Knight, Hatter, and Dodge will also accompany you," said General Doppel, which was when they noticed that Dodge was no longer among them.

"Where did he go?" asked General Gänger.

To find The Cat. Alyss sighted him in her imagination's eye, cautiously picking his way down a hall. *If he crosses paths with Redd, he'll try to engage with her.* She cast her worried eyes toward Bibwit. He too knew why Dodge had left them. And Dodge's selfish desire for retribution might compromise the Alyssians' chance for victory.

"We'll split the pawns between us," said General Doppel.

"Meet us at the Heart Crystal," Alyss said. "Look for a spiral hall."

The generals bowed. "By which time, may the peace of White Imagination have descended on the queendom."

Using her imagination's eye as guide, Alyss led Homburg Molly, Hatter Madigan, and the chessmen through the fortress. It was as if she had been there before, the way she maneuverd without hesitation through the passageways, heading straight for Redd while elsewhere, avoiding detection by the packs of card soldiers that patrolled the gloomy rooms and halls (it was easy to avoid the enemy when he worked alone), Dodge hunted for The Cat.

"Here, kitty, kitty. Here, kitty, kitty, kitty."

He had already crept around the fortress' lower floors, visiting the seekers' cave and the empty hall of the Glass Eyes, and was now systematically working his way up, floor by floor. Ahead of him, the hall curved up and out of sight like a corkscrew. He could have taken any of the corridors that branched off to the left and right of him, but something—a feeling, an instinct—propelled him forward. Not three spirit-danes' lengths away from the ballroom in which Redd waited for Alyss, he heard urgent, hushed voices coming from behind a door on his right. He didn't care if it was to be among his last actions in life. He didn't care about anything except confronting his whiskered nemesis. He kicked open the door and found—

 Not The Cat, but Jack of Diamonds and the walrus-butler, hiding from the violence. They both jumped, startled at Dodge's sudden entrance, but Jack was quick

to recover. He took a small knife from his waistcoat pocket and jabbed the air in the general direction of the walrus.

"Ha-yah! Yah! We've got you now! Thank Issa you've come," he said, to Dodge. "I thought I'd have to kill all of them myself. Hoi! Cha! Cha!"

Jack went on jabbing the air, but Dodge wasn't fooled, especially because Jack was trying to shove the key to the Looking Glass Maze into a pocket of his pantaloons.

To Dodge, anyone who had collaborated with his father's murderers was an enemy. "There's only one reward for a traitor," he said and raised his sword to strike Jack of Diamonds a fatal blow, when—

The unmistakable sound of purring. He spun around, saw The Cat standing in the doorway.

"And what is my reward?" asked the beast.

Dodge gave voice to no warrior yell, no cry of attack. He simply ran at The Cat, sword first. The creature leaped to the side and Dodge's blade missed, clanged against the stone wall just as The Cat swatted his shoulder with a claw, tearing his Alyssian uniform. Dodge himself was only grazed; four thin lines of blood formed on his skin. It could have been worse.

"A little something to match the ones on your face," The Cat said, indicating the scars on Dodge's cheek.

Dodge feinted left and, as The Cat moved right to avoid him, he spun and stabbed the beast with the knuckle-blade on his free hand—an ancient Wonderland weapon, the tops of its ring holes sharpened to a blade that spanned the width of four fingers.

A patch of The Cat's fur matted with blood, but it wasn't a fatal wound. The Cat lunged—a balletic move, landing on his front paws and kicking Dodge with his hind ones, the claws making shallow puncture marks in Dodge's chest and sending him stumbling to the floor.

Seeing that the doorway was clear, Jack of Diamonds and the walrus ran out of the room, each hurrying on his own way in search of a new hiding place.

~

Alyss was fast approaching the spiral hall, sandwiched between Hatter and Molly for protection, but she paused.

"What is it, Princess Alyss?" Molly asked.

In her imagination's eye she saw The Cat pounce. She saw Dodge roll clear and get to his feet, ready to face whatever might come next, battered and bleeding but as determined as ever.

"It's Dodge," she said. "He's—"

But just then a patrol of card soldiers spotted her and rushed forward. In a wall to her right, Alyss imagined a doorway opening into one of the fortress' many unused rooms, and just as she, Molly, Hatter, and the others passed through it, with all of the card soldiers but one a few steps behind them, and that one—a Three Card—in the doorway itself, she imagined it gone. The doorway vanished, leaving the Three Card half sealed in the wall and the rest of the card soldiers stranded on the other side of it without their quarry.

Dodge. She focused her imagination's eye on him, saw him punching The Cat in the face with the handle of his sword. *I won't risk losing him a second time.* She created another Dodge.

"I'll do this myself!" he screamed when he saw his double.

He slashed at his conjured self, which gave The Cat a chance to shove him away and gain some room. The double disappeared and The Cat went at Dodge with his front paws poised to strike. Bad move. Dodge used the paws as targets; with his sword in one hand and the knuckle-blade on the other, he stabbed them both simultaneously, and before The Cat could retreat, he sunk his sword deep and hard through the beast's rib cage. The Cat crumpled to the floor, lifeless.

"Get up!" Dodge shouted. "Get up, get up, get up!"

It felt as if he waited nine lifetimes for The Cat to regain consciousness. He saw the beast's eyelids tremble and again sank his sword into that furry chest. He didn't know that Genevieve and Hatter had each already taken one of The Cat's lives and that Redd herself had taken three more. Now that he'd begun it, now that he'd tasted the revenge for which he'd waited so long, he was in a frenzy of rage and impatience for it to be over.

"Come on! Get up!"

Dodge understood that a soldier's reflexes were fastest when he was relaxed, but his emotions were getting the better of his training and he failed to anticipate The Cat's cleverness. He stood over the creature, watching for the slightest movement. But upon again regaining life, The Cat held himself as still as death, so that his first move wasn't a flicker of eye muscle but the swipe of a claw across Dodge's thigh, inflicting the deepest wound yet.

"Aaaagh!"

Dodge fell back. Blood pumped through his shredded trousers and down his leg.

Slowly, almost leisurely, The Cat stood. His wounds were healed and he grinned. He appeared revived, stronger than ever, while Dodge's injuries were beginning to make themselves felt—his reactions slower, his shoulder and leg and chest pulsing with pain. The Cat stepped toward him and, for the first time in the fight, Dodge moved backwards, a whisper of defeat in his head, as—

Alyss at last came upon the ballroom where Redd waited. *I send you wishes and hope for survival, Dodge, since you won't let me send anything else. Please try not to let your darkest urges overtake what's good in you.* She was about to enter the ballroom when a horde of Glass Eyes ambushed her soldiers, and suddenly Hatter, Molly, the knight, and chessmen were fighting for their lives all around her. *Redd wants me to face her alone.*

Clangk! Skrich-onk!

The way Hatter and Molly fought, the particular manner

336

in which they spun, kicked, twirled, punched, and used their Millinery weapons, was very similar. *She fights more like a full-fledged member of the Millinery than a halfer.* But the thought was as fleeting as thoughts can be, and as Alyss entered the ballroom, she left the Alyssians to fight for themselves, her entire being focused on her aunt, with whom she was about to come face-to-face for only the second time ever.

CHAPTER 53

REDD HAD watched her niece's progress through the fortress with mounting intolerance. The interloper—for that's all Alyss was to her, just a once-coddled brat playing at a sovereign's game—had some nerve. How could Alyss possibly believe herself the crown's heir? By what twisted reasoning had she convinced herself? If Genevieve should never have assumed the throne in the first place, then how could the daughter be queen? No, thought Redd. She herself was and had always been the rightful monarch and on this day she would prove it for all time!

Alyss stepped into the ballroom. Finally: Alyss Heart in the flesh. The problem was, there were eight of her, eight Alyss Hearts. Which was the real one?

"Do you think your little games will save you?" Redd spat,

and from her scepter a bouquet of flesh-eating roses on a long vine shot toward one of the Alysses. It passed through her without effect. A second vine of roses, their toothy mouths gnawing the air, flew at another Alyss—but again, no harm done.

The real Alyss stood third from the left in the row of Alysses, thinking it lucky that she'd conjured her doubles, because she found herself momentarily paralyzed, unexpectedly affected by the sight of Redd. *I can't be angry. Won't be. I conquered my anger in the maze. Must control myself.* But the heat of her temper was rising, the old feelings of abandonment after her parents' deaths, the unfairness of just about everything.

"I don't have time to dillydally," Redd said. "Let the real Alyss Heart step forward."

The queen sent enough bouquets of thorny-vined roses to attack all eight Alysses at once. The roses passed through seven of them without effect. The real Alyss tilted her head in a certain way and the attacking bouquet wadded up, strangled itself, withered, and died.

"We're family," Alyss said.

Redd snorted. "Is that supposed to mean something?"

"Family," Alyss said again, trying to convince herself more than Redd.

"Don't talk to me about family! *You* were never disowned by your parents!"

"I'd rather have been disowned by them than seen them murdered."

"Goody for you!"

Redd opened her mouth and exhaled a jet of flame, out of which stomped two jabberwocky, breathing shoots of fire directly at Alyss. The princess diverted the flames to either side of her and, wielding the white crystal scepter, scattered the jabberwocky into countless particles of energy. As the particles were floating and eddying in the air, fading from sight, Alyss fired a series of orb generators at Redd, who was not yet committing too much of her power to defending herself in order to draw Alyss out and discover her strengths and weaknesses. With the attitude of a grouchy governess extinguishing candle flames, she snuffed out the orb generators before they reached her, repeatedly pinching her thumb and forefinger together in the air. Each time—*zzz!*—an orb fizzled into nonexistence.

Alyss could feel the Heart Crystal's energy radiating out to her, infusing her. *It's behind the far wall.* Redd, by staying close to it to realize her full strength, had ensured that Alyss' powers would also be increased.

Alyss shot two orb generators at the quartz and agate mosaic and—*kerboosh!*—it fractured apart. The red glow of the Heart Crystal filled the room.

Redd shed caution like an outgrown skin. "It's mine!" she shouted. "The crystal's mine!"

She sent X-shaped blades cartwheeling toward Alyss, and it was all the princess could do to avoid getting sliced or run over by them; she darted left and right and back again, but as

soon as she safely avoided one batch of X-blades, more came at her: an army of weapons not needing soldiers to man them. She conjured a cocoon of White Imagination around her as protection. An X-blade cartwheeled into her and knocked her to the floor. She tried blunting the blades' edges, but that didn't stop them from cartwheeling toward her.

Have to get on the offensive.

Still dodging the X-blades, she dealt decks of razor-cards from her sleeves, and a couple of cannonball spiders, but she was too taken up with defending herself to see if they had any effect. She made a fist with one hand and brought it down in the palm of her other. The cartwheeling blades fell flat on the floor, harmless. But now she had another problem because the room was alive with enormous, heavy, black, spike-covered wheels rolling rampant. Alyss wasn't so slow this time. She imagined the nightmarish wheels turned into squares and they locked in place, anchored by their floor-gouging spikes.

Can't let Redd bombard me. Must do more than retaliate.

She conjured a curious bomb—one that didn't destroy but create. It burst at Redd's feet and a shimmering cage of White Imagination–enforced alloy built itself around the queen.

"You think you can contain me?" Redd laughed and stepped out of the mini-prison as if it weren't there. Behind her, the Heart Crystal no longer glowed uniformly red but changed color constantly, from pink to white to red to a marbled red and white.

Aunt and niece stood in a cyclone of Black and White

341

Imagination, the winds of both scudding around them, popping and sizzling with electrical charges and lightning fragments shooting every which way.

Give me strength, Heart Crystal. Give me . . .

One of Alyss' cannonball spiders must have completely missed its target, because Dodge and The Cat were visible through a large, jagged hole in the wall to her right. She hardly took her eyes off Redd for a millisecond, but when she turned back, a large orb was coming toward her. She conjured one of her own and the two orbs collided.

Wuuumpf!

The impact sent shockwaves of displaced air reverberating throughout the room. Redd stood her ground but Alyss was thrown back and slammed to the floor. How had things gotten so turned around? One moment she was on her feet, holding her own against her aunt; the next she was laid out, looking the picture of defeat. One moment Dodge was fighting The Cat as an equal; the next The Cat was rearing back to lance him with a claw through the gut, Dodge defiantly facing his demise as—

"Dodge!" Alyss shouted, and in a reflex, she conjured an AD52 into his hand, just as something knocked her on the head. A black shroud fell over her vision and she lost consciousness, giving Redd the only advantage she needed to put an end to the upstart princess.

CHAPTER 54

ALICE AWOKE in her bed, cold and sweating. Prince Leopold, Mrs. Liddell, and the dean were looking down on her with expressions of mingled concern and relief.

"What is this?" Alice asked, befuddled.

"This," said Mrs. Liddell, "is your bed. You're at home, dear."

"You've given us quite a scare, my love," said Prince Leopold. "Do you remember anything of what's happened?"

Do I remember? She was afraid to answer.

"You fainted in church and have been in some sort of delirium ever since."

No! Impossible! "I've been in Wonderland," she said.

Mrs. Liddell's face tightened. Dean Liddell cleared his throat.

"Like in Carroll's book?" Leopold asked good-naturedly.

"It's nothing like the book!"

Her vehemence frightened them. She wasn't well. She was too weak to be upsetting herself so.

"Alice," Mrs. Liddell said, "you've been very ill. Perhaps we'll let you rest."

"I'll check on you shortly," the prince said.

Leopold and the Liddells turned for the door. *But they can't leave. Not yet.* Not when she was so confused, so—she had to admit it to herself—disappointed. *None of it real? The grown-up Dodge, my consultation with the blue caterpillar, the Looking Glass Maze?* She sat upright in bed.

"But . . ."

"What is it?" asked the dean.

"Have I really been here this whole time?"

"Of course."

Can it all have been a fever-dream? She fell back against her pillows. *It was so vivid. How can it not have happened?*

"It's a trick, Alyss!" Dodge shouted, appearing through the wall armed with an AD52. "Whatever you're seeing, it's a construct! It isn't real!"

He was gone as suddenly as he'd come—back through the wall. Neither the Liddells nor Leopold had noticed the intrusion. Alyss studied them more closely and now that she knew to look for them, she could see the energy bits of which they consisted. She felt something in her hand: the white heart scepter. *So Dodge is all right. He survived The Cat.* Indeed,

344

facing imminent death, Dodge had not hesitated to use the AD52 when it materialized in his hand. Instead of losing his own life, he took another of The Cat's, leaving the beast with only one.

Alyss swept the construct away. The bed and furniture, the Liddells, Prince Leopold—all vanished and she found herself on the ballroom floor at Mount Isolation. Redd stood over her, swinging her scepter down to cut off her head.

I'm not mad, I'm not, I'm not mad, yes I am!

With Redd's scepter only a few Wonderland inches from her lovely neck, she blew hard at the evil Queen, sending her flying backwards, and then jumped to her feet. Redd was still in the air when Alyss released a bolt of energy from her index finger. It latched on to Redd and, wagging her finger back and forth, Alyss smashed the queen against the ballroom's two remaining walls. Disorientated, Redd's imaginings fizzled and faded, less and less of a threat to Alyss, whose abilities seemed to be increasing in direct proportion to her confidence.

Unrealistic not to be angry, to never get angry or upset. It's a matter of degree.

Alyss' anger informed her, but it didn't rule her, although she seemed willing to beat Redd against the walls until the malicious woman died—a rather brutal death had it come to pass, but Redd managed to free herself from the energy-spear that held her, severing it with the pointed end of her scepter and dropping to the floor.

It was Alyss' turn to put her aunt on the defensive. She

sent deck after deck of razor-cards at Redd. She conjured exploding cannonball spiders, the giant arachnids taking up all her aunt's attention. The black, hungry roses that Redd sent snaking toward the princess were easily squashed, the orbs and unmanned, airborne blades effortlessly waved off, and the spears of black energy (Alyss was flattered, her aunt borrowing this idea from her) pinned motionless to the air by Alyss' own white spears with no trouble.

Both Alyss and Redd may have been strengthened by their proximity to the Heart Crystal, but Alyss could see that she was the stronger of the two. It must have dawned on Redd too because, frustrated and annoyed beyond all measure, she gave up on her fancy imaginings and ran at Alyss with scepter raised.

They brandished their scepters like swords, two powerful warriors engaged in good old-fashioned hand-to-hand combat. The space above and around them glittered and popped and sizzled and smoked with the thunderstorm of their imaginative powers. Then, with the speed of a gwynook's flapping wing, Alyss hooked the white heart of her scepter in a gnarled crook of Redd's scepter and yanked the latter to the floor, where she exploded it with a jolt of white hot imaginative energy.

Do I kill or . . . but what's to be done with her if I don't? She'll pose a threat as long as she lives.

Redd balled her hands into fists, making fleshy clubs of them.

346

"I'm stronger than you are, Redd."

"You will not defeat me!" Redd screamed.

Alyss braced herself for another attack, realizing only too late what was happening. She watched with disbelieving eyes as Redd launched herself into the Heart Crystal.

Krrrrrkkkkchsss! Hissszzzzll! Krrrch! Zzzzsssz!

The crystal crackled and smoldered. It began to vibrate, to emit a low, steady hum that deepened and grew in volume.

~

Cornered by an AD52-armed Dodge, and with only one life remaining to him, The Cat saw which way the imaginative energy was flowing. He hissed, and sprinted for the crystal. Dodge shot a spray of razor-cards at him, but the beast was too fast and leaped into the crystal, its violent internal motions causing the entire Mount Isolation fortress to shake ominously, threatening collapse, when—

The noise stopped. All was still. The Heart Crystal glowed a steady white.

The faction of Alyssians headed by Generals Doppel and Gänger had converged on the scene and, together with Hatter, Molly, and the others, had defeated The Glass Eyes. All stood dumbstruck in the silence that inevitably follows great and unexpected events. For in the queendom's long history, no one had ever jumped into the Heart Crystal and no one knew what it augured for the future.

CHAPTER 55

GENERAL DOPPEL was the first to recover himself. He saw Dodge sitting on the floor, panting, covered in blood— his own and The Cat's. "Call a surgeon!"

"Not necessary, sir. Oh no. I'm here and I have just the thing." The walrus-butler stepped over dead Glass Eyes and waddled across the room carrying a kit that contained a glowing rod to clean wounds and stop their bleeding, a sleeve of interconnected NRG nodes and fusing cores, and a spool of lab-grown skin with laser cauterizer. The walrus bowed to Alyss, pleased that fate had granted him the occasion. "I welcome your return most heartily, Queen Alyss," he said.

That brought Alyss around. No one had ever called her "Queen" before.

The walrus began ministering to Dodge's wounds.

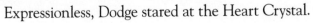

Expressionless, Dodge stared at the Heart Crystal.

Impossible to know what he's thinking. Has vengeance been served or—

There came a sudden disturbance at the ballroom's entrance as the Lord and Lady of Diamonds, the Lord and Lady of Clubs, and the Lord and Lady of Spades pushed their way through the gathered chessmen and hurried up to Alyss with looks of great relief.

"We heard such a commotion," said the Lady of Diamonds, "and when it stopped, we came as fast as we could, hardly daring to hope—"

"Your victory fulfills our deepest hopes for the queendom," finished the Lord of Spades.

"Yes," the Lady of Diamonds went on, "absolutely. It has been horrid—the tyranny we've suffered at the hands of *that woman!*"

"Redd has kept us hostage, Queen Alyss," offered the Lady of Clubs.

"Is that so?" Alyss said with a doubting look at Bibwit.

"Well, our bodies weren't held hostage so much as our minds," said the Lady of Clubs. "If we didn't obey Redd as every Wonderlander had to, we would have been sent to the Crystal Mines."

"And I'm ashamed to say," said the Lady of Diamonds, "that we Diamonds, a titled family dating back to the earliest epochs, were treated the most poorly by the former queen."

"You?!" guffawed the Lord of Clubs. "My wife and I certainly suffered more than any of your clan, and I daresay—"

"Say nothing but the truth, why don't you?" interrupted the Lady of Spades. "If anyone can claim the title of the most abused under Redd, I think it is my husband and I."

The lords and ladies began talking all at once, arguing about who had been the worst off under Redd's rule, until Alyss put a finger to her lips—*shhh*—and they fell silent.

"As soon as circumstances allow, a tribunal will be established to determine whether you behaved honorably during Redd's reign or whether you are, in fact, guilty of war crimes," Alyss said.

"War crimes?" spluttered the Lady of Spades.

The white knight and his pawns surrounded the suit families.

"But the one who is perhaps most guilty is not here," said Bibwit Harte.

"You mean this fellow?" It was the rook. All heads turned to see him leading Jack of Diamonds into the room. "I found him holed up in a wardrobe, avoiding all the fun."

"Unhand me, you . . . you chessman!" Jack shook himself free of the rook, straightened his waistcoat with a tug, patted his wig, and bowed to Alyss. "Queen Alyss, I have done nothing but try to serve you to the best of my ability. I risked my life to infiltrate this fortress on your behalf. Long reign White Imagination!"

The walrus had by this time finished tending to Dodge, who limped up to Jack of Diamonds. Without a word, he

removed the key to the Looking Glass Maze from the portly man's pocket.

"How'd that get there?" Jack asked falteringly.

"How could you, Jack?" the Lady of Diamonds gasped. "Shame! Oh, shame!"

"What deceit from our only son!" the Lord of Diamonds lamented, although he and his wife had both known about Jack's activities.

Alyss pointed at Jack's feet and a building bomb exploded there, erecting a mini-prison around him.

In the thrust and parry of battle, Redd's crown had fallen on the floor. Bibwit picked it up.

"Walrus, if you please—"

"Oh, I do!" said the walrus.

"—polish this and make it ready for Alyss' coronation."

The tutor then turned to the young queen. There was little he could teach Alyss Heart that life-experience hadn't already taught her. She was gazing thoughtfully at the Heart Crystal.

"Alyss?"

"What will happen? Should we send someone after them?"

Bibwit considered his answer for a long time before speaking. "Redd as we knew her may no longer exist. But just as when an invention passes into the crystal to inspire imaginations on other worlds, so her spirit will certainly pass down and remain for all time an animating force. Jumping into the crystal has made her immortal. As to what forms she may take in the future, I can't presume to say. But I do fear for the universe."

Alyss said nothing, lost in thought.

"Now . . . for the family that nurtured you in that other world."

"Yes?"

"Something tells me that they are worried about their missing daughter." Bibwit's ears twitched mischievously. "Understand that I'm just an extremely learned albino and you needn't listen to me, but I suggest you conjure an Alice Liddell of genuine flesh and blood and personality. Birth your twin with the fertility of your imagination and send her to live out the life that is no longer yours."

"But how? Am I ... capable?"

Bibwit smiled. Perhaps there were things he could still teach Alyss after all. "Look around you," he said. "Look at what you've accomplished. I would have thought you'd learned by now that you're capable of anything."

At his instruction, Alyss placed her hands on the crystal and—

Pop! Zzzz!

—a burst of white light, everyone covered their eyes, and standing at the center of it, locked in a synergic hug with the crystal, Alyss imagined the billions of life-giving particles that made up Alice Liddell—the cells of her blood, the pores of her skin—until somewhere outside Oxford, England,

352

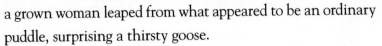

a grown woman leaped from what appeared to be an ordinary puddle, surprising a thirsty goose.

After weeks of residing in London at Prince Leopold's expense, the Liddells had arrived back in Oxford. They were sitting down to supper when Alice let herself in the front door. To a background of gasps and exclamations of relief, amazement, joy, and every other positive emotion that Alice's miraculous return could give rise to, she told of how she had escaped from her captors (a gang of Scottish stevedores looking to blackmail the royal family, she claimed), a feat which she herself pooh-poohed as nothing very astonishing.

In Alice's absence, and having convinced himself that he would never see her again, Prince Leopold had fallen in love with another—Princess Helen of Waldeck. Alice proved less upset than her mother by Leopold's new love. In a matter of years, she would marry a man better suited to her station in life—Reginald Hargreaves, treasurer at her father's college. Prince Leopold and Princess Helen would wed soon afterwards.

For as long as they lived, Alice and the prince harbored an affection for each other. And perhaps in memory of their near union, Alice named her firstborn child Leopold, and the prince named his firstborn daughter Alice. All involved lived contentedly ever after, except perhaps Mrs. Liddell, who liked Reginald Hargreaves decently enough, but oh, how splendid it would have been if only Alice had married a prince!

CHAPTER 56

THE DISARRAY of the queendom didn't lend itself to pomp and circumstance, so Alyss kept her coronation ceremony short and to the point. Her one concession to fanfare was to broadcast the event on the government-sponsored billboards and poster crystals of Wondertropolis. She wanted the populace to understand that they had a new queen. None of the billboards and posters would ever again feature reward offers for Wonderlanders who betrayed followers of White Imagination, or advertisements for Redd's numerous products and inventions.

The new queen and her retinue—Dodge, Bibwit, Hatter, Molly, General Doppelgänger, the rook, and the knight—retired to Mount Isolation's Observation Dome after the coronation.

"What's that?" Homburg Molly asked, making a face at the big, hairy thing taking up space near a telescopic panel.

The walrus was waddling around the room, offering goblets of wine from a tray. "Oh yes, that's the Wig-Beast," he said, "a plaything of Jack of Diamonds. Haven't you ever seen a Wig-Beast before?"

"It's ugly and I don't like it," Molly said.

The walrus quite agreed. It *was* ugly.

In time, a new Heart Palace would stand in place of the old, its garden featuring the grave of Sir Justice Anders as well as memorials to Queen Genevieve, King Nolan, and the numerous brave Alyssians who lost their lives during Redd's tyrannical rule. But Wonderland's recovery would require vigilance. Glass Eyes and soldiers from The Cut would have to be hunted down and destroyed. The principles of White Imagination might once again be foremost in the land but, as in Genevieve's era, problems would remain. Followers of Black Imagination would have to be monitored; members of the population addicted to artificial crystal or imagination stimulants rehabilitated; those thriving by corrupt business practices would comply with more ethical modes of professional conduct or be shut down.

"Queen Alyss?"

"Yes?"

It was Hatter Madigan. He seemed to have trouble finding his words. "I have given . . . devoted my life to the protection of you and your mother. I've done everything within my power and if ever I didn't meet the requirements of my duty . . ."

"You've done more than any queen could reasonably ask."

The Milliner bowed in thanks. "And I wish to continue in service, but I have an unorthodox request. I would like . . . to take a temporary leave."

Alyss thought of him sitting near the fire that night when she first exercised control over her imaginative power—how he had looked so ordinary without his weapons. *He is not consumed by duty after all, has interests and loves outside of it.*

"I had hoped you would rebuild the Millinery," she said.

"And I will, my queen. Upon my return to active duty." He thought to tell her of his reason—the loss of a certain Wonderlander whom he hadn't yet had a chance to mourn. But words failed him. Sorrow momentarily swelled his tongue.

"Who will look after me in the meantime?" Alyss asked.

Hatter focused his gaze on Homburg Molly. "All the protection you need is right there."

Molly beamed, surprised, then tipped her hat.

"Hatter, if you need time for personal matters, you may certainly have it. Your leave is granted."

"Thank you, Queen Alyss."

He excused himself from Alyss' company, and Molly, almost bouncing with pleasure, followed him across the room. The youngest personal guard to a queen ever! The

girl bombarded Hatter with questions as Alyss cast a look at Bibwit Harte and General Doppelgänger, who were involved in a debate about the health benefits of squig berry juice. The white knight egged on the tutor while the rook took the general's side, neither chessman caring about the subject but doing it for the enjoyment of watching the two celebrated Wonderlanders argue. Then Alyss' eyes fell on Dodge standing alone at a telescopic panel, looking out at the rubble of Heart Palace. She approached him.

"It *will* be rebuilt," she said.

Dodge nodded.

"No one will be forgotten, Dodge. Not Sir Justice, not the lowliest card soldier, no one."

Again, he nodded. "I owe you a thanks." He patted the AD52 strapped to his thigh.

"I'm only glad you weren't too proud to use it."

"I should have used it more."

She understood. He had killed The Cat but, in essence, The Cat had escaped. Whether or not Dodge's confrontation with the beast had been enough to loosen the noose of Black Imagination around his throat, to pluck free the barb of hatred that had given his life purpose for so long, only the future would show. But Alyss hoped he could put his anger behind him. She longed for the boy she once knew to take up the body of the man.

We might get to know each other again, refresh the love we once had—a love that although we were young was by no means childish. The jabberwock tooth he'd given her . . . *I'll wear it around my neck to show that I've not forgotten and I still care for him, a talisman against his darker urges.*

She turned from Dodge Anders and glimpsed her reflection in a looking glass. She remembered her time in the maze when she stood in this very room and saw, in place of her own reflection, Redd's face staring back at her from that same glass. But now her image rippled and faded, and there stood Genevieve and Nolan with their arms around each other, smiling with pride. The progress of the queendom, the Alyssians' victorious coup, whatever successes and failures awaited them in the future—it all began with her, Genevieve and Nolan's presence seemed to say, the power and wisdom that resided within her, the most powerful queen ever to lead Wonderland.

"It's all in your head," Genevieve said.

"I know," said Alyss, and despite the traumas of the past, the uncertainty of the future, she wouldn't have given up this moment for anything. "Isn't it wonderful?"

358

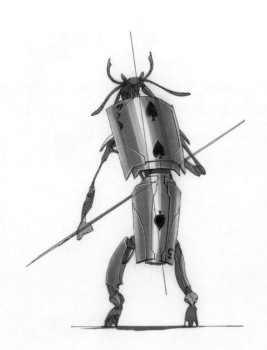

"Alice" arrives on Earth ——— **MAY 4, 1859** ➤ 13th day of the 13th rotation of the 1313th revolution of the thurmite moon since the founding of the queendom. Redd's coup

Henri Dunant inspired to found ——— **JUNE 1859** ➤ General Doppelgänger reunites the Red Cross by the horrors of the broken Hearts to form the the Battle of Solferino in Italy rebel resistance, the Alyssians

Queensland established ——— **JULY 1859** ➤ Redd's coronation ceremony in Australia

The largest solar storm in ——— **SEPT 1859** ➤ Redd moves the Heart Crystal recorded history impacts Earth, to Mount Isolation overloading telegraph machines, starting widespread fires and aurorae as far south as Hawaii

France and England invade ——— **OCT 1860** ➤ Redd demolishes the Valley of China and burn the Gardens of the Mushrooms Perfect Brightness

France and England force China ——— **OCT 1860** ➤ Redd orders everyone to use to allow opium to be sold Black Imagination Stimulant

Billy the Kid born ——— **NOV 1860** ➤ Homburg Molly born

James Clerk Maxwell takes first ——— **MAY 1861** ➤ Redd declares all art must use color photograph the color red

Observation balloons used in ——— **JULY 1861** ➤ Redd invents Glass Eyes to hunt the American Civil War Alyssians

First steam-powered ironclads ——— **OCT 1861** ➤ First of Redd's Rose Rollers roll clash in battle off the assembly line

Pasteur proves the existence of germs	**APRIL 1862**	Redd invents infla-rice, causing an epidemic of infla-bloatarhea
"Alice" tells her story of Wonderland to Charles Dodgson	**JULY 1862**	Redd Rose Acting Troupe premieres a new show, re-enacting the palace coup. It premieres at the Turquoise Amphitheatre.
Union forces forbidden to capture runaway slaves in the Civil War, annulling the Fugitive Slave Act	**JULY 1862**	Redd declares the death penalty for anyone who doesn't turn in fugitive Alyssians
First section of the London Underground opens	**JAN 1863**	Redd moves orphanages underground, according to the new law: Children should be heard screaming, not seen
Battle of Gettysburg	**JULY 1863**	Battle of Blaxik
Draft riots in New York City because of conscription for service in the Civil War	**JULY 1863**	Redd invents The Cut, an enhanced, ruthless private army of card soldiers, loyal only to her
San Francisco Call runs story on mysterious stranger in a top hat passing through the city	**OCT 1863**	*The Redd Flag*, Wonderland's premier newspaper, proclaims a new public holiday, called Alyss is Dead Day. Celebration is mandatory.
Charles Dodgson presents Alyss with a manuscript copy of *Alice's Adventures Underground*, his version of her story	**NOV 1864**	Redd commissions a rock opera dramatizing her victimization at the hands of her malevolent family

Alice's Adventures in Wonderland published	**JULY 1865**	Redd completes removal of all mention of her sister Genevieve from the monuments and libraries of Wonderland
Henry Wortz, commandant of Andersonville prison where 13,000 out of 50,000 prisoners died, is executed for war crimes	**JULY 1865**	Redd awards the Crimson Sash of Success to the wardens of Krag prison, where no prisoners survived
Climbers complete the first ascent of the Matterhorn mountain, on the border of Switzerland and Italy	**JULY 1865**	Redd begins construction of The Five Spires of Redd, intended to be the tallest structure in the universe
Alfred Nobel patents dynamite	**MAY 1867**	Redd invents Naturcide
Karl Marx publishes *Das Kapital*	**OCT 1867**	Redd orders Bibwit Harte to begin a total rewrite of *In Queendom Speramus*
United States signs Treaty of Fort Laramie with the Lakota tribes	**MAY 1868**	Redd signs treaty of non-aggression with King Arch of Boarderland
Reno, NV, incorporated	**MAY 1868**	Redd creates Redd's Hotel and Casino, where you can gamble your life on one roll of the dice
Last public hanging in Britain at Newgate prison	**MAY 1868**	First execution under Redd's law outlawing silence. Silence breeds independent thought, which breeds dissent.
Defeated Japanese swordsmen commit mass suicide in the Boshin War	**SEPT 1869**	A squad of surrounded Alyssian Chessmen "resign the game" by using deadly pink mushrooms rather then be captured by Redd

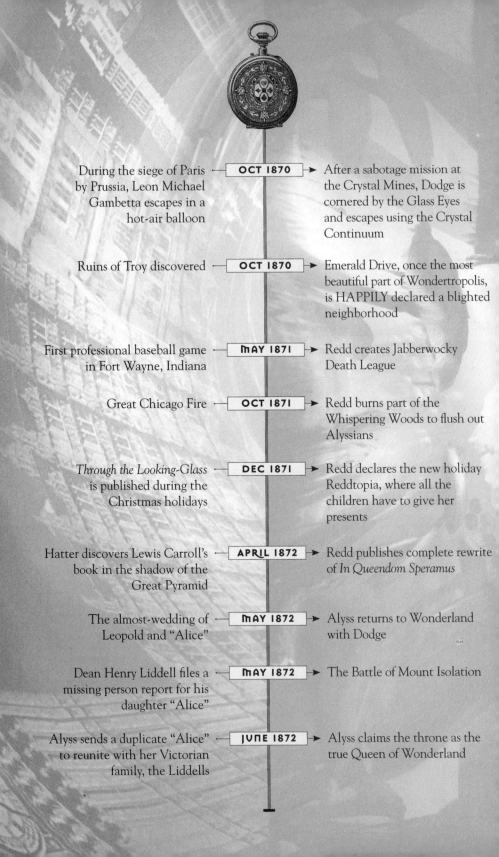

During the siege of Paris by Prussia, Leon Michael Gambetta escapes in a hot-air balloon	**OCT 1870**	After a sabotage mission at the Crystal Mines, Dodge is cornered by the Glass Eyes and escapes using the Crystal Continuum
Ruins of Troy discovered	**OCT 1870**	Emerald Drive, once the most beautiful part of Wondertropolis, is HAPPILY declared a blighted neighborhood
First professional baseball game in Fort Wayne, Indiana	**MAY 1871**	Redd creates Jabberwocky Death League
Great Chicago Fire	**OCT 1871**	Redd burns part of the Whispering Woods to flush out Alyssians
Through the Looking-Glass is published during the Christmas holidays	**DEC 1871**	Redd declares the new holiday Reddtopia, where all the children have to give her presents
Hatter discovers Lewis Carroll's book in the shadow of the Great Pyramid	**APRIL 1872**	Redd publishes complete rewrite of *In Queendom Speramus*
The almost-wedding of Leopold and "Alice"	**MAY 1872**	Alyss returns to Wonderland with Dodge
Dean Henry Liddell files a missing person report for his daughter "Alice"	**MAY 1872**	The Battle of Mount Isolation
Alyss sends a duplicate "Alice" to reunite with her Victorian family, the Liddells	**JUNE 1872**	Alyss claims the throne as the true Queen of Wonderland